WIZARDMATCH

Lauren Magaziner

DIAL BOOKS
FOR YOUNG READERS

Dial Books for Young Readers
Penguin Young Readers Group
An imprint of Penguin Random House LLC
375 Hudson Street
New York, NY 10014

Printed in the United States of America

Library of Congress Cataloging-in-Publication Data

Names: Magaziner, Lauren, author.
Title: Wizardmatch / Lauren Magaziner.
Description: New York, NY : Dial Books for Young Readers, [2017] |
Summary: Twelve-year-old Lennie Mercado's grandfather, the current
Prime Wizard of Pomporromp, is retiring and decides to host a tournament
for Lennie and her cousins to compete to win his title, land, position, castle,
and unlimited magical powers, but when Poppop introduces new rules to
eliminate sibling rivalry, Lennie decides the games are unfair and makes plans
to sabotage the event.
Identifiers: LCCN 2017012731 | ISBN 9780735227781 (hardcover) |
ISBN 9780735227804 (ebook)
Subjects: | CYAC: Magic—Fiction. | Contests—Fiction. | Families—Fiction.
| Sibling rivalry—Fiction. | Fantasy.
Classification: LCC PZ7.M2713 Wi 2017 | DDC [Fic]—dc23 LC record
available at https://lccn.loc.gov/2017012731 1 3 5 7 9 10 8 6 4 2

Design by Mina Chung • Text set in Fournier MT Pro

To Michael, my brother, bestie, and inspiration. Our deep
friendship, our playful rivalry, is the bond I treasure
most in this life. This book was always yours.

And to Stacey, my editor, pillar, and visionary.
Every book we do together is magic.
Thank you for each adventure.

The POMPORROMP FAMILY TREE

Three Generations of Pomp!

Mortimer de Pomporromp

Philip #1

- Emma
  Age 17
- Ethan
  Age 14

Lacey

- Bo
  Age 13
- Danielle
  Age 7
- Alice
  Age 6
- Jordan
  Age 3

Philip #2

- Jonathan
  Age 15
- Anya
  Age 10
- Mollie
  Age 5

Philip #3

- Julien
  Age 13

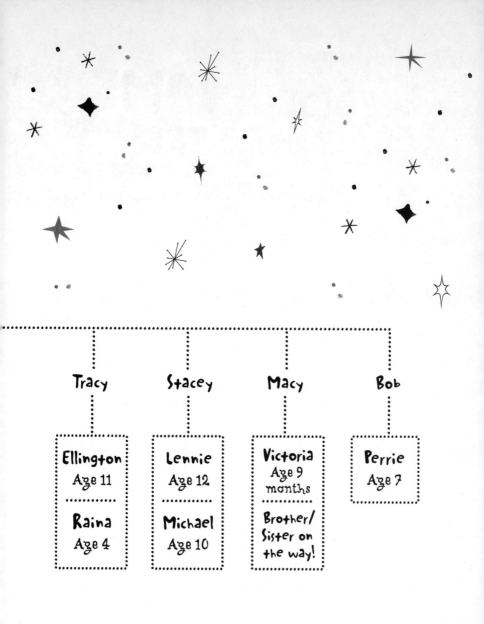

Tracy

Ellington
Age 11
....
Raina
Age 4

Stacey

Lennie
Age 12
....
Michael
Age 10

Macy

Victoria
Age 9
months

Brother/
Sister on
the way!

Bob

Perrie
Age 7

An Ill-Conceived Decision

Mortimer de Pomporromp—the oldest, most powerful, most celebrated wizard in his entire family—had the sniffles.

He groaned as he rolled over in bed, his back cracking and muscles aching as he reached for the staff propped up against his nightstand. With one tap of that magical stick against the floor, Mortimer could summon a whole factory of tissues. Which was just what his runny nose needed.

Almost, almost . . .

He stretched out his arm. His fingers closed around the staff, and his nose twitched. Already, it was too late to summon a box of tissues—they'd never reach him in time. He banged his staff on the floor just before . . .

"Ah—Ah—ACHOO!!!!!!!!!" Mortimer sneezed. Only instead of snot, chocolate pudding came flying out of his nostrils. It sailed across the room and landed with a *splat* all over the floor.

Footsteps clomped up the stairwell to his bedchamber; moments later the door burst open, and his assistant, Estella, blew into the room, waving a piece of parchment in the air.

"Mortimer de Pomporromp, what in *heaven's name* is this preposterous memo you just—"

"WATCH," Mortimer cried, trying to warn her. But it was too late: Estella slipped on the puddle of pudding-snot, flipped backward, and landed flat on her back.

Mortimer cringed as his assistant lay in the goop. It was sticking to her corkscrew curls, crusting on her brown skin, and was most certainly going to stain her lilac pantsuit.

"I've always wanted a booger bath, thank you," Estella said drily.

"Be thankful I had time to bewitch it!"

Estella glared at him as she wrung out her hair. "Yes, I'm thanking my lucky stars."

Mortimer turned to look out the window. It was a soggy, stormy day, filled with the crackles of lightning and the rumblings of thunder. Just like the stormy rumblings inside his soul. Of course, it wasn't coincidence; he controlled the weather with his magic . . . but *still*.

"This crazy memo!" Estella said. "Are we going to discuss it?"

"Woe is me, I'm sick!" Mortimer complained. "Life is *horrible*! Awful, just awful! Dreadfully appallingly grievously monstrously tragically shuddersome. Beastly and ghastly and rotten—"

"Stop being so dramatic," Estella said, and she whacked him with a pillow. "You just have a head cold."

"WOE!" Mortimer wailed. He thrashed beneath his fuzzy

blankets and held on to his stuffed animal for comfort, which—despite being filled with cotton—was a much better companion than Estella in times of distress. True, Estella was a loyal assistant, but in the twenty years she'd been by his side, she remained rather unconcerned with his emotional turmoil.

"All your complaining won't get you out of talking about this." She laid the parchment on his chest. *To Estella, please inform my children (Lacey, Tracy, Stacey, Macy, Philip #1, Philip #2, Philip #3, and Bob) that I am stepping down from the post of Prime Wizard, Earl of Pomporromp, Viscount of Netherly. I will host a Wizardmatch competition among my grandchildren to find the next successor.* It was written in his own handwriting, smudged a bit because he was a leftie.

"ARE WE GOING TO DISCUSS THIS OR NOT?" Estella said.

"Alas, the end of my days is near!" Mortimer moaned. "I see a bright light!"

"Shall I turn off the lamp above your bed?"

"Not *that* bright light! The other one! The deadly one! I shall never recover!"

Estella sighed. "You say that *every* year when you get a cold. And every year you recover just fine."

"Will you plan my funeral, youthful Estella?"

"Mortimer, you are *fine*. Other than being *melodramatic* and *ridiculous*—"

"My dear! Do not speak ill of the ill!"

Estella sighed and sat on the side of his bed. "Are you sure you're ready to pass on your powers? It's a big decision to step down, and I don't want you to take this lightly."

"Lightly! *Lightly!* Why, it's the heaviest decision I've made in my life! Nothing shall compare to this incessant skirmish between my brain and my heart! Why, the inner agony I've had to endure—"

"Mortimer!"

He waved his hand. "Estella, I came into my position at the age of twelve. Most of my grandchildren are between the ages of seven and fourteen. I *could* wait to hold Wizard-match. But I don't want to. Whoever is going to be the next Prime Wizard of Pomporromp is going to need at least ten years to study under me. I want to leave enough time for years of thorough training . . . and time enough to retire somewhere south and warm before my bones become brittle and frail and infirm—"

"Mortimer," she said with a sigh. Then she rested a hand on his own. "This isn't just because you're feeling sick, right? This is something you truly want to do?"

"This is no snap decision, Estella." He puffed his chest out. "Sir Mortimer de Pomporromp, Prime Wizard, Earl of this castle, Viscount of Netherly does not *make* hasty decisions."

"If you say so," Estella said, unconvinced.

But it didn't matter what his assistant thought—he knew in his bones (his nearly *infirm* bones) that it was time to have another Wizardmatch. Time to put his grandchildren through the ultimate test. The one winner would take it all: his land, his title, his castle. And most of all: his unlimited magical powers.

Mortimer tugged on his floor-length beard and said, "May the best kin win."

Preparing for Poppop

Once again, Lennie Mercado was practicing magic.

"Okay," she said to her reflection. Her brown eyes stared back at her, twinkling with determination from behind her glasses. "Sixteen seconds. You can do this."

She took a breath so deep that her lungs smarted, and she watched as her image in the mirror went from hazy . . . to completely invisible. Chills prickled on her skin, and her head felt tingly, like someone had cracked an egg on her skull, and the yolk was running down her neck.

One, she counted to herself, *two, three, four, five* . . .

"I can do it!" she said through gritted teeth.

Six, seven, eight, nine, ten . . .

"COME ON!" she cried, feeling the beads of sweat on her forehead. Her magical energy was low, and her whole body was aching.

Eleven, twelve, thirteen, fourteen, fifteen—

Lennie visibled again, popping back into view. Loose strands of hair were matted to her clammy forehead, and she was panting as though she'd just run a marathon.

"AUGH!" she aughed. Fifteen seconds was her record,

and no matter how hard she tried—and she *did* try—she just couldn't beat it.

Lennie plopped down on a beanbag in the corner of her room, thinking of that *awful* thing her mom kept saying to her every time she caught Lennie practicing her powers. Her mom had told her that there was only so much she could do to extend her magic. At some point, she was going to max out. Even her mom (who was thirty-nine and, like, *super old*) could only hold her invisibility for thirty seconds.

But Lennie practiced her hardest anyway. Even if she had to train for years before she even gained another second of invisibility, she'd do it. She'd do anything.

Lennie glanced out the window, scanning the redwood trees in her backyard, just in case Poppop Pomporromp decided to sneak in through the back door. She had gained one second since she'd seen him last summer, and she hoped he'd be impressed with her.

Except . . . Poppop was rarely impressed with anything but himself. Unlike Lennie (and her mom, and her brother, Michael), Poppop wasn't limited to just one fifteen-second power. He was the Prime Wizard of the family, which meant that he was special.

With just a tap of his staff, Poppop made spaghetti dinners dance on the table like synchronized worms. He levitated objects around the house. He once conjured a four-story tree house in the backyard in just a blink. And turned their living room into an ice-skating rink in the middle of July. He was the only person in the whole family who had no limitations on his powers. Lucky him!

Lennie squinted. But nothing did pop out of those redwood trees. Except a squirrel. And a chipmunk. And a possum . . .

Okay, nothing *unusual* was popping out of the redwood trees.

Squish.

The noise came from behind her.

Lennie whipped around toward the source of the sound— her mattress. There was nothing there. But her pillow looked a bit smushed.

"Michael!" Lennie shouted, reaching for a ball of socks and throwing it toward the pillow. "Get out of here!"

He flickered into view. He was sitting on top of her pillow, right where it was indented. He chortled, like invisibly sneaking into her room was the cleverest thing he'd ever done.

Lennie wasn't really in the mood. Yesterday he'd smashed a water balloon onto her head and never actually apologized for that. *And* he lied to Mom and Dad when Lennie tried to tell them about it. Just looking at him now, smirking at her, made her flush with annoyance.

"Go away!"

"What's the magic word?"

"Please?" she said impatiently.

"Nope."

"Abracadabra?"

"Nope."

"I do not have time for this," Lennie groaned. "And besides, I told you not to come in my room without asking!"

Michael held up a hand. "No, no, no. You said you didn't want to *see* me in your room again," he said. "So now you see me . . ." He went invisible again. "Now you don't!"

Lennie tried to stop herself from laughing, which turned into one extraordinarily loud snort. She could feel her anger from yesterday thawing.

"What are you doing?" Michael asked.

"I could ask you the same question, Mr. Room Intruder," Lennie said, glancing out the window again. Still nothing. "I'm looking for Poppop."

Michael crawled to the edge of her bed and hung upside down off the side. His hair wasn't very long—jet black, stick-straight, and silky, just like hers—but in this position it almost touched the floor.

"Does Poppop *have* to come over? He smells like earwax," Michael complained.

"But it's always so fun when Poppop does his magic!"

"Fun? Or BORINGGGGGGGG."

"Uh . . . *fun*," she said firmly.

Michael stuck out his tongue. "But then he naps for like ten hours in the afternoon and snores like an elephant! And then I'm doing *nothing* while we wait for him to wake up."

"Then spend time with me!"

"EW! GROSS! NEVER!" Michael shouted.

Lennie rolled her eyes. "Okay, I guess you're uninvited

to play with me. I take it back," she said, doing that sneaky *reverse psychology* thing her dad always pulled on her.

"Fineeeeeee," Michael said. But then his eyes lit up. "Invisibility standoff! If you win, you can make me do whatever you want for a whole hour. If I win, you have to do what *I* want."

Lennie grinned. "You realize I've been practicing every day for the past year."

Michael shrugged.

"And I always last two seconds longer than you."

"Sounds like you're chicken!" he taunted.

Lennie hopped on the bed and sat pretzel-style, facing her brother. "You're on."

"READY, SET, GOOOOOOOO!" Michael shouted.

She and Michael both vanished at the same time. And the odd sensation returned. Like a wave of chills traveling from the top of her head down to the tips of her toes. She held her breath and concentrated.

Her veins felt like they were pulsing. She wished she were Poppop—this would be *so easy* for Poppop. There wasn't anything he couldn't do. He could be invisible forever if he wanted to. And he *never* drained of magical energy. Unlike Lennie, who was feeling especially exhausted at that very moment. She had a second or two of invisibility left, and she could feel her skin begin to prickle. Invisible sweat formed again on her invisible brow.

She looked at Michael . . . his form was slowly becoming

translucent, the outline of his body wiggling like jellyfish tentacles.

She let out a breath, and her skin flickered back into view.

"AHA!" Michael shrieked. "I WIN! YOU LOSE!"

"WHAT?!" Lennie said. "ARE YOU KIDDING? You went visible *way* before I did—"

"KIDS! DINNER!" Lennie's dad called.

"LAST ONE TO THE TABLE IS A BIG LOSER!" Michael shouted, and he dashed out of her room, elbowing his way past her.

She tried to shove him back, but she was eating his dust. So she strolled to the kitchen coolly, pretending like she didn't care that she'd lost . . . or that Michael shouted, "I WIN! YOU STINK!" at her as she sat down.

Lennie reached for the dinner her dad had cooked, but he waved a spoon at her. "Wait until Poppop arrives!"

"Why would you call us down for dinner if you won't let us eat?" Lennie said, her mouth watering from the smell of garlic and chili peppers in the kitchen.

"Poppop will arrive any minute," her mom said, looking eagerly at the window for her own father to arrive. Then she turned to Lennie's dad. "Smells delicious, honey! Thanks for cooking."

Lennie's dad always cooked whenever Poppop Pomporromp was supposed to arrive because Poppop couldn't get enough of her father's sisig. It was his favorite— and Lennie's favorite, too. She put her chin on the table and stared over her empty plate, practically drooling.

But then, when her parents' backs were turned, she took a bowl of rice and hid it in her lap.

Michael wasn't as sneaky. He lunged across the table, grabbed a spoonful of the pork, and shoveled it into his mouth.

"Michael, we said to wait!" Mom groaned. "Look at how polite Lennie's being!"

Lennie rolled the rice between her palms, morphing it into a little rice ball under the table. When her mom turned again, she popped it into her mouth.

"LENNIE ATE SOMETHING, TOO!" Michael tattled in a singsongy voice.

Lennie kicked Michael under the table.

"AND NOW SHE KICKED ME!"

"Lennie, stop instigating!" her dad scolded. "Michael, stop being instigated! Both of you—save something for Poppop!"

Lennie glared at Michael, and he grinned at her as he took another bite of sisig. "Do you like seafood?" He stuck out his tongue, displaying a mouth full of chewed up pork. "SEE FOOD!"

"Gross," Lennie said.

"He's running late," her dad said, looking at his watch.

Her mom rubbed her temple. "He better not have gone hippo hopping again—"

"Hippo hopping?" Lennie said.

"When Poppop goes jumping on the backs of hippos. Very dangerous."

"I want to hippo hop!" Michael said.

"You do NOT!" their mom said firmly. "I can't tell you how many times Poppop's eluded authorities at safari sites and wildlife preservation centers."

"So . . . how *does* he escape?" Michael said carefully. Lennie was sure that he was taking mental notes on how to make a clean getaway.

"When he has his magic staff, your Poppop is invincible." She sighed. "I know that pesky staff helps amplify his powers, but it's more trouble than it's worth. Someone ought to smack him over the head with it every once in a while."

Lennie and Michael both laughed, though Lennie wasn't entirely sure whether her mom was joking.

"Don't worry," Lennie's dad said, bringing the last of the side dishes to the table. "He's supposed to arrive with Estella, right? She would *never* let him go hippo hopping. I'm sure he's just running late in Netherly. I bet he, uh, realized he forgot to pack socks."

"Or maybe he got stuck to the Jelly Floor!" Michael said, lighting up. "Mom, tell us again about the Jelly Floor!"

Their mom smiled. "You kids have heard that story *hundreds* of times."

"AGAIN! AGAIN!" Lennie and Michael both chanted. Lennie pounded her fists on the table, and Michael clanged his silverware against his glass—until their dad swooped in and stole his silverware right out of his hands before Michael could break yet another glass.

"Once upon a time," Mom said spookily, flickering invisible and uninvisible just for fun, which was *always* how she started a story about growing up in the Pomporromp Castle. Lennie clapped for her mom's performance. "When your aunt Tracy, uncle Philip #2, and I were *verrrrrrryyyyy* little, we snuck peanut butter and jelly sandwiches out of the kitchen and bewitched them with your grandfather's magical staff. And the sandwiches started growing . . . and growing . . ."

"And growing!" Lennie echoed.

"And growing!" Michael added.

"Until . . ."

"KABOOM!" all four Mercados said at the same time. They all knew the story by heart—Lennie knew it so well she felt like she had actually been there.

"The sandwiches exploded!" Mom continued. "Jelly was everywhere, high and low. Aunt Tracy, Uncle Philip #2, and I tried to clean it, and undo whatever spell we accidentally set off, but nothing worked. From that day on, the twenty-second story was floor-to-ceiling covered in jelly. So sticky that you can get stuck for days. So sticky that the jelly glued to the castle, and not even magic can get it unstuck."

"I love that story," Lennie breathed. She could listen to her mom's tales about Netherly every second of every minute of every hour of every day of every week of every month of every year. Netherly just sounded *so cool*. A whole separate realm where powerful wizards lived in harmony. A secret world where wizards were able to freely practice magic without fear of being discovered. Where every wizarding family had a castle and an estate. It was just too awesome to imagine. "Hey," Lennie said, not for the first time that week, "when are *we* going to visit Netherly?"

"Again," their dad said, "whenever your Poppop stops inviting himself over here and starts inviting us over there."

"I would like to go back home soon," their mom said. "It's been too long."

Michael tugged on the tablecloth. "Mom, Mom, Mom! Tell us another story about Netherly!"

"Do the ghoul story!"

"No," Michael said, "the moon room story—"

"No," Lennie said, louder, "you already requested the Jelly Floor story! It's *my* turn!"

"Kids, stop fighting—"

Ding-dong! came the sound of the doorbell.

"I'LL GET IT!" Lennie yelled, but Michael was closer and he started running. Lennie slid on her socks and Michael put out a foot to trip her, invisibling his leg just a fraction too late. She hopped over his invisible foot and gave him a very visible elbow in the gut.

"NO FAIR!" Michael said, but he was laughing.

They reached the door at the same time and opened it, fully expecting to greet Poppop Pomporromp with a big hug.

Only . . . it wasn't Poppop Pomporromp.

It was someone who was about to change everything.

A Special Invitation

At the door, there was a cat.

But no ordinary cat.

It was a cat wearing a bow tie and a monocle. And it was floating in midair.

Lennie's jaw dropped. She looked around the road for her poppop—it *would* be his idea of a joke to hide in a bush somewhere and levitate a cat in front of the door to spook them.

"What are you looking at, girl?" the cat snapped.

Lennie jumped in surprise. "It can talk!"

"I'm not an *it*, I'm a *him*. And are you going to invite me in? Your manners are truly abysmal." It—*he*—looked annoyed. Lennie thought cats pretty much always looked bothered, but this cat looked more bothered than any cat that Lennie had ever bothered to bother.

Besides a miserable expression, the cat had a black-and-white coat, which looked very much like a fur tuxedo. The red bow tie around its neck helped give the illusion that the cat was dressing up. It blinked up at Lennie with brilliant yellow eyes, one of which was hidden behind a monocle.

"You're not Poppop! Where's Poppop?" Michael asked.

"Your manners are equally awful. Also," he said with a sniff, "though I shudder to suggest such a horrific thing, you could use a bath."

From behind them, their mother darted up, her steps quickening as she saw who was standing—or floating—at the door.

"Fluffles?" Mom said in surprise. She snatched the cat and kissed him on the head, which the cat shook off. "What in the world are you doing here?"

"I prefer *Sir Fluffington the Fourth*, Stacey, for the last time," the cat said, glowering at her. "I have been knighted by your father, and you disrespect my title. Now, are you going to let me in?!"

Her mom knew this strange, magic cat?

The cat floated to the kitchen, and Lennie, Michael, and Mom followed.

"This is my childhood cat! Fluffles—"

"SIR FLUFFINGTON THE FOURTH!" the cat hissed. "I come bearing a message of the utmost importance from the Prime Wizard Mortimer de Pomporromp!" Fluffles said majestically. "Wait . . . hold on." He arched his back. *"Wock! Wock! Wock! Wock! HNGUH!"* And he expelled a giant pile of vomit on the kitchen floor. "A present for you," Fluffles said with a small bow. "You're welcome."

Her mom side-eyed Lennie's dad, which was her way of telling him to get a mop.

"What's the important message?" Lennie asked.

"Mortimer's not coming."

"Yay!" Michael cheered.

"What?!" said her mother in a huff. "That's just typical, isn't it? Changing plans at the last minute."

Fluffles held up a paw for silence. "He's not coming to you . . . because *you* are going to *him*."

Lennie stood up. Were they being invited to Netherly? To Poppop Pomporromp's castle? To his world of magic?

Her mother folded her arms. "Why the change of plans?"

"Well," Sir Fluffington the Fourth said, with an undeniable air of smugness. "The next Wizardmatch has officially begun."

The word *Wizardmatch* meant nothing to Lennie, but instantly, her mother blanched and gripped her chair. Tight. And Dad had deep lines on his forehead.

"Well, that's not the reaction I hoped for—I wanted cheers and whistles and maybe someone to pet me for eight hours."

"What is Wizardmatch?" Lennie asked in almost a whisper.

"It's a wizard dating website," Michael said matter-of-factly.

Her mom swooped down and grabbed the cat by the scruff of his neck, dangling the animal like a shirt on a clothesline.

"No, Michael," their mom said firmly, plopping the cat on her lap and petting him. "Before we talk about Wizardmatch, you kids have to understand something about Poppop. Something I've never told you."

Lennie held her breath.

"My father—your grandfather—Poppop Pomporromp," Mom said, "is a Prime Wizard."

"We know that," Lennie said.

"Duhhhhhhh," Michael added.

"There is only one per wizarding family, and he has both power and duty—"

"Doodie!" Michael giggled.

Mom gave him a pointed stare. "This is serious. The Prime Wizard is the heir to the family's powers and is the caretaker of the Pomporromp Castle in Netherly—"

"We know," Lennie said.

"I know you know," Mom said. "I'm trying to tell you what you *don't* know: Prime Wizards aren't born. They are *selected*."

Selected? Lennie had always thought that Poppop had just been born lucky.

"When Poppop was your age, his only power was the ability to control small amounts of fire. But his powers were very limited, much like yours are."

"So how did he get to be so strong?" Michael asked.

"Just listen," Dad said. "Mom is trying to explain."

Mom nodded at Dad before continuing. "Magic is in our genes. It gets passed down from generation to generation. So all of Poppop's kids—my siblings and I—inherited a small piece of the Prime Wizard's magic. And then I passed that piece of magic on to you. And then you'll pass a sliver of magic on to your kids. And so on."

"This is confusing!" Michael said.

"This is genetics," Dad said.

"You both inherited my invisibility, and the chances are likely that your kids would have that same ability. But *occasionally*, a different power is awakened. Your children, for example, could have the power to make things fly, instead of invisibility. In simple terms: Most of your magic is sleeping. But whoever becomes the Prime Wizard gets all their magic woken up."

"And," Lennie asked carefully, "how do you become the Prime Wizard?"

"You have to win Wizardmatch."

"But what *is* Wizardmatch?" Michael said.

"Only *one* person can be the Prime Wizard. When it's time to choose a new one, the old one hosts a competition to select the next one," their mom explained. "Wizardmatch tests magical ability, creativity, wit, and determination. If one of you were to win, not only would you be able to go invisible . . . you'd have ALL of Poppop's powers."

Lennie was smiling so hard her cheeks ached.

"So . . . whoever wins becomes the new poppop?" Michael asked. "I could totally do that. All I'd have to do is bathe in oatmeal and stick my dentures out at people."

Lennie jumped to her feet. Tears were brimming in her eyes—joyful tears. Exultant tears. Jubilant, delighted, happy-beyond-happy tears. "This is *literally* my dream come true!" Lennie yelled. Her skin was tingling with excitement.

"You know I've been practicing to increase my powers!"

"Of course we know! You've been ignoring your homework for magic practice, *neneng*," her dad said with a smile.

"*I* could be the next Prime Wizard!"

"Well, hey!" Michael said, hands on his hips. "What about me?"

"One of us could be the next Prime Wizard," she corrected herself. But inside, her heart was singing *me, me, ME!*

Mom frowned and shared a glance with their father across the table. Lennie didn't understand . . . this seemed like *good* news! Get-up-and-dance-around-the-kitchen kind of news!

Dad cleared his throat. "Don't you want to know how Poppop Pomporromp's story ended?"

"We know how it ended," Lennie said. "He won Wizardmatch!"

"In one way, yes. But in another way, he lost a lot," Mom said. She frowned. "I don't know all the details, but apparently, the last Wizardmatch competition shattered Poppop's relationship with his siblings."

"Wait, what?" Lennie said. She scoured her brain for any mention—any *whisper*—of Poppop's siblings in one of her mom's stories, but nothing was coming to mind. "Poppop doesn't have siblings!"

Her mom stopped petting Fluffles for a moment. Fast as a snapping turtle, the cat turned and gave her hand a sharp bite. "OW!" Mom yelped. "What'd you do that for?!"

"That's a love bite," Fluffles said.

"I'm bleeding!"

"But he *can't* have siblings," Lennie said, shaking her head. "Do I know them?"

Their mom glared at the cat as she massaged her bitten hand. "Lennie, *I* don't even know them. I didn't even learn about them until I was a teenager. I don't know what happened or why, but after your great-great-grandfather chose Poppop as the winner of Wizardmatch, Poppop never spoke to his sisters or brother again."

"It's the reason we never told you about Wizardmatch," her father added. "We didn't want you kids to feel competitive with each other. We're a family—that means we're all on the same team. Right?"

Michael stood up and put one foot on the kitchen chair. "I'm the team leader!"

"Feet off the furniture," Dad said automatically.

"We'd be so proud if one of you became the Prime Wizard," Mom said, "but it's more important to Dad and me that you two are lifelong friends."

The cat hopped off of her mom's lap and circled the kitchen table. "That's quite enough talking. I can't just wait around all day for you to share your *feelings* and all that. I have things to do, you know—I have about five naps to take!" the cat complained. "So if you'll *listen,* I'd like to share the rest of the Prime Wizard Mortimer de Pomporromp's message now."

The cat cleared his throat and hacked up a hairball in the process.

"Mortimer de Pomporromp is expecting you at the castle tomorrow morning."

Lennie waited eagerly for the rest of the message, but Fluffles went back to grooming himself.

"That's it?" her mom said.

"TA-DA," Fluffles added. "What do you want . . . fireworks?"

"We get to go to Mom's old house!" Lennie said to Michael, her heart fluttering. They were going to Poppop's castle! In Netherly! For the first time! Ever!

"You'll be living there for the summer," Fluffles said. "All three of you."

"But there are four of us," Michael said.

"Regrettably," Fluffles said, "only direct descendants of the Prime Wizard are invited to view Wizardmatch."

Lennie and Michael looked at Dad, who was smiling sadly. "It's okay," he said slowly. "I don't have that many vacation days anyway."

"I'll be there with you both," their mom said firmly. "Walking you through the competition, every step of the way."

"Don't worry! You're going to have such a good time, you won't even notice I'm gone!" Their dad winked. "You two have to promise me you'll have fun!"

Lennie looked at Michael and grinned. This was the best

thing to happen to her summer—and maybe to her life. All her practicing was going to pay off. The competition would be, well, competitive, but she was going to make her dreams come true. Hope blazed within her, and she had a real fire in her belly, a fire as strong as the sun.

And like the sun, Lennie was going to shine.

Pomporromp Castle

Lennie couldn't sleep. Her body was exhausted, but she couldn't quiet her brain. *Finally, finally, finally,* she kept thinking. She was finally going to see Poppop's castle up close—travel to Netherly, visit a world of wonder and secrets. She'd see magic. But not just see it—she'd *acquire* it. Become the next Prime Wizard. The first female Prime Wizard in a long, long, ridiculously long line of male Prime Wizards. And—as far as she knew—the first half-Filipino Prime Wizard.

In the dark, Lennie glanced at the shadowed outline of her suitcase in the corner of the room—she'd never packed so fast before. She was READY! She could go at a moment's notice! She could run a marathon! She could do fifteen cartwheels in a row. . . .

Lennie didn't remember dozing off, but suddenly a paw pressed on her face. It felt like a cat was dancing on her cheek. Actually, a cat *was* dancing on her cheek.

"What are you doing?"

"Hip-hop. Because it's *hip* to *hop* out of bed," the cat said. Lennie groaned in response. "Now I'm doing the cha-cha. Because you should feel fully *cha-cha*-charged. Now the waltz. Because it's time to *waltz* on over to Pomporromp Castle."

Lennie popped up so fast that Fluffles tumbled off the bed with a thump.

"OUCH!"

"Ooops!" Lennie said, putting on her glasses. She reached out to give Fluffles an apology back scratch, but he hissed at her and raced away.

Lennie got out of bed. It was still mostly dark in her room, but a tiny sliver of sunlight was reaching through her blinds. It was earlier than the time she got up for school. But she wasn't even tired—just excited.

She dragged her suitcase out of her room. She grunted and panted as she lugged it to the top of the stairs and then paused for a minute to catch her breath. It was much heavier than she remembered, seeing as she only packed some clothes and books and her clarinet, even though she knew she wasn't going to practice anything but magic. A trickle of sweat slid down her forehead.

Michael jumped out of his room, swinging his suitcase around with ease. "Hi, sis!" he whistled. "Whatchya doing?"

"Resting," Lennie said through gritted teeth.

Michael blinked a few times. "Why? Is your suitcase mysteriously heavy for some unknown reason?"

She studied him—his eyes were tiny unreadable slivers. He bit his lip, but the corners of his mouth were upturned in an unmistakable smirk.

"What did you *do*?" she said, flipping her suitcase and opening it up.

Michael sniggered and snorted and chuckled and chortled as she removed three bricks and a bowling ball from her suitcase.

"Not funny," Lennie said, lunging forward and grabbing him in a headlock. She mussed up his hair with her fist.

"Get off!" Michael laughed.

"Say UNCLE!"

"UNCLE!"

"Say UNCLE HUMPHREY."

"UNCLE HUMPHREY! UNCLE HUMPHREY!"

She let go of him and admired her handiwork—he looked like a porcupine.

"One day I'm going to be bigger than you," Michael said. "And you'll never be able to get me again!"

"Dream on, pip-squeak!" Lennie snickered.

She dragged her suitcase out into the yard, which was essentially a forest. They lived in the middle of the woods, with redwood trees for miles. They had to live somewhere private because of their powers.

But Netherly was a safe space for wizards. According to her mom, there were so many different wizarding families that lived in Netherly that the Pomporromp Castle was just one estate out of hundreds.

"Lennie?" her mom called from across the yard. "Are you ready?"

Her mom had twisted her caramel-colored hair into a fancy

updo, and her brown eyes shone as she looked at Fluffles. "Are we ready?" her mom asked again as Lennie approached. "Can we go now? What are we waiting for?" She was practically leaping with excitement—and no wonder! Her mom grew up in Pomporromp Castle, and hadn't been back since Lennie was a baby.

Lennie's dad bent down and put a hand on each of his kid's shoulders. "Now remember you two—you're on the same team. The Mercado team. So work together and support each other as much as you can. No matter what happens, I'm proud of you both."

First, he hugged Michael and whispered something to him before kissing him on the cheek. "Blech!" Michael said, walking away with Mom and Fluffles.

When it was Lennie's turn, her dad said in her ear, "I'm always rooting for you, *neneng*!" and kissed her on top of her head.

Lennie looked up at her dad. "I wish you could come! I'm so nervous."

Her dad laughed. "You? Nervous?! I don't believe it!" he said with a wink. "You don't practice every day for nothing! I don't know much about magic, but I know you. And *you* are extraordinary."

Lennie hugged him tightly.

Fluffles twitched his whiskers impatiently. "Are you just about finished over there?" he said. "I don't have all day, you know!"

Lennie skipped over to Fluffles, her mom, and her brother, and her dad helped carry her suitcase the rest of the way.

"I ingested the transport to the Pomporromp estate yesterday," proclaimed Fluffles. "Let's see if I can dig it back up." Fluffles arched his back and began to cough. *Wock! Wock! Wock! Wock! HNGUH!* Vomit ejected from his mouth with an enormous *SPLAT* onto a redwood tree.

The spot glowed orange for a second—then began to grow in size, bigger and bigger and BIGGER until the whole tree trunk was glowing and translucent.

"COOL!" Michael said. "BARF DOOR!"

Lennie cringed. This was *disgusting*. She was hoping for something a bit more . . . majestic. Maybe a ball of light. Or a special orb.

Lennie looked at the cat. "This is going to take us to Netherly?"

"Is there a *problem* with the door I created?" Fluffles said, his voice a warning.

"Er . . . no, it's fine. Great. Beautiful, even," Lennie stammered. She never thought she would describe throw-up as beautiful.

"Good. Then you first, Stacey."

"GO, MOM, GO!" Michael shouted.

Mom smiled and touched her hand to the tree. For a moment, the vomit stain glowed beneath her hand. There was a sound like a bell chime, soft at first, getting louder and louder each second—so loud that Lennie and Michael both covered their ears. But it wasn't just the sound that vibrated—the air wobbled, too. At last, with a sound like a slurp, their mom disappeared right before their eyes.

"Mom!" Lennie said, running forward and grabbing at air. "She's gone!"

"Don't worry, she's fine," Fluffles said.

Lennie's stomach churned. That didn't *look* fine. It looked painful! Was Fluffles 100 percent sure it was safe? What if the door was broken? What if it transported her to the middle of the ocean? Or outer space, where she'd tumble through nothingness forever and ever and—

"Ladies first," Fluffles said with a little bow. "You're next, Lennie."

She tentatively stepped forward. Then she turned around and looked to her dad, who nodded in encouragement, while Michael said, "Chicken! *Bawk bawk!*"

She instantly swallowed her fear.

The moment she touched the tree, she felt cold. The portal was like icy slime beneath her fingers, and her whole body erupted in chills. Lennie tried to call for her dad or Michael, but the ringing was much louder now—not just around her, but as if it were coming from inside her.

Her navel lurched; an invisible fishhook was yanking her upward by her stomach. The world went black. And then, the feeling like she was on the biggest drop of the tallest roller coaster. Falling. She held her breath in fright.

At once, the feeling of dropping ceased, and Lennie

stood there, in darkness, as a cool wind prickled her skin. Then, the more Lennie blinked, the more Netherly came into focus.

And she was standing on the edge of a cliff.

"Lennie!" her mom shouted. "BE CAREFUL!"

Lennie immediately dropped to the ground, her heart pounding as her chin rested over the edge. She dared to peek straight down: She was staring out over a dark and murky sea, as black as oil. The rough waves crashed against the wall of the cliff, the water splashing back with violent spittle. The salty air tickled her nose.

"Get away from the edge!" her mom said. Lennie was still lying down, but her mom took it upon herself to drag her by the feet.

Lennie got to her knees and looked left to see a swimming pool, right up against the edge of the cliff. But it was filled to the brim with smooth brown goop. She eyed it warily.

"Don't worry," her mom said, sensing her hesitation. "It's only pudding."

"Pudding?"

"You know how your grandfather likes his food." Her mom dipped her hand into the pool and licked the pudding off her fingers. "Mmmmmm!"

"Wait, we're here?" Lennie said, perking up. "This is the Pomporromp estate?" She squinted into the ocean, looking for some dramatic palace in the middle of the inky water. "Where is the castle?"

Her mom laughed. "Len, you're looking the wrong way!" Then she turned Lennie around by the shoulders.

Lennie's heart fluttered as she stared. Pomporromp Castle looked to be fifty stories tall—at least! It was shaped a bit like a tornado—thin on the bottom, then funneling out. As Lennie looked up at the castle, up up up toward the sun, she *swore* it looked like it was teetering and tottering like a spinning top.

The castle was smack-dab in the middle of the estate grounds, which seemed to stretch from the ocean-side cliff to a wall of trees all the way across the property. Near the trees seemed to be a muddy patch of land, but the rest was just grass as far as the eye could see. A color of grass so fresh, so green, so bright, so vibrant that it made Lennie's eyes water.

She'd been dreaming of this her whole life, but it was even better than what she'd imagined.

"Where's your brother?" her mom said. "He should have been here by—"

POP! Michael flickered into view. *PLOP!* Michael dropped right into the pudding pool.

"I'M COVERED IN POOP!" he cried, thrashing around. "Delicious poop, but POOP!"

"Michael, get out of there!" Mom barked.

"Here, take my hand," Lennie said, reaching out to help him.

But instead, he yanked her in.

"YOU JERK!" she cried, splashing him with pudding.

Fluffles appeared on the side of the cliff. When he saw Lennie and Michael in the pudding pool his ears went back. "This is *hardly* time for a swim!" he sniffed. "You are about to see Estella—and possibly the Prime Wizard! I demand you groom yourselves! Allow me to demonstrate," Fluffles said, sitting on the ground and licking himself all over.

Fluffles paused. He looked up and glared at them until they both began licking themselves. Michael slurped pudding off his kneecap; Lennie sucked pudding out of her hair. Michael consumed the pudding around his mouth; Lennie ate pudding out of her toes.

They did pretty well, except for their elbows. Lennie knew it was scientifically impossible to lick her own elbow. But it didn't stop her and Michael from trying.

"Much better," Fluffles said at last, staring up at them through his monocle. "Why, you two are practically glowing!"

"That's saliva," Lennie said.

"It's a good look on you," Fluffles said. "Now, there will be a family reunion feast at seven in the fancy dining room. Don't be late. Stacey, I have to get more families. Can you handle taking the kids into the castle from here?"

"Of course!" Mom said, swinging her duffel bag. "This way, Team Mercado!"

Lennie followed, dragging her suitcase across the grass. The weather was perfect—a strong, warm sun and a fresh sea breeze. With the faint smell of chocolate wafting from her elbows.

As Lennie got closer to the castle, she realized that it was so much more complicated than she first thought.

The entire castle was a mix of different buildings cobbled together. There were parts of stone cottages, clock towers, igloos, huts, Tudor houses, castle turrets, brick chimneys, gothic rooftops, and fancy columns. Some parts were right side up, and some were sideways. The longer she looked at the castle, the more details she seemed to find. She wondered how many pieces of architecture her poppop must have transported here to stitch together this masterpiece.

"Pretty interesting, right?" her mom said. "It's actually an old family tradition—whenever a new Prime Wizard is selected, he gets to add a new piece to the castle."

"He?" Lennie said, folding her arms.

"Or *she*," her mom corrected herself.

"She?" Michael said, folding his arms.

Their mom sighed.

"When I'm Prime Wizard," Michael said, "I'm going to turn the whole building into a hot dog."

"Mom, what's that?" Lennie asked, pointing just ahead. There were gravestones all over, with writing too small to read from this distance. And now that she was getting close, she could see that the ground looked like chunky sauce.

"Ah, yes," her mom said. "The Garden of Goulash."

"What's goulash?" Michael asked.

"It's like a stew with meat and tomato sauce. This ground is made of it, but, well, don't eat it. We're not exactly sure where the meat comes from. The fact that it's next to the graveyard isn't too promising."

Lennie gagged.

"Disgusting!" Michael said with glee.

"And more important than not eating the mystery meat," her mom said, "is *do not* go into the borderlands." She pointed to a line of trees beyond the Garden of Goulash that made a fence at the edge of the property. "That is the area between the Pomporromp's estate and our neighbors' estate: the Oglethorpes. Another powerful wizarding family."

Lennie and Michael stood on their tiptoes, trying to see their next-door neighbors' house—but the line of trees may as well have been a brick wall.

"It's dangerous in there," their mom said, pulling them both into a hug. "Poppop and Madame Oglethorpe both fire a lot of spells into the borderlands, so it's become a booby-trapped area. No going in there without an adult, okay?"

Michael grinned at Lennie, and she knew what he was thinking: that booby traps sounded like a lot of fun.

"I can't wait to show you the inside!" Mom called, holding the front door open for them, and they all squeezed inside the narrow doorway.

And then Lennie was in the lobby of Pomporromp Castle. Looking inside, she knew that she was instantly home.

The whole interior of the castle was perfectly circular and was made of shiny cherrywood that glowed almost golden. There were no stairs, just a spiral ramp that wrapped around the castle like a giant Slinky. The banisters were thick—perfect for sliding down. Lennie tilted her head back to see the ceiling far above. A round glass roof—like an open eye—gave her a clear view of the cloudless sky.

Just then, a whirring noise grew louder and LOUDER. Someone wearing a full-face helmet was skateboarding down the ramp. The rider stopped directly in front of them, popped off the board with a wheelie, and took off the helmet.

It was Estella, her poppop's assistant. She sometimes came with Poppop on his visits to Lennie's home. She always snuck them magical candy that made them sneeze sparkles.

She shook her springy hair out and kicked the skateboard across the open atrium. Then she pulled a scroll from out of her pocket and began to read in a monotone voice.

"Welcome," she said, "to the glamorous, grandiose, gargantuan, beautifultacular, wonderfulicious, megamazing Pomporromp estate. I am your greeter, Estella Jane Wixson—"

"We know who you are, Estella!" Lennie said.

"Duh!" Michael added.

She looked around warily. "I have to read this, or Mortimer will have a croc."

"You mean, have a cow?" said Mom.

"If only!" Estella said. "A cow would be much easier to handle! Fewer teeth." She looked around warily. "But," she whispered, tucking the scroll into her pocket, "I won't tell if you won't! Now . . . hold out your hands," she said to

Lennie and Michael. And then she began piling things on. "Here's your map, magnifying glass, compass, sundial, telescope, quadrant, astrolabe, and—oh yes—your protractor."

"Protractor?" Lennie groaned.

"Of course! To help you navigate the castle."

"TOO MUCH STUFF!" Michael said, wobbling under the weight of all the tools.

"Here," Estella said, handing them each a fanny pack. "Everything's designed to fit inside this."

Lennie gingerly put her items on the floor, while Michael flat-out dropped his load. They both clipped on the fanny packs.

"These look dorky," Lennie said.

"No, you look . . . trendy," their mom said halfheartedly.

"You can walk up the ramp to get to where you're going," Estella said. "But I don't recommend it. Mortimer has this horrible habit of poking people who are walking. A slow poke for the slowpokes. So, I recommend using the skateboards." Estella smiled. "Your poppop is very excited about them. He wanted to make the castle more hip."

Lennie didn't know anyone her own age who skateboarded. She wondered if Poppop had missed the mark on this one.

"When I'm Prime Wizard, we'll all roll on giant meatballs," Michael said.

"To summon a skateboard, all you have to do is whistle, and one will come zooming your way. Stacey, you'll be staying in your old room, of course. Lennie, Michael, you two are staying in the Cheeseburger Chamber. Now if you excuse me, I have a few errands to do before the next family arrives!" Then she put her helmet back on and zoomed up the ramp on her skateboard.

Once Estella was gone, their mom put an arm around each of them and led them to the bottom of the ramp. She whistled three times, and three skateboards came rolling down to them.

"Let's hope I don't break my neck on one of these things," said Mom, tentatively stepping onto the skateboard. But the moment her foot touched the board, she zoomed off.

Lennie jumped after her. She found she didn't even have to pedal herself up the ramp—the skateboard defied gravity, moving upward with magic. And it was *fast*. So fast that Lennie lost her breath somewhere around the second floor and didn't find it again until the fifteenth floor.

"WHEEEEEEEEEEEEE!" Michael shouted from behind her. "NO HANDS! NO FEET, EITHER!" He jumped up off his skateboard and back onto it again without losing a beat.

As they rolled up and up and UP, each floor looked identical. There was always a landing—and then an archway— that led into whatever was on each floor. *I'll have to study my map later*, Lennie thought. There was no way she'd be able to navigate without it. Luckily her mom was leading the way.

"THERE IT IS!" Lennie suddenly shouted as she rocketed past the twenty-second floor. "THE JELLY FLOOR! LOOK, MICHAEL! LOOK!"

The floor, the myth, the legend. It was the only level in the cherrywood castle that looked different—because it was sopping with thick, purple jelly. The landing, the archway, and the hall beyond—all of it was glopping and glistening. She could tell, even without touching it, that it was just as sticky as her mom always said.

Michael shrugged. "Whatever. It's okay I guess."

"You're crazy," she said. "It's the best thing in the world." She bent her knees and her skateboard began to roll faster— away from Michael and closer to her mom.

"I *love* this castle!" Lennie breathed. "It's like no place I've ever seen before."

Her mom smiled warmly. "You know that the Prime Wizard becomes the head of the Pomporromp estate, which includes the castle, the grounds, the Garden of Goulash, the pudding pool . . ."

"I could live here?"

"You *would* live here, Lennie."

Lennie grinned. Her mom had so many magnificent memories in this enchanted castle. And now, she'd get to make her own memories.

If she was lucky, maybe she'd make a lifetime full of them.

Family Reunion

Lennie and Michael spent the afternoon unpacking. Well, *Lennie* spent the afternoon unpacking. Michael shoved everything in drawers like he was stuffing a turkey, all of his clothes rolled up into little wrinkled balls.

Then he sat on the bottom of a bunk bed that looked like a cheeseburger. The whole room was bizarre. The wardrobes were shaped like ketchup bottles, the mattress resembled beef, the sheets were ruffled and green like lettuce, the comforter was round and tan like a bun, and the windows were red and in the shape of a sliced tomato. The wallpaper even had a bunch of dancing cheeseburgers with smiley faces on them.

Michael watched as Lennie meticulously folded her shirts, shorts, dresses, socks, and even her underwear, and placed them neatly into the dresser's drawers.

"Don't waste your time," Michael said. "Everything wrinkles when you wear it anyway."

Lennie crawled over to the wardrobe on her side of the room—she began to line her shoes up across the bottom, and she even fixed Michael's shoes, which were dumped in a heaping mess on the floor. "If I organize now, I'll save time later."

"Time for what?"

"Time to train, obviously. Invisibility flexes, stretches, squats . . ."

Michael hopped up on his knees and scooted his way to the edge of the bed. "Can I train with you?"

"Oh, *now* you want to train with me?" she said, hands on her hips. "I've been asking you to practice with me every day!"

"You're kind of a boring teacher. Whenever we practice magic together, you want me to do *work*."

Lennie rolled her eyes. "Imagine that! Well, I'm planning to train a lot. I want to be in tip-top shape to beat our cousins."

She sat down on the foot of Michael's bed. Even though Michael was technically her competitor, she knew it wouldn't hurt to train with him, or to have a friend in the competition. Besides, he was no match for her. He couldn't hold his invisibility nearly as long.

"Look," Lennie said. "As much as I love our cousins, I love you more."

"Ew," Michael said.

"Michael, if you're struggling during Wizardmatch, I'll help you. And you'll help me. And we can both get to the final round . . . and have better shots at actually being named the Prime Wizard."

"So . . . we're in an alliance? A SECRET ALLIANCE!"

"Sure, secret alliance. But it doesn't really have to be secret—"

"OF COURSE it has to be secret!" Michael said. "Secrets are sneaky. Just like being invisible!"

It was good to have an alliance, she thought. Lennie trusted her cousins Ellington and Raina, who she basically grew up with. But she knew her other cousins Jonathan, Anya, and Mollie would betray her the first chance they got. She loved them, but their whole family was ruthlessly competitive. Visits with them usually ended up with tossed board games and temper tantrums over "friendly" sports. Lennie didn't want to imagine what they'd be like when the stakes were so high.

And Lennie definitely couldn't trust her cousins that lived in Netherly. She'd never *actually* met them!

"We should seal our secret alliance," Michael said, "with an invisible high five."

"Yeah!" Lennie said, firing up her power. She and Michael both went invisible and high-fived—but as her hand swiped through empty air, her nose suddenly hurt.

"Owwww! Michael!" Lennie cried, visibling again. "You hit my glasses!"

"Oooops!" He giggled, clearly not sorry at all.

"There seems to be a lot of fun coming from this room," Sir Fluffington the Fourth said, peeking his face in. He sauntered inside and sat down on the carpet, resting his black-and-white face on his paws. "We felines don't have much fun—not unless there's a laser pointer around. Or a piece of string."

"I have a piece of string!" Michael said, pulling a shoelace off his shoe and dangling it in front of the cat.

Fluffles's whiskers twitched, trying to resist. But his pupils grew wide, and he swiped at the string with glee.

"So, have you finished transporting all our cousins?" Lennie asked.

"Indeed. It was an awful job, fetching everyone like a *dog*, but I had to do it," Fluffles continued, grooming himself. "I'm such a warm presence. I make everyone feel comforted with my charming personality."

Lennie and Michael blinked at him.

"Don't you think I'm friendly?" Fluffles snapped.

"Oh, yes," Lennie lied.

Michael smiled stiffly. "So. Very. Friendly."

The cat seemed satisfied with their answers, sticking his butt proudly in the air and prancing around the room.

"We're your favorites, though," Michael said. "That's why you're here!"

"My favorite is whoever's petting me," said Fluffles, nuzzling up against Lennie's leg. He arched his back and waggled his tail a bit. "Cough cough hint hint wink wink."

"There's no time for petting," Lennie said. "The family reunion dinner starts in fifteen minutes." She dug into her fanny pack for the map of the castle—and a magnifying glass to peer at some of the small lettering up close. "Here we are," she said, pointing to Cheeseburger Chamber on the map. "And we have to get . . ."

"Here!" Michael said, pointing to the nineteenth floor on their map, which was labeled Fancy Dining Room. According to the map, there was a Fancy Dining Room, a Casual Dining Room, and an In-Betweeny Dining Room. There were also three casual kitchens, one fancy kitchen, and a Dessert Turret—which was labeled on the map in red. *Warning: Exposure to This Tower May Cause Cavities. Proceed at your own risk!*

In the hall, as they edged to the ramp and the open atrium, all three of them whistled for a skateboard, though Sir Fluffington's whistle was much more like a howl. When three skateboards magically stopped in front of their feet, they hopped on and began to roll down the ramp.

Going down was a lot more terrifying than going up. The skateboard was fast and felt totally out of her control. Lennie was *certain* she was one wrong knee-bend away from being bucked off and dropping thirty stories through the open atrium right onto the floor.

"WHEEEEEEEEEEE!" Michael cried.

"AHHHHHHHHH!" Lennie responded. She closed her eyes, which possibly only made things worse. Her shrieks rang throughout the atrium as she whipped around the castle—round and round, like a teacup ride.

When they began to slow, Lennie opened her eyes. They sailed past the Jelly Floor and came to a wobbly stop on the nineteenth story. Lennie hugged the banister—she nearly kissed the floor!

Once she calmed, she took a few steps forward and looked around. There was a wooden archway ahead, leading into one enormous octagonal room. It seemed to hang off the side of the castle—since, when Lennie looked down, she could see a field of grass straight through the clear floor. The walls were vines, tangled up in one another. And the ceiling was sparkling and bright. Lennie tried to look at it, but it made her eyes burn.

"Avert your eyes!" Fluffles said. "It's made of pure sunlight."

She looked away, but Michael stubbornly stared at the ceiling. Lennie shook her head. Telling Michael *not* to do something pretty much guaranteed that he did it.

Across the room, in the far back, stood a table with serving plates on it. Next to the table was a throne engraved with jewels that spelled out: POMP FOR THE RUMP OF MORTIMER DE POMPORROMP. *Obviously where Poppop sits,* Lennie thought. For everyone else, there were two long tables. Even without a sign or label, Lennie knew that one had to be for the adults, and the other was for the kids.

There were already lots of people in the dining hall, chatting. Some Lennie knew well, like Ellington's mom (Aunt Tracy) and Anya's dad (Uncle Philip #2), who were both tucked away in the far corner of the room. Some Lennie recognized from pictures, like her oldest cousins Emma and Ethan, who had red hair, and Perrie, her young cousin with a purple pixie haircut, who was supposedly a genius. And some relatives she didn't recognize at all. Everyone was white, just like her mom, which shouldn't have surprised her—it *didn't* surprise her. She'd seen pictures. But still. Now that she was actually standing here in person, she was uncomfortably aware of how much she and Michael stood out. She wished her dad were here.

"Len, Michael, come here!" their mom called out, waving them over.

She was standing next to a woman who looked familiar, but Lennie couldn't remember *which* aunt she was. She and her mom both had the same long nose and round face, but her aunt's hair was so long it brushed the floor, and her eyes were blue instead of brown.

Mom put her arms around Lennie and Michael. "We have a big family, and it might take you some time to learn who's who, and that's okay. Don't worry if you can't remember everyone at first."

"Who's this?" Lennie asked, pointing to the woman next to her mom.

"I am your Aunt Lacey! And here are my children," she said, gesturing to four kids standing beside her. They looked very much like siblings, with sharp, icy blue eyes and hair so white it looked almost silver.

"Hullo!" said a boy who was clearly the oldest. "I'm Bo."

"Jolly-ho!" said the next oldest. "I'm Danielle."

"Good morrow!" said the third child. "I'm Alice."

"Salutations!" squeaked the youngest. "I'm Jordan."

"Er . . . hi," Lennie said. "I'm Lennie."

"We already know," said Danielle. "Our mom told us."

"Yes," Lennie said. "Our mom told me and Michael about you, too."

"No," Bo said. "Our mom can see the future. So it's different."

"She can see the future?" Michael said in awe.

"Well, she can see what's currently happening," said Bo in a voice that was light and airy.

"My, my, look what the cat dragged in!" said a man, suddenly butting into their circle. He put his hands on their mom's shoulders and said, "And Fluffles really must have dragged you! Just look at the bags under your eyes—"

"Philip #3! Hellooooooo," her mom replied in a chipper voice that was *so fake* Lennie almost laughed.

Lennie wasn't sure how she'd keep all three Uncle Philips straight, since they all had the same name. This particular Philip was a short man with a tricornered hat and a smug-looking face.

"Welcome back," he said, popping his hat off, and giving them an ironic bow. "It's been so long I didn't think you'd *ever* return! Do you even remember your way around the castle?"

"Good to see you, too," her mom said, smiling through gritted teeth.

"And *this* must be your progeny," he said, tipping his hat at Lennie and Michael.

"No, we're her kids," Michael said, folding his arms.

"Come, meet my son, Julien—the next Prime Wizard of Netherly."

Lennie could already feel herself scowling as Julien walked over. He seemed to be Lennie's age, with freckled cheeks and messy, mousy hair. He smirked.

"Hey, I'm Lennie," she said, trying to be nice. "This is my brother, Michael. Nice to meet you!"

"Pleasure," Julien said, in a way that sounded like it was most certainly *not* a pleasure.

Clang! Clang! Estella banged on a pot to get everyone's attention. "EVERYONE, TAKE YOUR SEATS!" Estella shouted.

Uncle Philip #3 turned to his son. "Julien, go show your cousins over to the kids' table."

Julien rolled his eyes as they trudged over.

"It's okay," Lennie said, trying to let him off the hook. "You don't have to lead us. We'll just sit there." She pointed to the end of the table, where she'd be close to the food, and her stomach let out a roar of approval. She started walking toward a seat, but Julien stepped in front of her.

"No," he said, pointing to the chairs closest to the exit. "That's where you sit."

"Oh, are there assigned seats?" Lennie asked.

"No. I'm sitting here. And I don't sit next to *bummers*," Julien sneered.

"Excuse me?" Lennie said, stepping protectively in front

of her brother. She didn't know what *bummers* meant, but from Julien's tone it was something nasty. "*What* did you just call us?"

"Bummers. You're wearing the bum-bag," he said, pointing at her fanny pack. "You're not from Netherly. And you've never been to Pomporromp Castle. I practically grew up here. This is my house. And I'm going to be the next Prime Wizard of the family."

Lennie scrunched her fists.

Julien took a menacing step closer. "*No offense,* " he said.

"No offense, but you are very offensive," Michael said, poking his finger in Julien's chest.

"No offense, but we're going to wipe the floor with you," Lennie added.

Julien smirked. "I'd like to see you even *try*. Bye-bye, bummers!"

He walked away and was graciously welcomed into a circle of cousins that included Bo and his siblings, and the older redheads, Emma and Ethan.

Lennie huffed as Julien sat down.

"What a booger!" Michael said, grabbing a chair near the exit.

Lennie sat next to her brother and glared down the length of the table at Julien. "I hate him, I hate him, *I hate him*," Lennie growled.

"Hate who?" said her cousin Ellington, plopping down on Lennie's other side.

"ELLINGTON!" Lennie yelled, wrapping her arms around her favorite cousin. Ellington's four-year-old sister, Raina, sat on Michael's other side; she hugged him around the neck as tightly as she could and pressed her cheek against his with incredible force, while he squirmed. "CAN'T! BREATHE!"

Then Raina and Ellington switched. Lennie picked up her little cousin and spun her around as Raina giggled.

Lennie hadn't seen her cousins since the holidays, and Ellington's wavy auburn hair was longer than ever, practically brushing her butt. Raina's was long, too—she always tried to copy whatever Ellington was doing. And although Lennie was only a year older than Ellington, she towered over her. Ellington was even tinier than Michael.

"Seriously, what was that about?" Ellington said, gesturing toward the Netherly cousins.

"We just met *Julien*," Lennie said.

"And he's the worst," Michael added.

Ellington winced. "Don't tell me! I don't want to know. I don't want to start a fight."

"Don't get involved!" added a voice she recognized. Lennie looked up to see her cousin Anya hovering above her, her curly hair framing a halo around her face. "Don't let *anything* distract you from the competition, or you'll lose. And we can't lose."

Anya and her teenage brother, Jonathan, both sat down across from Lennie, and Anya's younger sister, Mollie, sat with Raina, since they were almost the same age—and best of friends.

"Our dad's been really tough," Jonathan explained. "Ever since Fluffles told us about Wizardmatch, it's been nonstop *Winners win, kids. Winners don't lose. And what are we? We're WINNERS!*" he imitated in a deep voice.

That *did* sound like Uncle Philip #2. Their whole family was only happy when they were winning. And when they weren't winning, it was like hanging out with a hurricane.

Lennie didn't mind losing, occasionally, when the game was soccer or Monopoly or kickball. But when the game was Wizardmatch, Lennie'd be bringing nothing but her best. It was different, now that magic was on the line. This time, Anya and Mollie and Jonathan were just going to have to get used to losing.

"Long time, no see!" Anya said, nodding at Lennie and Michael. "Hey, where's Aunt Stacey?" she asked, looking around for Lennie's mom.

"Somewhere around here," Lennie said. "All the adults are catching up, I guess."

Lennie looked over at the adult table, and it seemed like the adults were all mixed together, no matter where they lived. But at the kids' table, there were *two whole empty chairs* between Lennie's group and the Netherly cousins. It was non-Netherly versus Netherly. The bummers versus the butts.

Lennie was going to comment, but suddenly the sparkly, sunlit ceiling dimmed. It was the moment everyone had been waiting for: her poppop, Mortimer de Pomporromp, the Prime Wizard, was making his grand entrance.

Sparkles of light erupted in the entranceway, and at first Lennie could only see Poppop's outline as he stood dramatically in the shadows. But then he pirouetted into the room and posed grandly, his staff held triumphantly in the air. Lennie stared at the long piece of wood with the rubber duck sitting on top. It was amazing to think that one day she might get to hold the staff, and that it would amplify the strength of *her* powers, just like it did for Poppop.

Her poppop looked exactly the same as he did last summer. Strands of his thinning gray hair were matted to his forehead, which was wrinkled and marked with liver spots. His long beard was slung over his shoulder like a scarf. And his woolen robes were an impressive shade of lavender.

"I say!" Poppop said. "I've been standing here frozen for thirty seconds, and no one is clapping! Clap, I SAY! CLAP!"

Lennie applauded for her poppop, as the whole family chimed in, too.

"Much better!" he said, walking in the aisle between the tables. When he reached the *precise* middle of the room, he waved his staff, which emitted a purple mist.

Cutlery came flying in from the hallway. The plates spun like tops; the floating glasses tossed their water into the air and caught it again; forks and knives and spoons were clanging together to a beat. Lennie's mouth hung open as she watched.

Her awe grew even greater as the food followed the cutlery. The potatoes rolled on the floor with a rumble. The chicken drumsticks swung through the air like pendulums. The broccoli casserole spun into the room like a tornado.

Poppop stood in the middle like a conductor, directing them all. Then, as the last dessert came straggling in, Poppop groaned and shed his woolen outer robe.

"WHO THOUGHT IT WAS A GOOD IDEA TO WEAR WOOL IN JULY?" he shouted, stamping on his robe.

"Um . . . *you*," Estella said. "You said, *Estella, fetch me my wool robe out of the storage closet,* and I said *Mortimer, it's far too hot, I think you should wear silk,* and you said, *Estella! I shall wear my finest, most impressive wool, and that is the end of the conversation!*"

"Right well," Poppop said, clearing his throat loudly. "I don't recall—"

"And then I said, *I think you'll regret it,* and you said *You're not the boss of me! Nah-nah-nah-nah boo-boo!*"

"OHHHHH-KAYYYY!" Poppop said, his cheeks growing red above his gray beard.

Then her poppop—the great Prime Wizard Mortimer de Pomporromp—took his spot on the throne.

Lennie sat up straight, trying to look every bit as graceful and powerful as a future Prime Wizard *should* look. Even though she'd seen Poppop every summer for as long as she could remember, there was only one chance to make a good eleventh impression.

Poppop stared out at his descendants. The silence was so loud and so long, it was almost painful. Lennie could cut the tension with a knife. Or a spoon. Or even with a stuffed animal. Michael began to twitch next to her, and she knew that if someone didn't break the silence soon, he'd yell out something totally inappropriate.

At last, Poppop cleared his throat. "Well, don't let the food get cold!" he said. "I spent three whole minutes whipping it up!"

Then, at once, it was a mad rush to the serving table. Kids and adults alike pushed and shoved for the chance to load their plates up with dinner. And right when Lennie reached for one of the serving spoons, Anya cut in front of her.

"Hey!" Lennie said.

"Snooze you lose!" Anya said, sticking her tongue out.

Lennie huffed. Anya had to be first at everything, and it was the most *annoying* habit.

Lennie waited until a few people got in between her and Anya before she turned back to the serving plates. There was a chocolate cake that exploded whenever someone tried to cut a slice. There were noodles that danced and meatballs that rolled away from your spoon.

And—most disturbingly—there was a plate full of carrots that talked. ("Take that other guy! He's sooooo much more delicious!" "Look at the bruising on my side—you definitely don't want to nibble on this!" "Please don't eat me! I have baby carrots!")

Lennie grabbed herself a turkey leg, potatoes, and a chocolate chip cookie. Only, when she got back to her table, she found that the turkey tasted like apple pie, the potatoes tasted like orange juice, and the chocolate chip cookie tasted like rotted fish.

"MADE YOU EAT!" Poppop shouted, chortling with laughter as family members all up and down both tables began spitting out their foods. "FOOLED YOU GOOD!"

Lennie spit the fishy cookie into her napkin and folded it into a ball. She was suddenly homesick for her dad's adobo.

"He did that every day he was at our house last August," Anya said, shaking her head. "He kept switching tastes around on us and laughing at our grossed-out reactions."

"It was disgusting," Jonathan said. "And the worst part about it was that there was no way to get him back!"

Ellington poked at her roast beef tentatively. "I don't even want to try this anymore." With a twist of her wrist, she floated the roast beef off her plate and back to the serving table, using her magic.

"Well, I think it's awesome," Michael said, shoveling handfuls of brussels sprouts in his cheeks. "I wish I could do that to people."

"You do *enough* damage," Lennie said. She turned to her cousins. "He broke two glasses in the past week."

"HEY!" he said.

"Careful, Len, or he'll break a third!" Jonathan joked, pointing to the glasses on her face.

Michael's eyes lit up, and he reached for her glasses with an invisible hand—but Anya froze Michael into place with her magic. His eyes darted around in panic, but the rest of him was stuck solid. Mollie clapped for her older sister, and Raina giggled.

"Thank you, Anya!" Lennie said. "And *don't you dare!*" she said to her brother. "You know I can barely see without these! And I need to see for Wizardmatch!"

At the reminder of the upcoming competition, Lennie glanced over at the Netherly side of the kids' table, where redheaded Ethan was changing his hair shape, growing it and shrinking it into different styles. Even the baby was giggling as Ethan morphed his hair into the shape of a walrus.

As Lennie observed the other cousins, Poppop Pomporromp stood up grandly, holding his arms in the air.

"HEAR YE, HEAR YE!" he shouted, stomping his rubber ducky staff on the floor. His voice was ten times louder than normal and echoing around the dining room. At once, everyone hushed. "Welcome to the magnificent Pomporromp estate. As you all know, I am ready to retire, which means I need to find the next Prime Wizard among my grandchildren. I shall explain the rules and provide insight into the mysterious challenges that are to come." He swung his beard onto his shoulder and cleared his throat. "Wizardmatch consists of THREE different tests, with one test every few days. After each test, I will eliminate a handful of contestants. And I shall determine—once and for all—

the winner of Wizardmatch after a third and final test."

Lennie took a deep breath. No matter what challenges came her way, she could handle them. She'd *have* to.

"So without further ado. That's a funny word," Mortimer said, scratching his beard. "Ado, ado. You know, I could say nonsense for hours and you'd *have* to listen to me!" He let out a great belly-shaking laugh before turning to Estella. "What was I saying again?"

"Nonsense."

"Ah, yes, now I remember—I was choosing a Prime Wizard!" Poppop continued. "Once the next Prime Wizard has been chosen, I will gift them my powers. They will get stronger and more powerful, while I get weaker and more brittle until I shrivel away and die."

"Mortimer!" hissed Estella.

"Honestly, Estella, what's the point of even hosting Wizardmatch if I don't get to be dramatic? Okay, I'll lose all my magic, but will retire to a nice beach in the neighborhood of Snorkenblossom."

Michael turned to her. "Where's Snorkenblossom?"

"Shhhhhhh!" she said, careful not to take her eyes off her grandfather.

"The competitors must be under the age of fifteen, of course," her poppop said.

Lennie looked around the table. Emma was scowling, and Jonathan was sulking.

She felt a pang of sympathy for them. It must be awful

to be the only two cousins not allowed to participate.

"I hope you are ready," Poppop said. "Because this summer you will fight to the death!"

"Mortimer!"

"Okay, fine! You will fight until you are severely injured or maimed."

"Mortimer!"

"Okay, fine! You will all be returned perfectly safely to your homes. ARE YOU HAPPY NOW, ESTELLA?" he shouted, stamping his foot. "Wizardmatch will push you to the brink physically and mentally. It will be challenging and cutthroat, and only one of you will walk away satisfied. And . . . well, it's time to admit: I have a little surprise for you all. A change in the rules. A twist."

A twist? The whole Pomporromp family erupted into whispers, and Lennie's stomach swooped. She didn't like the sound of a *twist*.

Poppop grinned, his dentures sparkling. "When I was a boy, Wizardmatch destroyed my relationship with my family. We were never able to recover from bitter competing. Henceforth, and from now on, we shall have no sibling against sibling in Wizardmatch!"

He turned to the adult table.

"Only one child per family can compete. And, my sons and daughters, you will choose the contenders."

Lennie's brain was spinning. Dread struck her. "But wait a

second!" she whispered to Michael. "If we can only have one competitor in our family, then . . ." She stood up and looked over at the adult table. Seeing her mom's tormented face, she suddenly knew:

Her mom was going to have to choose between Lennie and Michael.

Playing Favorites

The dining hall erupted into outrage.

Lennie felt sick. This was the worst news she'd ever heard in her whole life. She was prepared to compete against Michael. But now, one of them wouldn't get the chance to compete *at all*. Lennie stared at Poppop, who was holding up his hand for silence. *How could he do this? What is he thinking? Who is Mom going to pick?* Michael was quiet beside her, and she could tell he was just as anxious as she was.

"WHY!?" cried Uncle Philip #2. "Why are you doing this?"

"To save you from yourselves!" Poppop said dramatically. "I care about family. Family is all I've got—well, besides talent and power and fame and fortune."

Her aunts and uncles had begun to shout. Some of the cousins, too. Lennie sat there, stunned.

"My decision is final! SILENCE!" Poppop bellowed. Then he smacked his staff on the floor, and a white fog rolled out from the rubber ducky's mouth.

Lennie murmured to Michael, "This is not fai—"

But as the fog reached her, she found she could not finish her sentence. Her voice was gone—stolen by Poppop's spell!

And it wasn't just her: The whole dining hall had hushed. It was so silent Lennie could've heard a mouse poop.

"I *said* silence!" Poppop said. Then he addressed the adult table. "My sons and daughters—if you have multiple eligible children, then together we will privately discuss which child should compete. I will make my recommendations, but the final choice is ultimately up to you. You will announce your decision tomorrow evening."

All the adults looked steaming mad.

"Ahhhh . . . this silence is nice! Perhaps I should keep you like this!" Poppop said. "GOOD DAY, GOOD-BYE, GOOD RIDDANCE!" Then he stomped his magical staff on the floor again and POOFed into thin air.

The moment he was gone, the spell was broken, and everyone began complaining again.

"See the list outside the dining hall for your appointment time!" Estella shouted over the murmuring as they all shuffled toward the exit.

After dinner, the adults crowded around the appointment list, and out of sheer curiosity, Lennie took a peek, too. Her mom's appointment was at nine that night. Her stomach dropped a bit when she saw it.

Lennie and Michael headed back to their room in silence. Every time they caught each other's eyes, they looked away. She didn't know what to say. What would happen now that only one of them could compete?

All sorts of complicated thoughts burst in Lennie's head.

To be Prime Wizard—to awaken her magic and get to live in the Pomporromp Castle—was her dream come true. She wanted it hungrily, deep in her bones. She wanted it more than unlimited ice cream. More than a million dollars. More than a PUPPY—and she'd been asking for a puppy her whole life!

Finally, they reached their room and closed the door behind them.

"What are we going to do?" Michael said.

"I don't know," Lennie said, climbing onto the top hamburger bunk and pulling Michael up with her. Together, they lay on their stomachs, staring out through the red tomato window. From this distance, Lennie could see the pool of pudding wobbling in the wind. And she gnawed on her lip as she thought deeply about their situation.

She *had* to stand up for her dreams. Would it be a betrayal to Michael if she begged her mom to compete? As her mom always liked to remind them, she wasn't a mind reader—and if they wanted something, they had to use their voices and ask nicely for it.

But maybe Lennie didn't even have to worry. She was two years older than Michael, clearly more interested in magic—and better at it, too. Her mom knew how hard she practiced her magic. Her mom had to know how badly she wanted this.

"This is *sooooooo dumb*!" Michael said.

"I know," Lennie said gently, "but it's Poppop's decision. He runs the competition, so he makes the rules."

"It's still a dumb rule!" Michael said. "One of us isn't even going to have a chance!"

There was a pause.

"You're going to get it," Michael finally said. "You're older. Also, you're *perfect*. You're Mom's favorite."

"Mom doesn't have a favorite."

"Favorite, favorite, favorite!" Michael chanted.

"Stop saying that—"

"Faaaaaavvvvveeee," he said, *"rit!"*

"You're being obnoxious!"

"You're being obnoxious!" he mimicked.

"Stop copying me!"

"Stop copying me!"

Lennie sucked in a deep, angry breath. *Mimic this.* "I'm a huge poop face," she said.

"You're a huge poop face!" Michael said.

Ugh! She slid off the bed in a huff. "Fine! I'm leaving!"

"BYE!" he said, and she slammed the door behind her.

What's his problem? she thought. She skateboarded down the ramp, her dark hair flapping in her face. She figured she'd find Ellington in her room on the third floor and talk this out with her. But when she reached Ellington and Raina's cinnamon-roll-themed room, no one answered the door.

Rats, she thought. Where could her cousins be? Were they somewhere together, as a family? Ellington's mom was going to have to talk to Poppop at some point tonight, just like all of her aunts and uncles and mom . . .

She perked up. A wickedly brilliant idea had popped into her head. Why didn't she think of this before? She could go invisible and listen in on Mom and Poppop's meeting!

Peering at her map, heart pounding, Lennie scanned for any clue of where Poppop might hold these top-secret meetings. Her eyes locked on the Pomporromp Penthouse, which took up the top three stories.

That was it! That was where she needed to be!

She checked the clock in the hall: 9:03.

The meeting had already started. She had to hurry before she missed all of it!

She ran back through the hall so quickly that she slipped and banged her knee, but she didn't care. She was in a rush!

The skateboard whirled her up the ramp, past the fancy dining room, past the Jelly Floor, past the Cheeseburger Chamber, past many more floors that Lennie hadn't yet explored. At the forty-seventh story, she hopped off the skateboard.

There was a big, glittery, golden door at the top of the ramp. It was the entrance to Poppop's penthouse. Carved right into the gold itself was: DOOM AND DEVASTATION AND DEATH AWAIT ALL WHO ENTER!

Which was such a Poppop Pomporromp way of saying, "Please keep out."

Lennie put her ear to the door. There were two voices, but they were muffled.

"*Mumble mumble mumble* Lennie *mumble mumble*," came the sound of her mother's voice.

"But Michael *mumble mumble mumble whisper*," replied Poppop Pomporromp.

"*Grumble grumble* magic *mumble grumble* Wizardmatch," said her mom.

She *had* to get closer!

Lennie took a deep breath. If she used her invisibility, she had fifteen seconds to get inside and hide before her magical energy drained and she became visible again. *I can do this, I can do this, I CAN DO THIS*, she thought.

She flickered invisible. *One.* Very slowly, very carefully, she pulled the door open. *Two.* She tiptoed inside. *Three.*

She looked around. *Four.* The room was lined with hundreds of pictures of Poppop. In the center of the room, there was something that looked like an enormous screwdriver, twisting into an upstairs floor. *Five.* And behind the giant screwdriver was a desk—where her poppop was seated. A plushy chair faced the desk—where her mom was sitting with folded hands. *Six.*

But where to hide?

Then, Lennie saw it: a window curtain behind Poppop—one that draped to the floor, long enough to cover her feet. *Seven.* Lennie rushed forward. *Eight.*

Step, step, step. *Nine.*

Step, step—*creeeeeaaaaak.*

She froze.

"Did you hear something?" her mother asked her poppop.

Ten! Eleven! Twelve!

"It's an old house," her poppop said. "Now back to Wizardmatch."

Lennie held her breath. She was an arm's length away, with only three seconds to reach the drapes without her mom noticing. She crept forward—as quickly and quietly as she could. *Thirteen!*

She peeled back a side of the drapes. *Fourteen!* She tucked herself behind them just in time. *Fifteen!* Lennie flickered back into view. Sweat dribbled down her back. Her muscles ached.

But did she get away with it? Did her mom see the drape move?

Lennie held her breath and listened.

"But they're not matched, Dad," her mother said. "Lennie is stronger."

"By what, a millisecond?" Poppop said with a snort.

"Actually by two seconds. And every second counts."

"Pfffffffffftttttt!" Poppop said, blowing a raspberry. "Six of a dozen, half a dozen of a dozen!"

"What does *that* mean?"

"It's all the same," Poppop said. "Two seconds of a difference is no difference to *me*! Once the winner gets my unlimited powers, it won't matter that Lennie had two seconds on Michael."

"But Lennie is stronger," her mom said softly. Lennie's heart fluttered with pride. "Len has more focus—and she really cares about magic. I swear, Pop, you've never met anyone more determined. Lennie would excel in this competition. And more importantly, she'd be an amazing Prime Wizard."

"But Michael is more like *me*. And I want someone like me to be the next Prime Wizard," Poppop said firmly. "Lennie? Well, she's a sweet girl, but she's just . . . *not right*. She doesn't have that Prime Wizard look."

Didn't have the Prime Wizard look? *What* look? When she looked in a mirror, she saw a Prime Wizard! Lennie felt sick to her stomach.

There was a too-long pause in which no one said anything at all. At last, her mom spoke icily. "What are you saying, Dad?"

"I'm saying that you should select Michael. I think he's a more serious competitor. He makes me laugh, he has my nose, and he reminds me of myself. Besides, I can easily picture him wearing my collection of Prime Wizard robes. Michael has what it takes—I just know it."

Lennie gripped the drapes, feeling like she'd been punched in the gut. Or socked in the face. Or smashed over the head with a dinner plate. What did Poppop mean—*a more serious competitor*? Just last week, Michael was sticking peanuts up his nose and shooting them out with a big sneeze!

Lennie invisibled again so that she could stick her head out of the drapes to look at her mom and Poppop. Since Lennie was behind Poppop, she could only see his hair and neck—but she could see, dead-on, the flush creeping up her mother's cheeks.

Her mom sighed. "I know you identify with Michael . . . but I'm just not sure he's ready for this responsibility. He's very unpredictable. And with two seconds longer on her invisibility, Lennie's definitely more qualified. She's even been tutoring Michael on how to grow his powers. She's been working every day for the past year on her invisibility, and growing her magic is her lifelong dream. And she's—*here?*"

Her mom was looking right at her.

Shoot!

"Excuse me?" Poppop said.

"I mean—she's HERE for the long haul!" her mom said loudly. Lennie ducked back behind the curtain again, her stomach twisting into knots. "She's HERE for hard work! She's HERE for responsibility! She's HERE to be the first female Prime Wizard—and the first wizard of color! She's HERE for it all!"

"Look, Stacey, the final decision is up to you, but trust me . . . if you don't put Michael in the competition, you will be DOOMED."

"Are you just being dramatic, or . . . ?"

"DOOOOOOOOOOOOOOOOOOMED!" Poppop howled.

Her mom stood up. "Well, I'm going to go now," she squeaked. "Thanks for the meeting. I'm just going to stand by the door. And hold it open for a bit. Because it's warm in here, Dad, and you need a good draft. Yes, you need a nice cross breeze. I think it will help. By the way, *loooooove* what you've done with the place. What interesting new pictures you have on the walls. . . ."

Lennie invisibly scurried to the door, ducked under her mom's arm, and tapped her on the shoulder to say she was safely out of the room.

"Well, that's enough of that!" her mom said. "Bye!" And she closed Poppop Pomporromp's golden doors. Then she whipped around to Lennie.

"Lennie!" her mom said. "That was supposed to be a private meeting! Were you there the whole time? What were you thinking?!"

Lennie didn't say anything. If she opened her mouth, she knew she'd start crying, and she *would not cry*.

Her mom tucked a lock of Lennie's silky black hair behind her ear. "I—I really wish you weren't there to hear that." Her mom rubbed circles on her back, and Lennie blinked back tears. "He doesn't know what he's saying, your poppop. He doesn't mean it. He's a good person on the inside. He loves you very much, you know."

Lennie closed her eyes, and a single tear slid down her face.

Her mom pulled her into her arms. "Don't cry, Len! I love you. You know I believe in you—I think you'd be an amazing Prime Wizard." But when Lennie's tears didn't stop, her mom grabbed her shoulders. "Hey! Remember what I always taught you: Sticks and stones can break my bones, but words can never hurt me."

But they did hurt. Poppop's words were like a virus that gnawed on Lennie's insides, eating her up, making her flush and feverish. She'd much rather be smacked with a stick or pelted with a rock.

Was this really how he thought of her? He didn't seem to love her. He didn't even seem to *like* her.

There were so many thoughts swirling around in her head that she didn't know what to say. Her legs were wobbly, and her voice felt shaky, and her eyes were burning. *Keep it together, keep it together,* she told herself.

Her mom kissed the top of her head. "I don't want you to worry about this, sweetheart. Put it out of your mind." She grabbed Lennie's hand, and together they walked back to Cheeseburger Chamber. Her mom tucked her into bed above Michael, who was sleeping comfortably, with no idea what had just happened and no cares in the world.

But Lennie had a sleepless night. She tossed and turned, replaying the conversation between her mom and Poppop over and over and over, haunted by all the things he said— and all the things she *didn't* say back.

Opening Ceremonies

In the morning, the day looked exceptionally bright through Lennie's tomato-tinted window. From her spot in bed, she could see that the pudding pool had melted a bit. It looked a little like chocolate soup, but it didn't seem to stop Anya, Jonathan, and Mollie from going for a morning family swim.

As Lennie rolled off the top bunk, she found a note slipped under their door.

ATTENTION POMPORROMP FAMILY:
What: Wizardmatch Opening Ceremonies
Where: The Open Lawn, behind the castle
When: 4:00 p.m.
Who: YOU!

Lennie had the sudden urge to crumple the note as all the feelings and thoughts and worries from last night came crashing back to her. Instead, she placed it facedown on Michael's bedside table. She couldn't bear to look at it a moment longer.

Michael let out a snore as she approached, but he didn't wake up. Lennie tiptoed to her ketchup bottle–shaped dresser, and as she quietly changed out of her pajamas, she thought about the *Prime Wizard look*. She glanced down at her arms. Michael had skin just as dark as hers. Did Poppop say those things last night because she was a girl? But what did *that* have to do with anything?

She didn't know what his comment meant—only that it cut her deeply.

Once she was dressed in a T-shirt and shorts, she tiptoed out into the hallway. She set out to find her mom, but she wasn't in her room or in the dining room, where Lennie glumly grabbed some sort of pretzel that kept folding and unfolding itself. The dining hall was mostly empty—except for a really enormous man who was by far the tallest and broadest one in the family, and Perrie, the young cousin with short purple hair. Lennie hadn't met her yet, but she knew Perrie from the pictures.

"Hi," Lennie said, walking over to them. "I'm Lennie."

The man surveyed her. "Lennie? Stacey's kid, Lennie?"

She nodded.

The man laughed. "I was looking to meet you and your brother last night, but with all the chaos at dinner . . . I'm your uncle Bob!"

Uncle Bob? This enormous man was her mom's *baby* brother? He was probably twice her mom's size. Lennie turned to look at Perrie, who bashfully hid her face behind a thick book she was holding.

"And this is my daughter, Perrie. Don't be shy, Pear-bear!" Uncle Bob said, giving the girl a little nudge.

Perrie must have been six or seven. Lennie couldn't even believe that Perrie would be competing so young—how would she fare against cousins twice her age?

Perrie took a deep breath, and it was like suddenly a whole bunch of words she'd trapped inside her got loose all at once. "Lennie, hi. I've been wanting to meet you I don't know any of my cousins since dad and I live so far away and I've only been to Pomporromp Castle four times mostly before I could even remember and this is my fifth time isn't it beautiful I'm so obsessed with it," Perrie said quickly, all in one breath.

"Oh, yeah, me too," Lennie said, trying very hard to keep up with how quickly Perrie talked.

"I even like my bedroom, Lobster Lodge, even though I'm allergic to shellfish, and my lips swell up every time I lay on my pillow!"

"You should switch rooms!" Lennie said.

"Well, Poppop says he's going to fix that tonight, so I should be good for tomorrow. But it's making me talk *really slowly* right now, don't you think?"

If this was slow, Lennie was afraid to see fast.

"Anyway, I was just headed outside, if you want to come—"

"Sure!" Lennie said, practically jumping to get a word in.

Uncle Bob looked at his daughter. "Remember what I said, Perrie: no wandering into the borderlands."

Perrie nodded.

"If you need me, I'll be on the fourteenth floor. Okay?"

"Okay!" Perrie said.

As Lennie and Perrie headed downstairs, Perrie continued to nervous-chatter about the castle and all the things she'd read about magic in her favorite textbooks. Lennie couldn't help but wonder what Perrie's power was.

"Lennie?"

"Huh?" Lennie said, snapping to attention.

"That kid is calling your name."

From two stories up, Michael was waving wildly at them.

"That's my brother," Lennie explained. "COME DOWN HERE!"

For once, he actually obeyed, and when they all met on the ground floor, Michael and Perrie smiled at each other.

"Hi!" he said. "I'm Michael. What's your name?"

"Perrie Arabella Monina de Twickenham."

"Twickenham?" Michael snickered.

"That's the name of the cottage where Daddy and I live. In Netherly everyone is named after the property they live in, not their family name."

"You sure have a lot of first names, though!" Lennie said.

"And you don't have nearly enough!" Perrie replied. Then she ran out the front door. "Come on!"

The sun was so bright that it was almost blinding. The short grass glowed a neon color—and to their left, the Garden of Goulash burbled and gurgled and burped in the heat. It smelled like slimy hot dogs.

"IT'S ALIVE!" Michael shouted as a sauce bubble erupted with a *pop*.

The smell from the Garden of Goulash was making Lennie queasy—even queasier than she had already been feeling, thinking about last night. And so Lennie pulled her brother and cousin in the direction of the pudding pool.

At the edge of the property, they sat next to the high dive, which must've been fifteen feet tall. Lennie faced outward, looking at the sea beyond the cliff. The three of them huddled together, dipping their fingers into the chocolate and licking the pudding right off.

"So how old are you?" Michael asked Perrie, his mouth full.

"I'm seven and one-sixth years old! That's 2,616 days," Perrie said. "How old are you?"

"Ten!" Michael said smugly. "And I turned ten ages ago . . . it's practically been years! You think you can beat a ten-year-old in Wizardmatch?"

"Twelve," Lennie said. "I'm *twelve*."

"Who's talking about *you*?" Michael said, sticking his tongue out at her.

"Of course I can beat a ten-year-old and a twelve-year-old! I can do it with my hands tied behind my back." Perrie stood up defiantly.

Nothing happened at first, but then! Perrie's arms started getting longer. And longer. And *longer*. They were stretching out like taffy, all gooey and wiggly. And they kept growing. Perrie's arms hung so low that her knuckles brushed the ground.

Then Perrie swung her loosey-goosey arms behind her back and tied them into a figure-eight knot.

"Wow!" Lennie marveled. "Impressive knot work!"

"So you can lengthen your arms," Michael said. "Big whoop!"

Perrie grinned. "And that's not all I can do!" she said, untying her hands. She reached forward, and grabbed Michael's shirt.

"HEY, LET ME GO!"

But she didn't. Perrie lifted Michael up in the air, her arms extending—up, up, UP—until they were ten feet tall. Michael wriggled and shouted and even tried invisibling, but there was no escaping Perrie's grip.

"UNHAND ME!" Michael bellowed. "OR ELSE!"

Perrie was so impressive that Lennie could only gawk. Flexibility, limb extension, *and* super strength? It was almost unfair that one person could have so much magic!

"DON'T DROP ME IN THE PUDDING!" Michael yelped.

"Just say: *Perrie, I give up, and when you're the Prime Wizard champion of the family I will kiss your butt!*" Perrie said.

"NEVERRRRRRRRRR!!!!!" Michael howled.

"Then I hope you like to swim," Perrie said. Suddenly, she grew pale. Her arms shrunk back to normal. She placed Michael back on the ground gently, and her arms retracted with a soft *hiss.*

"You're lucky I decided to be nice to you," Perrie said sheepishly, rubbing her short hair.

Lennie knew instantly that Perrie's powers had limitations, just like hers and Michael's. She knew Ellington's and Raina's powers didn't last very long, either. Did *everyone* in her family have limited powers except for Poppop?

Perrie hummed. "So do you both have the same powers, or is it different, because I'm wondering what I'm going to be competing against for the next few weeks, or who."

"Mom's going to pick Lennie. She's the *faaaaaaaavorite!*" he said.

"Am not," Lennie muttered. Worry gnawed at her, and she was not in the mood for this fight again. She lay on her stomach, peering over the edge of the cliff.

"Look!" Perrie said.

Poppop was scurrying out of the castle, Estella and Fluffles both trailing in his wake. Lennie watched, feeling the need to punch her poppop—and at the same time, she wanted to prove him wrong.

Once Poppop was in an open grass field behind the castle, he stopped to stroke his beard and look out in the distance. He didn't seem to notice Lennie, Michael, or Perrie at all.

"What's he doing?" Michael asked.

Moments later, Poppop wiggled his staff around. Something silvery poured out of the mouth of the rubber ducky that sat atop the staff—and formed itself into the shape of bleachers.

Then Poppop made a podium to the side of the bleachers,

with a throne in the middle, a seat on his right-hand side, and a seat on the left. *He's preparing*, Lennie realized, *for the opening ceremonies tonight.*

Maybe, Lennie thought, she just needed to get Poppop to like her more. And what did Poppop appreciate more than anything in the world? Being showered with compliments.

"I'll be right back," she said, not even giving Michael or Perrie the chance to come with her. She needed to do this alone.

"Hi, Poppop!" Lennie said, reaching him. "Estella! Fluffles!"

"Are you here to pet me?" Fluffles said, cuddling up to her leg.

"Good morning, Lennie!" Estella said cheerfully.

"Is it a good morning?" Poppop said. "I can change that!" And with a tap of his staff, clouds formed in the sky. As goose bumps appeared on her arms, Lennie wished she had a jacket.

"Do you mind if I—um—have a moment with Poppop?" Lennie asked.

"Of course!" Estella said, bending over so that Fluffles could leap into her arms. She massaged his neck as she carried him away to examine the bleachers and podium Poppop had just made.

Poppop stroked his chin as he stared at her. "Did you have something to say to me?"

"I just wanted to let you know how *amazed* I am! The castle, the grounds, they're all fantastic!"

"And don't I know it!" Poppop boasted. "It's difficult to maintain, but years of honing my craft, and I've finally mastered it. I mean, for a while there *was* that one room that kept floating away . . ." He zoned out for a moment. "Good thing you didn't visit while we were having *that* pesky problem. The last thing I want is for my family to float away in an unstable room to meet their UNTIMELY ENDS." He put the back of his hand to his forehead dramatically.

Even though he was talking about death and stuff, it actually kind of sounded like he was happy about it.

"And YOU!" Lennie said. "You are sooooooo powerful! And sooooooo impressive!"

Poppop bashfully tugged on his beard. "Stop that—you're making me blush!" Then Poppop frowned. "No, no, I didn't mean *stop*! Do go on!"

"Right!" Lennie said. "You are so clever and brilliant and brave. You're so good at magic. And your feast was delicious. I, er, like your purple robe today. And you hardly have any ear hair. And . . ." she was running out of compliments. "Your beard is so floofy!"

"Want to know my secret?" he whispered. "Olive oil. It works wonders on detangling my chin tresses. Also, it makes me smell like garlic bread. Though, sometimes I do wake up to find myself gnawing on my beard."

"Ew," Lennie said out loud, then covered her mouth. She quickly started talking again. "So, I just wanted to let you know how excited I am about Wizardmatch. You're my role model! I want to grow my powers, just like you! Being Prime Wizard is my ultimate lifelong dream! I can't wait for you to teach me all you know!"

"Well, don't get too hasty. There are many tests that still have to happen before I select a Prime Wizard." He pulled up his sleeve to check his watch, but there was nothing on his wrist. "Oh my! Look at the time, gotta run! So much to do before the opening ceremonies this evening!"

"Okay. I . . . I love you, Poppop!" she said. She never really said that to him before, but it seemed like a thing she *should* say to her grandfather.

Poppop blinked at her. "I don't blame you," he finally said. "I love me, too."

Then Poppop skipped away, across the field, with Fluffles and Estella scampering behind him.

Lennie had no idea whether Poppop liked her more now— but it couldn't have hurt, right? She turned around and headed back toward the pudding pool, but Michael and Perrie were both gone. In fact, the grounds were empty except for one family: Aunt Lacey, Bo, Danielle, Alice, and Jordan.

Out of curiosity, Lennie trailed behind them, from a distance, just to see where they were going. They were tromping through the Garden of Goulash, headed toward the borderlands between the Pomporromp property and the Oglethorpe estate. *Why would they need to leave Pomporromp estate? What are they doing?*

"Boo!" said a voice behind her.

Lennie yelped as she whipped around to face Ellington.

"What are you looking at?" Ellington said.

"Bo, Danielle, Alice, and Jordan. Where are they going?" She fished in her fanny pack for her map. "My mom said it's too dangerous to go out there."

"*We* went out there," Ellington said before Lennie even laid a hand on the map. "Mom took Raina and me there last night. Mom wanted some place to strategize for Wizardmatch. She didn't want to be overheard, just in case one of our cousins has supersonic ears or something."

Lennie's stomach flipped. "Strategize?"

Ellington nodded. "She told me that I'd be the family champion, and gave me some tips on—Uh, Lennie? Are you okay?"

Lennie was certain she must've been a sickly green color. She leaned up against the cool exterior of the castle. "Your mom told you you're competing?"

"Yeah. Hasn't yours?"

Lennie looked down. "No . . . she hasn't."

There was a pause.

"Well, that doesn't mean anything," Ellington said, patting Lennie awkwardly on the back. "There, there! Of course it's going to be you. You're so smart. And you work so hard on your magic. You were born for this!"

For a moment, Lennie considered telling Ellington about the conversation she'd overheard between her mom and Poppop. But she didn't even know where to start. And something about that conversation made her cheeks flush—like she was ashamed. Even though she had nothing to be ashamed about.

"You know what I think?" Ellington said. "Your mom probably hasn't had a chance to break the bad news to Michael yet. But don't worry. Anyone with a brain would choose you. I mean, I love Michael," she added, "but she's going to choose you."

That's right, Lennie thought. *It should be me. Mom even said so to Poppop.* But still, she couldn't shake a nagging little worry in the back of her head.

To distract herself, Lennie went exploring with Ellington. They stopped at the thirteenth floor, which was so unlucky that Poppop put caution tape all around it and warning signs not to go down the hall. Floor twenty-four had a violent library—when Lennie and Ellington shouted out what kind of books they were looking for, *every* book on that topic came zooming off the shelves, pummeling them in the chest until they cracked open the spines. (Though the books purred with glee whenever they were opened.)

There was the twenty-seventh floor that had a room full of money: hundreds of different currencies, some from their world, some from Netherly. Lennie opened the glass display cases and reached in, but every time she tried to touch the money, the currency transformed into already-chewed bubble gum. Floor thirty-one was a giant game room—but it wasn't as fun as it sounded, since Poppop had put a slow-motion spell on everything there. When Lennie and Ellington tried to play table tennis, a single rally took a half hour.

They climbed up farther. The next floor was a music room, where all the instruments were playing themselves—and right in the middle of the room, headbanging to the music, was her redheaded cousin. Ethan.

The music screeched to a halt. Ethan turned to look at them, his green eyes lined with black makeup. Lennie noticed his sneakers had little skulls on them. He regarded them with a nod.

"Hi. I'm Lennie. And this is Ellington."

"Nice to meet you," Ellington added.

"Mmm," Ethan said.

"So . . . what are you doing in here?" Lennie prompted.

"You wouldn't understand," Ethan said, growing the hair over his eyes. "Nobody gets me. Nobody at all! Nobody except Mittens!"

"Awww! Your pet cat?" Ellington said.

"My pet tarantula."

Lennie shuddered. "Well . . . we'll see you later!"

They retreated into the hall, and as a clock chimed three times, Lennie realized they only had an hour to get ready and meet outside for the opening ceremonies.

"I have to change," Ellington said. "Come with me?"

Lennie followed her cousin back to her room on the third floor—where everything smelled like ooey-gooey deliciously sweet cinnamon buns.

"I don't know how you can stay in here without getting hungry," Lennie said.

"I can't!" Ellington laughed. "I'm hungry all the time. Now help me pick. This one?" she said, displaying a frilly pink dress that looked like a poodle's worst nightmare. "Or this one?" she asked, holding up a white poofy thing. Ellington had always loved dresses, but Lennie had never actually seen *anything* this lacy before. It was like Ellington was dressing herself in a doily.

"Uh . . ."

"You're right," Ellington said. "The pink one."

Ellington slipped into the dress and began wrapping her long hair with thick pink bows.

"Okay . . . *what* are you doing?" Lennie asked.

"Preparing for the competition." Ellington smiled. "It's all part of my losing strategy."

"Losing? What in the world are you talking about?"

"I don't want to be the Prime Wizard," Ellington said, fluffing up her hair. "I want to be a veterinarian."

"Since when?"

"I rescued a bird with a broken wing a few months ago."

"But being a vet doesn't have anything to do with your powers!" Lennie said.

Ellington coiled a lock of hair around her finger to give it extra curl. "So what?"

"But what about Wizardmatch? You could live in this amazing castle and have all your powers unlocked!"

"I don't care about all that," Ellington said with a wave of her hand. "I'm only participating in Wizardmatch because I have to."

Annoyance flinched through Lennie. Here she was, worried that she wouldn't get a spot in a competition that meant *the world* to her, and Ellington had a spot and didn't even want it!

"It's just a shame I have to compete in the first place," Ellington continued. "Raina and I both don't want to, but last night, Poppop *demanded* Mom pick one of us. He said we couldn't say no. So we came up with a plan to lose."

"Which is?" Lennie said stiffly.

"If I look dainty enough, maybe Poppop will think I'd be a bad Prime Wizard and eliminate me early. I want him to think I'm weak."

"Wearing a *dress* doesn't make you weak!" Lennie growled.

"Obviously," Ellington said. "But it's not me—it's Poppop's stupid, old-fashioned way of thinking."

At that very moment, a voice resounded in the castle: "ALL POMPORROMP DESCENDANTS, PLEASE MAKE YOUR WAY TO THE COURTYARD FOR THE OPENING CEREMONIES."

"I'm not ready!" Ellington whispered. "I don't want to do this!"

"At least you know you're getting a chance!" Lennie snapped.

Ellington's eyes grew wide. "Don't get mad at me, Len. Please?"

"Sorry," Lennie said gruffly. "I'm not mad at you."

At least . . . she didn't *think* she was mad at Ellington.

When they arrived at the bleachers outside, it was clear everyone was sitting with their own immediate families. Ellington's family was, thankfully, all the way on the end— and Lennie felt oddly relieved when her cousin walked away.

Lennie scanned the rest of the seats. Anya's family was in the back, and all of them had their heads together in a huddle. Bo and his blond-haired, icy-eyed family were seated in the middle of the bleachers in height order; they sat with rigid posture, staring straight ahead. Julien and his father, Uncle Philip #3, had plopped in the front, sprawled out, like they owned the bleachers. Perrie and Uncle Bob were sitting next to them, and Perrie kept looking nervously to her left.

Lennie couldn't find her brother or her mom. But then someone tapped her on the shoulder.

"Hi!" Michael said. "Guess what? I went in the border-lands!"

"You did *what?*"

"Shhhhhhhhhh!" Michael said. "Anya dared me. Don't tell Mom. It was only one second, anyway—it was too dark in there. I couldn't see a thing. It was actually really *boring.*"

"Michael, what were you thinking?"

"I wasn't!" he said cheerfully. "And it was fun! I think I'll not think *every* day!"

"Come on," Lennie said, leading him up the bleachers. Mom still hadn't arrived, and already, there were barely any seats left. Lennie and Michael squeezed together, next to the only relatives she hadn't met yet: a pregnant woman with shoulder-length brown hair, who must be her aunt Macy, and her very round and very bald baby. "Hi," Lennie said to her aunt. "We haven't met yet but I'm—"

"Lennie!" Aunt Macy said, pulling her in for a hug. "And Michael! Of course I recognize you two! I've been so looking forward to meeting you. And so has little Victoria, here. Say hello, Victoria!"

The baby reached out and yanked Lennie's hair.

"OUCH!" she said as Michael snickered at her.

"And in here," Aunt Macy said, patting her stomach, "is Victoria's little sibling."

Suddenly, Victoria burst into tears. As Aunt Macy fumbled with a pacifier, Lennie continued to look around for her mom. She was the only one missing from the family gathering. Did she just lose track of time? Was this a bad sign? Or was this a good sign?

Lennie took a deep breath, trying to exhale all her nerves. The sun was setting, and the sky had begun to turn brilliant shades of oranges, reds, and purples. The Pomporromp Castle looked even more dazzling in this light—with some of its golden towers and metal rooftops catching the sunset in all the right ways. *I'm going to make you mine,* she thought to the castle. *No matter what! And I'll take care of you like you were my own puppy!*

At last, her mom came running in, but with no spots left

near Lennie and Michael, she was forced to sit in the back—from this angle, Lennie could only just make out the top of her head.

Lennie considered getting up to squeeze into a spot near her mom, but right at that moment, Poppop Pomporromp took his place at his podium and blew into a foghorn.

WOOOOOOOOONK!!!!

"Hmmm," echoed the sound of Poppop's voice, which seemed to be coming from everywhere at once. "I thought a foghorn would sound happier. . . . Next time we'll try a tuba. Or a triangle. Or a duck . . . Perhaps we should have used a duck, Estella!"

"The *champions*, Mortimer," Estella reminded him pointedly, tapping on her clipboard.

"Ah, yes!" Poppop Pomporromp said, grandly sticking his pointer in the air. "It's time to have my sons and daughters select their champions. For some, there is only one potential champion. Will only-children Julien and Perrie please make your way to the arena?"

Julien stood up with—*ugh*—that smug smile again. Lennie wanted so badly to be the one responsible for making that smile slide off his obnoxious face. Perrie hugged a book to her chest as she followed Julien down to the grassy arena.

"Excellent," Poppop said. "Now, Philip #1, you have two children: Emma and Ethan. Macy, you have two children: Victoria and Mortimer Junior—"

"I'm *not* naming this baby Mortimer Junior," Aunt Macy said, rubbing her pregnant belly.

"Sleep on it. You may change your mind. Mortimer is a *very* snazzy name!" Poppop insisted. "Emma is too old to participate. That unborn baby is too young to participate. Which means you both have one eligible competitor. So, Ethan and Victoria join Julien and Perrie in the arena."

Ethan walked down glumly, head down and hands in his pockets. Victoria stayed put.

Poppop clapped his hands. "Estella, fetch Victoria and bring her to the center!"

"Aren't you going to say please?" Estella asked.

"Please?" Mortimer said, scandalized. "*Please?!* A Prime Wizard de Pomporromp needs not use such frivolous things as *manners!*"

Estella simply glared at him.

"Okay, fine, *please*," Poppop said in a small voice, and Estella hopped up the bleachers to fetch baby Victoria.

Everyone applauded halfheartedly as Estella carried the baby down and laid her in the grass, where she immediately fell over onto her back. Fluffles nudged her with his head to prop her up again.

Lennie felt worried for baby Victoria. What if the tests were too dangerous for someone so young?

"Four down, four to go. For my remaining children, now is the time to make your pick! And we shall begin with. . . ."

Lacey! You see? You thought I'd be predictable and go in age order, but YOU DON'T KNOW ME!" Poppop bellowed. "Lacey, you have the greatest number of children, all of them eligible. So will it be Bo, age thirteen? Danielle, age seven? Alice, age six? Or Jordan, age three?"

Aunt Lacey looked around dreamily.

"Lacey!" Poppop said. "SNAP TO ATTENTION!"

"What? Oh, right," Lacey said, her voice breathy. "Eenie, meenie, miney, mo, catch a tiger by the toe," she said, pointing back and forth between her children. "If he hollers, let him go. My mother says to pick the very best—"

"LACEY!" Poppop bellowed. "In this century, please!"

Lacey pointed at her oldest. "Bo. He's very down to earth."

Bo was staring at the sky until Aunt Lacey elbowed him in the side.

"Right!" Bo said, suddenly looking down at his feet. "I am . . . grounded. Completely. In reality. Yes. That is me!"

"Oh, just go!" Poppop said, waving Bo down to where the other competitors were milling around. "Now Philip #2," he continued, turning to Anya's dad. Lennie's pulse quickened as she watched her cousins. "Jonathan is just a few months too old, so you must choose between Anya and Mollie."

"Dad," said Uncle Philip #2, rubbing Anya's shoulders like a boxing coach, "I'm picking the kid most likely to *crush* this competition. And that's Anya."

Mollie held out a towel for Anya, who wiped her face with it and handed it back to her younger sister. Jonathan, meanwhile, looked grossed out as he handed Anya her mouth guard.

"Welcome to the competition, Anya," Poppop said.

Anya pumped her fist in the air and soaked up the applause. She ran down the bleachers, throwing a few punches in mid-air to psyche herself up for the competition.

"You're going DOWN!" she growled at her competition in the arena. "NUMBER ONE! NUMBER ONE!" Anya chanted, trying to get the crowd to shout with her.

Lennie looked around the bleachers, her heart in her throat. There were only two families left . . . just hers and Ellington's. She tried to catch Ellington's eyes across the crowd, but she was twirling her hair around her finger, trying very hard to look dainty.

"Tracy," Poppop said. "Ellington, age eleven, or Raina, age four? Which one shall defend your family's honor to the death—*OUCH!* ESTELLA, DON'T PINCH ME!"

Aunt Tracy stood up. "Love my girls," she said. "And I want to make it clear that I know they'd *both* do a fantastic job. But as both Ellington and Raina already know, I'll be sending Ellington into the competition."

Lennie wiped her palms nervously on her shorts as she glanced at her mom, who was looking away and biting her nails, her nervous habit.

"Stacey," Poppop said, and just the sound of her mother's name made Lennie's heart float up through her mouth and leave her body entirely. She was glued, frozen.

Her mom should know by now whether or not Lennie

would be competing, right? But Lennie had no idea—not a single clue, not one iota—what was going to happen next. And that made her want to throw up.

"So . . . who will it be, Stacey—Lennie, age twelve? Or Michael, age ten?"

Her mother winced. "I—I don't . . ." she sputtered, a blush creeping up her neck and into her face. Lennie's stomach swooped.

"We don't have all day, now! Who do you pick? Or is it whom?" Poppop said, turning to Estella.

"To whom, for whom," she said.

"To whom do you select?" Mortimer asked, scratching his beard. "No, that doesn't sound right. Who taught you grammar, Estella? Or is it *whom* taught you grammar? Either way," he said, staring hard at Lennie's mom, "Who's your champion? Lennie or Michael?"

Lennie or Michael?

Lennie or Michael?

Lennie or Michael?

Her mother closed her eyes. "Michael."

After

The stadium applauded for her brother, but it all sounded like blurred noise to Lennie. It was like time itself had stopped. And there was just one word that repeated itself in her brain.

First, uncomprehendingly: *WHAT???*

Then, angrily: *WHAT!!!*

And finally, crushingly: *What.*

Down on the grass, Michael was elatedly running in circles, and Lennie felt like crying. Her mother walked across the bleachers to sit beside her, putting her hands on Lennie's shoulders, but Lennie shook them off violently.

This wasn't happening. THIS WASN'T HAPPENING. How could Mom do this to her? Without even warning her first.

"I still believe in you, Len," her mom whispered. "I love you so much."

Liar! she thought, folding her hands defiantly.

Lennie didn't understand—she could hold her invisibility for two seconds longer than Michael. It was a fact. They all knew it. *She* was the one who led invisibility drills with *him*. Why would they pick the student for this big competition when they could have picked the teacher? The unfairness of it all swallowed her up in a big wave.

Poppop Pomporromp was saying something about the competition, but Lennie wasn't even listening. She peered down at the nervous, excited champions with a fiery glare that could have melted all of Netherly.

"We'll meet here in forty-eight hours for the champion introductions. Be prepared . . . or BE SCARED," Poppop cackled. "Good night!"

Without a word to her mom, Lennie stormed away. It was dark by now, and she held her arms as she whipped across the courtyard and into the castle. The rest of the families were celebrating over dinner, but Lennie didn't feel like joining them. Up the stairs she went, until she was safely in her room.

But it wasn't safe for long, because she was sharing it with Michael.

"Lennie, Lennie, Lennie! Isn't this cool?" Michael said, bursting into the room after she'd snuggled under her covers. "I get to compete!"

"Congratulations," she said, trying her hardest not to let her voice wobble.

"I can't believe it! HA-HA-HA-HA-HA!!! This is so so so so awesome! The best thing that could ever happen—"

Lennie pulled a pickle-shaped pillow over her ears. Every word he said was a twist in her gut. She squeezed her eyes shut—she didn't want to look at him or hear him or even occupy the same space. She missed her room . . . she missed her dad . . .

Lennie fell asleep with the pillow on top of her head and didn't wake up until dawn—to the brilliant sun radiating through her tomato window. It was beautiful—and then, she remembered, it *wasn't*. Her chest tightened as she thought about yesterday. Her one chance to follow her dreams, completely shattered. She shoved the pillow over her face, blocking out another *perfect* day in this *perfect* world where everything was *oh-so-perfect*.

Eventually, she peeled the covers off her and dangled her feet over the bed. Michael was still snoring, content in his sleep; she couldn't stand to look at him! She changed hastily and got out of there as fast as she could.

She was hungry—no, *utterly and completely famished*—from having skipped dinner last night. But the thought of having to sit next to Michael, Ellington, and Anya at breakfast—at any meal, really—was too much to bear. Just seeing them would cause all these feelings to bubble up; even thinking about them made her feel like she was drowning.

And Julien—if he saw her, he'd be even more insufferable. She'd *always* be a bummer now, since she wasn't going to be Prime Wizard. And he actually might be! The thought of that made her kick her skateboard so hard it rolled down three stories. She had to whistle for it again and wait for the board to spiral back up the ramp.

And then, there was Mom and Poppop. Imagining running

into them made Lennie want to EXPLODE. And she couldn't—wouldn't—have a meltdown in front of the whole family. Examining the map in her fanny pack again, Lennie decided to sneak to casual kitchen #2.

Casual kitchen #2 was located on the forty-first floor, and it was filled with swirly wisps that transformed into delicious smelling food when Lennie got within arm's length. She walked around, drooling from the sweet smell of brownies suspended in midair, the savory whiff of hovering garlic bread, the spicy scent of floating chicken curry. Whenever she stepped out of range, the food transformed back into smoke again, taking the scent with it.

She finally stopped when she wandered near a cloud that transformed into a full stack of buttermilk pancakes, dripping with butter and oozing with syrup—complete with fresh fruit on top.

Lennie reached for the plate and found it was heavy in her hands: The food was piping hot and ready to eat. She sat on a stool at a high-top table in the corner of the room. Looking out a small window into the borderlands, Lennie folded the top pancake and stuffed her cheeks with it, like a chipmunk. It practically melted in her mouth.

Sighing, Lennie stared at her stack of magical pancakes.

She never thought any of this would happen. Sure, she had been worried about it, but deep down she never *actually* thought she wouldn't get to participate in Wizardmatch. Or that her mom would choose Michael over her.

How?

How did this happen? She tried to replay the moments leading up to the opening ceremony in her mind.

Was the problem that she was half-Filipino when he wanted someone white? Or was it that she was a girl, when Poppop wanted a boy? Or was it both, together, that made her too different? But she didn't *feel* too different. She felt just like everyone else . . . until Poppop pointed out that she wasn't.

She deeply, desperately missed her dad. He would have understood how she felt. He would've known exactly what to do in this situation.

It just wasn't fair. She didn't even have a chance to prove herself to Poppop.

She perked up.

Prove myself to Poppop! That's exactly what I have to do!

She ran to the ramp and took a skateboard all the way up to Poppop's penthouse. On the forty-seventh floor, she faced those golden doors again. *DOOM AND DEVASTATION AND DEATH AWAIT ALL WHO ENTER!*

Lennie knocked on the door.

"Ouch! Stop hitting me!" the door said. "You must have a password to enter."

A password! Lennie grimaced. "I didn't need a password last time. Can't you just tell my poppop I'm here to see him?"

"PASSWORD!" demanded the door.

"Uh . . ." she said. She didn't know her grandfather *that* well. She only saw him one week a year. What could his password be? He was very dramatic, and he loved being the Prime Wizard, and had a real pride in the Pomporromp estate . . . and himself.

"Pomporromp!" Lennie said.

"Really? *That's* your guess? You think he'd really pick his own name?"

"I—uh—!"

"I'm only teasing—you're right. He *did* use his own name," the door said, swinging open.

Lennie stumbled inside. It was the same circular room she was in when she'd eavesdropped on Poppop and Mom, with the giant screwdriver contraption in the middle and the desk in the back. But in the light of day—and without the time pressure of having to hide—she noticed things she hadn't noticed before. For one, the perimeter of the room had hundreds of pictures, framed and hanging.

She slowly walked around, mesmerized. There was Poppop smiling with a group of people wearing funny wigs and holding gavels. Poppop going hippo-hopping. Poppop cradling his rubber ducky staff. Poppop eating something that looked like a yellow balloon. Poppop doing a cartwheel. Poppop getting zapped by lightning. Poppop and some of Lennie's cousins—Emma and Ethan; Bo, Danielle, Alice, and Jordan; and Julien, looking smug as always.

She had the urge to rip that photo up. But instead she edged over to the desk hidden behind the screwdriver contraption.

Lying on top was an open piece of parchment. Lennie leaned over and read:

To Mortimer,

My my my. A little birdie (yes, an actual bird) has just told me that you will be restarting Wizardmatch.

ARE YOU DAFT?

Really, that's not a rhetorical question. I'd like to know.

Because if these rumors are true, then you really never do learn your lessons, do you, Morty? Don't even bother trying to write back; I am not leaving a return address because after sixty years apart, I rather enjoy not hearing anything that comes out of your face.

Best wishes for choking on a potato chip,

Humphrey de Cobblespork

Cobblespork! Lennie giggled at that. But then her fingers brushed over his first name.

Humphrey. . . . Humphrey . . .

She and her brother always shouted "Uncle Humphrey" when one of them gave up in a wrestling match or a game. It was her family's code word for surrendering. Lennie had learned it from her parents, but she had no idea that there was a real Humphrey out there somewhere. She thought it was just something her parents made up.

Suddenly the giant screwdriver began spinning, circling down automatically like a spiral escalator. Lennie jumped back away from the desk.

But it wasn't Poppop. It was Estella, reading a stack of papers while she descended, the escalator twisting her around. Estella didn't even seem to notice that Lennie was standing right there.

"Hi, Estella," Lennie said, and her poppop's assistant yelped, tossing all the papers into the air in fright. They sprinkled down to the ground like the world's most boring confetti.

"Sorry," Lennie said, bending down to help Estella pick up all the loose papers.

"What are you doing here, Lennie?" Estella asked.

"I want to talk to Poppop," Lennie replied. "It's important."

Estella swooped down to gather another paper. "Does this have anything to do with Wizardmatch?" Estella gave her a mournful glance, and Lennie flushed. She hated that look in Estella's eye. She didn't need Estella's pity—she needed a fighting chance! She *could* prove herself . . . if only someone would let her!

Estella sighed. "You want him to change the sibling rule, don't you?"

Lennie nodded.

"I don't think he's going to change his mind," Estella said softly.

"I don't care—I need to talk to him. Please!" she added, hating herself for begging.

Estella gestured to the spiral escalator. "He's up there."

Lennie stared up, but she couldn't see the floor above. She took a deep breath, then started up the steps two at a time.

"Lennie!" Estella called after her. "No matter what happens, you'll be okay."

Lennie didn't look back. At the top of the escalator, there was another door, silver this time. She knocked twice.

"Estella—it's too early! I *told* you I need my beauty sleep! This gray beard doesn't sparkle naturally you know—"

"Poppop, it's me. Lennie. Can I come in?"

"Oh! Er, yes, child!"

She opened the door. Poppop's room was really like an apartment—she could tell there were more rooms attached to this first one that stretched on. There was clutter everywhere, but lots of magic, too. He had pinwheels hanging from the ceiling that were whirring without any wind. On a table, tops were spinning ceaselessly. Lamps were turning themselves on and off.

One day, this could be mine! Lennie thought, before she crashed back down to reality again and remembered that unless she changed Poppop's mind, none of this would *ever* belong to her.

Poppop yawned and gestured to a chair underneath a wide window. "Make yourself comfortable." And without waiting for her response, he tucked himself back under the covers and started snoring.

"Uh . . . Poppop?"

"HUH WHA WHO'S THERE?!" he snapped.

"Still me," Lennie said. "I need to talk to you. Can you wake up, please?"

There was a long pause, and Lennie had the sneaking suspicion that Poppop was trying to fall asleep just to get out of talking to her.

She shook his shoulder until he peeked one eye open. "Are you still here?"

Lennie hopped off the bed and towered over him. His hurtful words ran through her head on a loop.

"Poppop," she said, squaring her shoulders and trying to sound confident and strong. "I've always been really excited about magic—I've been practicing my invisibility every day for over a year. And I get good grades in school! And . . . and being the Prime Wizard is what I want more than anything in the world! You have to let me compete—"

"NO."

"Please! Give me a chance to prove—"

"NO."

"You *have* to let me try—"

"Does *NO* mean something different in your world?" He leaned forward, grabbed his staff, and knocked it once on the floor. A book came soaring in from the other room.

"What are you doing?" Lennie asked.

"Consulting my dictionary," Poppop said as the book landed in his hands. "Just to make sure people in San Francisco understand the word *no*."

"Of course I understand what no means—I'm just not taking it for an answer!"

"If you won't take *no*, then maybe one of these will do

instead: Never! Nope! No sir-ee! Not on your life! Certainly not! Uh-uh! Nah! Hardly! Out of the question! Under no circumstances! No dice! Go harpooning!"

"Go harpooning?"

Her grandfather scratched his head. "Oh, that's right—*go FISH!*" Poppop slammed the dictionary shut. "The rules are here for a reason. A good reason, might I add."

What good reason?! she thought, her anger swelling. *No good reason!* She'd heard his excuses for supporting Michael, and they were stupid.

"Well it doesn't seem very good to me. Because of your rule, I don't get a chance to show you what I can do!"

Poppop Pomporromp stood up and paced the room. "When this competition is over, only one person's life will change forever. For everyone else, everything will have to go back to the way it was. But if I let siblings compete against each other, your relationship with your brother would *never* go back to normal. Once the claws come out, the scars are permanent. Get it?"

Lennie folded her arms defiantly.

Her grandfather sighed. "Once upon a time, *I* was entered in Wizardmatch. In test after test, my siblings and I fought and scraped and bickered and argued and backstabbed one another to get to the top. And when I won, Winifred, Bernadette, Ophelia, and Humphrey—"

"Humphrey?" Lennie said, perking up.

"My brother. The point is," her grandfather said, "I was

the best wizard among us, and my siblings were very mad and bitterly jealous of me. We never talked again, STORY OVER, THE END."

"But it should be ME, not him!" she blurted. And even though she truly believed and meant it, she immediately felt guilty for feeling that way. And then she felt guilty for feeling guilty because she couldn't really help how she felt. And she felt guilty for feeling guilty about feeling guilty . . . and so on until her guilt was just spinning all around her like a tornado. No . . . a guiltnado.

"I—I just don't understand why he was chosen," she tried to explain. "It doesn't make sense. My powers are stronger."

Her poppop shook his head.

Lennie took a deep breath. All this time she had been telling him about her talents . . . but maybe she had to *show* him. Once he saw her potential with his own eyes, he'd realize how unfair it was to keep her from competing in Wizardmatch.

Leaning up against the wall was Poppop's magic staff—the very thing that helped him harness his immense powers. Lennie edged over to it. She put her hand out and touched the smooth bark—

"NOOOOOOOOOOOOOOOO!!!!!!!!!"

Poppop stretched his arms out like taffy—just like Perrie could. His hands zipped toward Lennie and jerked the staff out of her hands so violently that it left a splinter in her palm.

"DO NOT!" he bellowed, his face turning purple and three forehead veins bulging. "NEVER. TOUCH. THE STAFF. NEVER EVER NEVER EVER NEVER EVER EVER *EVER*. IT IS NOT A TOY—IT IS A POWERFUL MAGICAL TOOL THAT COULD BLAST YOUR EYE-BALLS RIGHT OUT OF YOUR HEAD."

"I . . . I just wanted to show you some magic," Lennie whispered, trying desperately to keep her voice from wobbling. No one—not even her parents or her teachers—had *ever* yelled at her like that before.

"We are done here," Poppop said icily. "You will not be competing in Wizardmatch, but you *will* stand obediently in the wings and cheer on your brother. Support him if he wins; comfort him if he loses."

"But what about me?"

"There is no *I* in family," Poppop said. And then, after a moment of silence, he exclaimed, "Ah, wait, yes there is! What I'm trying to say," his voice sounding suddenly harsher, like the edge of a jagged tooth, "is the world doesn't revolve around *you*, Lennie."

Lennie sucked a deep breath in. Her eyes stung with the tears she dared not shed in front of Poppop Pomporromp. She pushed past him and fled from his room, down the spiral escalator, and out the chamber doors. Not at all stopping . . . not even when Estella called, "Lennie!" in her wake.

She couldn't talk to her poppop. She wouldn't talk to her

mom. Her aunts and uncles were busy with all of their own children. Her dad was far away. There was no one left to listen to her—no one who *really* cared.

She picked the splinter out of her palm with her nails—then skateboarded down to her room. But when she walked in, she was not alone.

Michael was sitting on the bed, tying his shoelaces. For a brief moment, she stood in the doorway, wondering what her poppop saw in Michael that he didn't see in her.

"Lennie!" Michael said, startled. "I almost didn't see you!"

"Here I am," she said softly. It took everything she had not to cry.

"I'm about to leave!" Michael said. "Mom is training me in one minute."

It was like a sack of stones had plunged into her stomach. Training was *her* thing. Now Michael was going to steal that, too? "Training you?" she said.

"You know, for Wizardmatch!" He hopped off the bed and flexed his muscles. "Mom says I've got to be in tip-top shape, so we're running drills and exercises and stuff. Just like you always do! It's so amazing, isn't it?"

"Amazing," Lennie said flatly.

Michael didn't seem to notice. "I'm so important now! I don't have time to even breathe anymore! I don't even have time to go to the bathroom! Mom thinks I have a real shot at winning this thing. Oh no! I'm late!" he said, looking outside. "Got to go! See you later, Len!" He dashed out of the room without a second glance at her, and she rushed to lock the door behind him.

Alone, leaning against the cold metal door, Lennie let it all out: her big blubbering snot-nosed snuffles.

She'd had the power to disappear all her life, but never before had she felt so invisible.

When It Rains, We Train

The next morning brought a downpour that sounded like a rattlesnake. It was like the sky was crying for her—not to mention raging with thunder and lightning. The rain poured onto the grass making mud puddles in different spots, and the pudding pool was watery and overflowing.

Lennie curled deeper beneath her blanket. She did not want to get up. She'd just lie in bed for days, or weeks, or years. It wasn't like anybody cared if she moved. *She* didn't even care if she moved.

Then, the door to the room opened, and Mom came in. Lennie purposely rolled over so that her back was to her mom.

"Get up," Mom said to Michael. "Come on, sweetie—time to train."

Michael yawned loudly. "Five more minutes."

Lennie pressed her lips together. *She* would have jumped right up at the opportunity to train.

"Now," her mom said sternly. "The champion introductions are this afternoon, and after that, Michael, you only have two days until the first test. Every second of training counts. Some of your cousins are very strong. Now, get up!"

"Ugh," Michael ughed.

"You too," Mom said, putting a hand on Lennie's back.

"What?" Lennie said, grabbing her glasses from the bedpost. She sat up so fast in her top bunk that she almost hit her head on the ceiling.

"I want to train both of you at the same time."

Lennie pulled the blanket back up around her head. She was cocooning and wouldn't emerge until someone told her this was all just a horrible nightmare that she would wake up from any second.

Her mom pulled the blanket off her and looked deep into her eyes. "Len, I know you're really hurting, but when life knocks you down, you have to get back up and keep going. Come on, now, sweetheart," her mom said tenderly. "You're stronger than this. Show me you can face life's hardships!"

Lennie reluctantly slid out of bed. It wasn't what her mom said that got her moving—her mom's advice was a bunch of baloney. It was the thought of training again that spoke to her. Practicing magic, Lennie realized, was the only thing that *might* make her feel better. It was hard to imagine feeling any worse.

"YAY! I'm so glad you're coming, Len!" Michael cheered as Lennie silently began to slip into her Wellies and raincoat.

Lennie smiled weakly.

As they headed outside, the rain hit her like a waterfall; she folded her arms and shivered.

"Is there an u-umbrella?"

"No!" her mom shouted over the rain. "Your poppop changes the weather all the time, on a whim! The conditions for Wizardmatch could be *anything*, so we have to be prepared."

No, Michael *has to be prepared,* Lennie thought glumly. *I don't have to be prepared for anything.*

Her mom led them across the lawn, pulling them to the left, through the Garden of Goulash. It was not an ideal day to start: The meaty goulash sauce was watery with rain, and it took great effort to pull her feet out of it. The storm was so rough, that within ten steps, she was soaked through, and the meat sauce splashed up and splattered on Lennie's raincoat. But despite everything, she trudged through, chilled and trembling.

Now that she was in the middle of the Garden of Goulash—and not just passing by the outskirts—she could finally read the unusual engravings on the tombstones (once she wiped the raindrops off her glasses):

Here lies Kimber, we sure will miss her. And there lies Scott, we sure will not.

"I can eat bath soap," Gladys said, and now she's dead.

RIP Horton de Pomporromp, who died on a dare. He bragged a lot, we thought him rude, he proved us right, now he's worm food.

"Lennie!" her mom said, pulling on her arm. "Come on!"

Lennie broke away from the tombstones and sloshed through the soupy ground. In the distance, Ethan was training with his equally mopey-looking father, Uncle Philip #1, near the bleachers from the opening ceremony.

Anya was running laps around the castle with Uncle Philip #2. And when Lennie turned around, she saw Julien and Uncle Philip #3 doing push-ups by the pudding pool. Aunt Lacey seemed to be lecturing Bo over near the borderlands—right on the edge of the Pomporromp property.

Lennie's mom had to holler to be heard over the storm. "WE'RE GOING TO RUN A FEW DRILLS! Both of you—run to that tombstone *way* over there, then run back halfway to me while invisible, touch the ground, run back to the tombstone visible, then run to me completely invisible. Ready? GO!"

Lennie and Michael ran. Lennie pumped her arms and pushed her legs—despite the rain, this was just like the training she did in her backyard. Her magic surged through her, and her skin tingled as she went invisible. It was like stretching a muscle she hadn't used in a few days, but it felt so good.

Lennie touched the tombstone, turned invisible, and ran halfway back. Then she repeated, losing herself in the wind and the rain, getting totally drenched in the process—until she completed the first exercise.

She reached her mom fully invisible, then turned around to see where Michael was. He was still a half a field away, flickering in and out of invisibility, panting as he held on to his side. She'd beat him by a mile.

Her mom didn't say anything; instead, she kept her eyes

on Michael, purposely avoiding Lennie's face. It made their silence even more awkward.

Michael trotted over. "That was soooooo bad."

"No, no, it was a good first try," her mom reassured him. "It's okay. We'll practice day and night before Wizardmatch. You'll be ready, sweetie. And maybe Lennie can teach you some tips. Right, Len? Come help out your bro—"

Lennie stomped her foot in the goulash so hard that it splashed all over her mom's coat.

"Lennie!" her mom scolded.

But Lennie didn't answer. She turned on her heels and clomped off.

"Lennie, where are you going?" Michael cried.

She stormed across the property. Rain pummeled her like a thousand tiny fists. She kept her head down as she slogged across the estate—

Thump.

She knocked right into Ellington.

"Lennie! I didn't see you!" her cousin said. "Wait . . . are you crying?"

"No," Lennie said, more defensively than she'd meant to sound. She adjusted her tone and continued. "What are you doing out here in the rain? Are you training right now?" she asked her cousin.

"Nope!" Ellington said. "Just wandering around."

"Let's go inside," Lennie said, linking elbows with her cousin.

Soggy as pieces of wet bread, they began to march back to the castle. Lennie looked back at her family. In the storm, Michael slipped on the goulash and fell flat on his face, turning visible the second he hit the ground. "You know," Ellington finally said, "I'm surprised your mom chose Michael."

Lennie shrugged, afraid that if she opened her mouth she'd start blubbering or sobbing or *blobbing*, which was some horrible combination of the two.

"Do you know why you weren't picked?" Ellington said softly. Ellington put a hand on her arm, and Lennie took a deep, sharp breath. "You can tell me," her cousin whispered. "It's okay."

Lennie walked faster, and tucked her head down. An intense sense of shame flushed in her cheeks. "It's because," she said, refusing to look at Ellington, "it's what Poppop wanted. He wouldn't listen when my mom tried to tell him how good at magic I am. He basically said I would lose if Mom entered me. So, she chose Michael."

Ellington patted her back, and Lennie felt both better and worse at the same time. "What are you going to do?" Ellington said gently.

"I don't know!" Lennie groaned. "I already tried talking to Poppop, but he wouldn't listen. And Mom doesn't understand how I'm feeling—she told me to get up when life gets me down, which is the most useless advice ever. What do you think I should do?"

They were back at the castle entrance now. Inside the

foyer, Ellington wrung out her long, chestnut brown hair and soaked the floor with rainwater. "I'm not sure getting into the competition is the answer," she said, her voice so soft it was almost drowned out by the pitter-patter of water dripping off the two of them.

"What do you mean?"

Ellington bit her lip. "Can I be honest with you? I think the best thing you could do is let everything having to do with this whole competition roll off your back."

"Let it roll off my back," Lennie said, deadpan. Her own grandfather didn't think she was good enough, and she was supposed to let it *roll off her back*?

"Yes. You know in your heart that they're wrong, Len, so let them think what they want to think, and don't let it bother you."

"I can't!"

"Sure you can."

"NO, I CAN'T!" Lennie said so loudly that she scared Fluffles upstairs, and his yowl echoed around the castle. If she stayed silent, it was like saying she was okay with this. And she wasn't. "I can't just sit back, Ellington. I need to stand up for myself! I have to do something about this!"

"But what?"

Lennie didn't know. But whatever it was, it had to be BIG.

Introducing . . . the Champions!

Later that day—in the aftermath of the rainstorm, in the glow of the setting sun—the Wizardmatch competitors were about to be officially introduced. Lennie sat on the bleachers, just like Poppop said she would. As Poppop had explained earlier, magically projecting his voice around the castle, there would be no elimination today. Just an exhibition of everyone's powers before they were put to the test.

Lennie arrived at the stadium very early, the intense and blustery wind sending a chill right through her. The bleachers were the same as the ones from the opening ceremony just two days ago, but it felt entirely different. Her world felt different. *She* was different.

She stared pointedly into the open arena as her aunts and uncles began filing in and taking seats. They were all chattering excitedly, while Lennie felt like she had her own personal rain cloud above her head.

No one sat near her. Not Ellington's little sister, Raina. Not Anya's siblings, Jonathan and Mollie. Not Bo's siblings. Not one of her aunts and uncles. She was all alone.

She glowered as Poppop took a seat on a plushy throne on his special judges' stage. Estella sat to his right, holding a clipboard, while Fluffles was scrambling to get up on his designated chair. He tried to claw his way up the leg of the chair, leaving scratch marks and rips in the upholstery.

"Len," her mom said softly, rubbing Lennie's back in a circular motion. She'd been so distracted by Fluffles she hadn't even noticed her mom sit down next to her. "I know you got upset this morning, and it hurts me that *you're* hurting. What can I do to make you feel better?"

Lennie stiffened beneath her mother's touch. Was she trying to be comforting? Because she was failing. Hard.

"Your poppop was just *so* insistent about Michael," her mom continued, when Lennie said nothing. "I was just going by what he wanted."

Lennie glared at her mom.

"Lennie, are you not talking to me?"

Lennie nodded.

Her mom's face fell. "I understand why you're upset. But I want you to know I would have sent both of you to compete if I could. And I really wish I could have."

Could've, would've, should've. They were all just empty words now. And after a day of giving her mom the cold shoulder, she wasn't going to stop now.

Lennie stood up and marched on over to the other side of the bleachers, closer to her older cousins. She recognized Emma, whose red bangs swept over her eyes; Lennie could only see the tip of her freckled nose and her black lipstick. And of course she knew Anya's older brother, Jonathan. Lennie hadn't talked with him since the first banquet, but she had seen him from a distance, shredding a storm on the magical skateboards in the Pomporromp Castle.

Lennie edged close to them, hoping they'd include her in their conversation. But Jonathan and Emma didn't seem to notice Lennie lingering by them.

"—absolutely ridiculous," Emma hissed. "I learned in bio class that your brain doesn't even stop developing until you're twenty-five years old. Our brains have *years* before they're done growing—that's plenty of time to learn Prime Wizard magic before we meet our *untimely doom, death, and demise*," she finished, imitating Poppop.

"I know," Jonathan said. "I mean, who made up that stupid fifteen-year-old age cap, anyway?"

"My brother, Ethan, is going to turn fifteen this summer," Emma said. "So right now, he's eligible for the competition . . . and in a few weeks he won't be? That's absurd. What's going to change between this week and next week? Absolutely nothing. Age is just a number."

"If anything, teenagers should be given a *greater* shot," Jonathan said. "My magic is much stronger than Anya's, but Anya is the one who gets to compete just because she's younger."

Lennie had been so wrapped up in her own issues that she had never even considered that Jonathan could be just as annoyed about Anya competing as she was about Michael.

It was these stupid rules that Poppop had made up—the

sibling rule, the age rule. The whole thing stunk more than Fluffles's throw up.

"HEAR YE HEAR YE!" Poppop Pomporromp said, his voice echoing around the stadium at ten times its normal volume.

Many of Lennie's aunts and uncles covered their ears, though she couldn't tell whether it was because of the volume or because they didn't want to have to listen to Poppop.

"It is time to introduce the challengers. Just now, they have all been given a single directive: IMPRESS ME."

Then Poppop sat down on his chair and clapped his hands, like some spoiled emperor.

The first contestant onto the field was Ellington, who timidly kicked her shoes the whole way to the middle of the arena. Lennie could only see the side of Poppop's face, but he didn't seem very impressed.

"Um—hi," Ellington said shyly.

Ellington stared deeply at Poppop's podium—until suddenly Sir Fluffington the Fourth let out a yowl. The cat was floating up in the air and gliding toward where Ellington was standing, all the while yelling, *"NO NO NO!!! HISSSSSS SCRATCH CLAW! UNHAND ME, YOU VILLAIN!"*

Then she floated the cat back to the chair and plopped him on his head.

Lennie frowned. She'd seen her cousin do *so much more* with her magic—lift multiple objects at a time with only her mind, juggling them and letting them soar in intricate patterns. Ellington was phoning it in.

"Oooooooooh!" Mortimer giggled, clapping his hands together. "Not a grand display—and you do need to rethink your presence—but I do love parlor tricks!"

Lennie winced. The way Poppop said *rethink your presence* reminded her of his comment about how she didn't have the *Prime Wizard look*. And all her hurt crashed through her again like an ocean wave.

Ellington curtsied low. Then with an obnoxious, high-pitched giggle, she ran back to where the other champions were waiting, near the pudding pool, away from the magical spotlight that was beaming out of the mouth of the rubber ducky atop Poppop's staff.

*If she wants to fail Wizardmatch, she'll have to do better . . .
er, worse.*

Lennie was secretly, shamefully, pleased that Poppop liked Ellington's performance. She almost wanted Ellington to succeed out of spite. If Lennie had Ellington's spot, she would *never* waste it like that!

Next, Bo ambled out onto the stage, his white-blond hair and light blue eyes sparkling. He whistled casually as he dawdled around the stadium for a bit. Then he picked up a rock. He took a long look at it. And then he swallowed it.

Lennie leaned forward.

"Did he just *eat* that rock?" Emma spluttered to Jonathan.

All of a sudden, Bo looked like he was going to be sick.

He sunk down to his knees and began to retch. *ECK*, he coughed. *ECK ECK!* And then he leaned forward like he was 100 percent definitely absolutely without a doubt going to vomit.

Except, instead of throwing up, he coughed up a small bluebird. Lennie tried her hardest to wrap her head around this . . . but her cousin just *ate a rock and barfed it back up as a bird.*

"TA-DA!" Bo sang. Then he ate a clump of grass, which he regurgitated back up as a pigeon. Then he took off his shoe and stuffed it whole into his mouth, which he regurgitated back up as a toucan. Then he ate his sock, which he regurgitated back up as a hummingbird. Then he reached for his watch—

"STOP!" said Poppop, who was starting to look a little ill. In fact, almost everyone watching this display was staring down at Bo with queasy expressions. "W-what *is* this exactly?"

"My power," Bo said. "I can eat anything and regurgitate it back up as a bird!"

"My! What a . . . um . . . interesting and . . . er . . . useful power," Poppop said.

"But I'm not done," Bo said. "I was about to make a flamingo."

"NEXT," said Poppop.

And next was the *very person* Lennie hated most: Julien. He grinned in that annoyingly smarmy way. And he looked at Poppop Pomporromp for a beat.

Then two. Then three.

Lennie held her breath, waiting for him to display his power.

"WOW!" Poppop said suddenly, rising to his feet. "Julien truly is most impressive! Everybody clap! CLAP FOR JULIEN!"

The whole stadium clapped awkwardly as Julien walked off the arena. And that was it.

Lennie was more confused than ever. What the heck just *happened*? He didn't even *do* anything!

Lennie was still replaying Julien's test in her mind as Estella carried the next contestant—baby Victoria—onto the field. Once the baby was nestled into a patch of grass, Estella rushed off again.

"Now, Victoria," Poppop said. "Let's see what you can do."

Victoria blinked. Then blinked again. Then scrunched up her face in a tiny ball. And that's when she began to cry.

All three judges ran out onto the field to check Victoria's diaper.

Poppop held his nose from the stink. "My goodness," he said, picking Victoria up and holding her to the sky. "THIS IS THE MOST IMPRESSIVE POO I HAVE EVER SEEN IN MY WHOLE LIFE. SUCH PERFECT SHAPE, SUCH HORRENDOUS STENCH, AND AT SUCH A YOUNG AGE, TOO. Well done, Victoria!"

That wasn't magic! Lennie thought sourly. *Everybody poops!*

"I feel bad for whoever—or is it whomever, Estella?—has to follow that act!" Poppop clapped his hands and Estella carried Victoria away. Poppop looked to Fluffles. "Now who—whom—*is* next?"

And of course, up next was Michael.

Lennie held her breath as her brother walked onto the field. He looked so confident—and more focused than Lennie had ever seen him before.

Am I rooting for him? Lennie wondered. *Of course I am—we're family.* Closer family than she could ever be with her cousins. If it came down to her brother getting Poppop's powers or any of her cousins getting them, then she would want her brother to win. To be happy and powerful and successful. Because she wanted the best for him.

Besides, it wasn't *his* fault that Lennie hadn't been selected. She *had* to be on his side. She was proud of him. She was proud of him. She was proud of him. . . .

"Now you see me," Michael began grandly. "Now you don't!" And he went invisible.

She was proud of him . . . *no.*

The truth was: she wanted *so badly* to feel proud of him. But something was gnawing inside of her chest.

It should have been *her.*

Everyone on the bleachers was whispering, *where did he go? What is he doing?* If Lennie knew her brother at all, she had an inkling of what he'd do next. And her suspicions were confirmed when Poppop's drinking water seemed to levitate off the table and spill right onto his head. Then Michael went visible again, and he was hysterically laughing, bowled over with maniacal giggles.

Typical Michael move. He'd done it to her about a million times, but drenching the judge of the competition? That was like asking to be eliminated.

Poppop blinked. "I suppose I was due for a good bath," he said, and then he guffawed, throwing his head back and letting his belly jiggle. "Very sneaky, m'boy!"

You have got to be kidding me! Her brother barely used his powers for five seconds. She didn't get it. Didn't Poppop want the most talented young wizard? Or did he simply want whoever—whomever (which was it?!!?)—was going to entertain him?

Everyone clapped politely, but Mom cheered loudest of all, practically falling over herself as she shouted all sorts of praise and admiration at Michael, and a cold, stony pit grew inside Lennie's chest.

Next was Ethan, who grew his hair fifty feet long and twisted into different shapes. It was a pretty impressive display, but Lennie couldn't even think about Ethan—or Perrie or Anya, who both went after him. Her thoughts were still stuck on Michael. She didn't want to be jealous . . . but it was impossible. He was clearly Poppop's favorite. And her mom chose Michael, so he seemed to be her favorite, too. Maybe everyone just secretly loved him way more than her.

And if he won the competition, how would she ever face

him again, knowing that he was given the chance to be someone great, and she wasn't even allowed to try?

"In two days, we'll meet at the pudding pool for the first individual test! Now, everyone give another round of applause for the champions!" Poppop Pomporromp said, clapping his hands together. The champions all ran out onto the field and took a lap around like prized show poodles.

Lennie closed her eyes—she couldn't watch this anymore, and they were still only *introducing* the contestants. How was she supposed to stand it when they were onto the first test or second or third? Or when Poppop was transferring his powers to the next Prime Wizard—as her dreams would be forever beyond her reach?

No, she couldn't watch—she just *wouldn't*. She had to get out.

She had to run away.

The Borderlands

At midnight, Lennie clicked her fanny pack on. She tip-toed through the castle, afraid that a rattling skateboard would make too much noise. It took longer than usual to get from her bedroom on the thirty-seventh floor to the ground floor, traveling the ramp by foot. But she had to make a quiet getaway.

Poppop must have gotten bored and changed the weather again because it was snowing. A very light dusting of snow that fell from the starry sky but didn't stick to the ground. The night air was rather chilly, and she rubbed her hands together as she made her way across the Pomporromp grounds.

She traipsed around the Garden of Goulash, not wanting to get her shoes all full of meat sauce. But beyond the ceme-tery and the garden, stood the borderlands.

It was her only escape. She had to cross the buffer zone between the Pomporromps and the Oglethorpes. Through the land where Poppop and Madame Oglethorpe threw in a mix of toxic spells to keep each other at bay. Where she'd promised her mom she wouldn't go.

But her mom had promised her for years that she could be anything she wanted to be. So . . . *neither* of them were keeping their promises.

At last, she reached the edge of the Pomporromp property. In front of her, the darkness was thick and complete. She knew there were magical tricks and traps in the land between her poppop's home and the Oglethorpes'—but beyond that, she didn't know what to expect.

A chill fell over her—and not just because of the snow. She took a careful step forward, and without another word or glance or breath or thought, she ventured into the shadows beyond.

At first, she could see the moonlight, but as she got deeper into the borderlands, the thickets got thicker and the bushes got bushier. Soon they formed a cocoon around her, and she could no longer see the sky.

Lennie dug into her bag for a flashlight and continued forward. Every so often, she'd hear a noise—a tree branch snap or a bush move—and she went invisible. *Calm down, Mercado!* she scolded herself.

The air was thick and heavy. She moved her flashlight around wildly. She had the intense feeling that she was being watched, and she invisibled again.

You're just paranoid. There's nothing to be scared of. Keep it together.

She shined her flashlight on a tree, which had colorful neon fruits hanging down from it, with a sign that said,

TRY THIS DELICIOUS ORANGEPINEAPPLEBANANA FRUIT (come on, you know you want to).

"Okay," Lennie said out loud, "clearly a trap."

She walked to the right and saw a long, thin Bubble Wrap pathway stretched out on the ground, with a sign that said *POP THESE (come on, you know you want to)*.

"Double trap."

She sidestepped around the path and walked through the flat, dark, tree-covered borderlands until she reached a bridge, hovering over a moat filled with liquid as dark and oily as the sea that surrounded Poppop's estate. Before the bridge was a sign that read *THIS IS A TRAP.*

"Triple trap!" Lennie whispered.

Unless . . .

Unless Poppop just wanted her to *think* it was a trap. It was very much like Poppop to say something was a trap, when it wasn't a trap—just to be tricky. But on the other hand, maybe that's what he *wanted* her to think. Maybe the real trap was that the thing that looked like a trap actually *was* a trap.

Her head was spinning.

Then she shined her flashlight left and right—the moat seemed to stretch on as far as she could see in both directions. For all she knew, it cut across all of Netherly, and she didn't want to walk all night. She could swim to avoid the bridge . . . but there was something cold and uninviting about the look of the slick water.

She peered at the bridge and—with a very deep breath—

Lennie took a tentative step forward. Nothing happened. She breathed a sigh of relief.

She was fine! Everything was fine.

She took another few steps forward—

Crack! came a noise, the sound of the wood splintering beneath her feet. And before Lennie could run backward, she fell in the moat.

The water was as icy as she'd thought it'd be. And at first it felt like regular liquid, but the more she thrashed, the thicker the water became. It was gummy and sticky—like glue or paste.

"HELP!!!!!" Lennie panicked. "SOMEONE HELP!"

But no help came.

She flailed her arms, trying to paddle herself to shore, and her flashlight slipped out of her grasp, landing in the sticky mess. She couldn't tell if she was swimming forward or backward, upstream or downstream, or even just paddling in place.

"HELLO?????!!!" she called into the forest.

Breathe, don't panic!!!

She went invisible—a gut reaction—but it was useless.

"USELESS!" she shouted in anguish.

With a gurgle and a few bubbles the sticky goop sucked her down even farther—she was up to her neck. And sinking ever quicker. She couldn't swim or wade or move—she was cemented to her spot.

"PLEASE! SOMEONE!"

The liquid was up to her bottom lip. Lennie took a deep breath—

Suddenly, the liquid erupted beneath her and spit her out the other side of the trench. The sticky goop was still caked to every single inch of her, but she was *free*. She caught her breath for a moment, panting as she lay on the solid ground.

What was she thinking, coming into the borderlands alone? That was too close for comfort—she was two seconds away from drowning. But at least she'd made it. She'd crossed the water.

This side of the moat was no different from the other side—just as dark and shaded. A thick canopy of trees still blocked the stars, and the land was still flat and cracked. Only, without her flashlight, she didn't feel quite so brave anymore.

Well, I can't cross that bridge again, she thought, her hands shaking. So there was no way to go but onward . . . Even the land seemed to nudge her along, rumbling beneath her feet. Like it was impatient. Was it another trap?

Turning invisible, Lennie carefully crept forward. Ahead of her, in a dark clearing under the shelter of hundreds of trees, was an enormous rock, taller than a giraffe and wider than an elephant. She edged toward it slowly.

Come hereeeeeeee, came an unnervingly, spine-chillingly, goose-bump-pricklingly, sweat-drippingly creeptacular whisper.

Lennie froze.

Comeeeeeeeeeeeeeee, the voice rumbled again.

It sounded like it was coming from *inside* the rock. Then the rock rumbled and broke apart in the center, leaving a crack just big enough for a single person to slide through. She edged closer to the dark and dodgy entrance and stared in, but she couldn't see anything. If only she didn't lose her flashlight!

Lennie backed away quietly. She would *not* go inside. No way, not-uh, never ever *nope*.

Comeeeeeeeeee in! the voice said, louder this time. It was also crisper. And clearer. And closer.

Lennie's heart hammered. This was not good. Not good at all. Words like DOOM and DEATH and UNTIMELY DEMISE popped into her brain.

Stop thinking like Poppop! she thought to herself. She took a deep shuddering breath to calm her nerves. If she *really* wanted to prove to herself that she had what it took to be the next Prime Wizard, then she had to be courageous.

She invisibled and tiptoed to the mouth of the cave. A puff of hot wind whooshed out. It was like someone was blowing a moist breath on her.

She jumped back, so scared that she accidentally visibled again.

There you are, came the chilling voice, and she could see the shadowy outline of a figure coming toward her from inside the rock. *Crunch, crunch, CRUNCH* came the sound of pebbles under the shadowy figure's feet, growing louder and closer! *You're just in timeeeeeee . . .*

"For tea!" said an old man, poking his head out of the rock.

"Huh?" Lennie said.

"I said . . . you're just in time for tea! Come on in!" The man smiled at her. He had thinning gray hair, a naturally downturned mouth, and eyes that gleamed in the darkness. He was shivering in his coat—a shabby brown thing with lots of pockets and frayed sleeves—and he hugged it tighter to himself. "Well? Come on! I don't have all day. And it's cold out here."

Lennie shook her head no. "I don't have tea with strangers."

The man chuckled, his voice deep and smooth. "I'm not a stranger. I'm family."

"What?!" she choked. "I've never seen you before in my life!"

"My name is Humphrey de Cobblespork. I'm your great-uncle."

The Deepest Darkest Secretest Cave of Secrets (DUM DUM DUMMMM!)

Lennie gasped. Her poppop's brother! The one who'd never spoken to Poppop again after he lost Wizardmatch. Could this man *really* be him?

"I see you've heard of me!" Humphrey de Cobblespork said.

"What are you doing here?" Lennie said. "My mom said that you and my poppop haven't spoken in, like, a hundred years."

"I'm not *that* old. Wait . . . I don't look that old, do I?"

Lennie stared at him, too dumbfounded to speak. Of all the things she thought she'd find on her run-away-from-home adventure, her estranged great-uncle would have been the *last* thing she'd have ever predicted. "What—how—who—why—"

"You *are* one of Mortimer's numerous grandchildren, yes?"

Lennie nodded.

"What is your name?"

"I'm, um, Lennie."

"Nice to meet you, *Um Lennie*. It is much too chilly outside at this hour! Come, come!" He waved her inside.

She hesitated. She didn't *know* Humphrey de Cobblespork. Maybe it wasn't such a good idea to follow him inside. . . .

He disappeared into the rock with a shrug, and the ground shimmied beneath her feet again. She looked toward Madame Oglethorpe's house, but it was still so far away—and who knew how many more booby traps were in the forest? Next time, she might not be so lucky to escape. It was probably safer to stick with her great-uncle. And without another thought, she scurried after him.

Inside, the rock was even bigger than it looked from the outside.

It was very dim; Lennie could only see the vague outline of stalactites pointing down from the ceiling and stalagmites sticking up from the ground. The walls inside the rock were gravelly and unshapen—twisting this way and that—and the dim light, she determined, came from the twinkle of geodes. The path seemed to stretch on for miles.

"Watch your step—don't break your neck on a pebble. Or get impaled by a stalagmite. Or get eaten alive by vampire bats. Also, beware of the centicentipedes and millimillipedes."

"Centipedes and millipedes?"

"No, *centicentipedes*. They're bugs with one hundred toes on each of their one hundred legs. Millimillipedes have twice that. Nasty little buggers. So leggy. So toey. They don't bite, but they *do* tickle."

She didn't even realize the inside of a rock could be so dangerous. But all this talk of impaling and getting eaten alive had her thinking that maybe her great-uncle Humphrey was just as dramatic as his brother.

"You live here?" Lennie said incredulously. "Right next to the Pomporromp estate?"

"It's my temporary abode. I call it 'The Deepest Darkest Secretest Cave of Secrets *DUM DUM DUMMMMM!*'" he sang.

"What secrets?"

"No secrets!" he said brightly. "I just thought it sounded like a good name for a hovel like this. No, the only thing I have back there is a nice fire. And tea. And electric blankets, which is truly your world's greatest modern marvel."

"You've been to my world?" Lennie said.

"Certainly! My friends got me passage. I have friends in high places! Also friends in low places! And friends in middle-of-the-road places, but they're rather dull."

"Uh-huh," Lennie hummed, ducking beneath a particularly low stalactite.

"Almost there," Humphrey de Cobblespork said. "Here we go!"

In one step, the cave went from darkness to overwhelming brightness. Lennie held her hands over her eyes as she tried to adjust to the sudden light.

"Ah, yes, I forgot how much of an eyeball shriveler this can be."

With her eyes closed, the room was rather hot. Well, *hot* was an understatement. It was more like blisteringly boilingly broiling. Scorchingly, scaldingly, swelteringly sizzling. Roasting and toasting and smoking and arid. She blinked rapidly, trying to push through every instinct telling her to keep her eyes closed.

Uncle Humphrey turned his back on her and began to fiddle around with something in the corner of the room.

"What are you doing?"

"Working my magic!" Humphrey said.

"What—what kind of magic do you have?" She coughed through the heat.

"You know how our family works—we inherit just a small version of our ancestors' powers. You have invisibility, as you exhibited outside. And I would love another demonstration in a moment. I am awed and inspired—your powers are truly wonderful, my dear!"

She blinked at him, stunned. *Did he just call her magic wonderful?* Lennie smiled slightly as her eyes finally adjusted to the brightness in the room.

She looked around. The first thing she saw was fire everywhere—Humphrey had five different fireplaces going at the same time. Then, outside of the fireplaces, there were mini-fires blazing all over the room, suspended in air. Some were hovering in little balls, dangling from the ceiling. Others were poking up from the tables, licking at kettles and pots full of bubbling liquid. Orange and yellow and blue flames—

like tiny suns all over the place. It was beautiful. Even more beautiful than staring at a sky full of stars.

"I can make fire," Humphrey said.

"These are magic fires!" Lennie said in awe.

Humphrey held out a chair for her, and she plopped down just as the teakettle began to screech. She observed her great-uncle carefully as he poured out two cups of tea. In the light of his cave, she could see him better. He had flashing hazel eyes, a frowny mouth, and a stubbly chin. Atop his head, Humphrey had grayish-brown hair that wasn't *bald* quite yet, but thinning a bit. And while her poppop had a bit of a belly on him, Great-Uncle Humphrey was tall and muscular; he looked strong.

But it was the difference in their attitudes that was most jarring to her. Poppop always had to make every little thing into a grand dramatic spectacle, from his entrances to his colorful robes. But her great-uncle was dressed in a worn, tattered coat. His pants had holes in the kneecaps from where they'd worn away. He didn't live in a fancy-pants castle; he was living in a cramped cave. He seemed to live a simpler life . . . and a tougher one.

Humphrey placed a teacup in front of her.

"I have so many questions," Lennie said.

"I figured you would," Humphrey replied. "Drink up, drink up!"

She eyed the tea warily. Tea always tasted like old socks to her.

"If you're really my poppop's brother, then why is your last name Cobblespork, and not Pomporromp?"

"Those aren't our surnames—those are the estates and lands we own. *De* just means *of.* Mortimer owns the Pomporromp estate. Therefore, he is Mortimer of Pomporromp—or Mortimer de Pomporromp. I currently own a cottage called Cobblespork—therefore, I am Humphrey de Cobblespork."

"But if you own a house named Cobblespork, then why aren't you there? What are you doing here, in this rock, in the middle of the borderlands?" she demanded. "And how is it that I just *randomly* ran into you here?"

"Oh, it wasn't random," he said, sipping the tea. "I sought you out."

"You *sought* me?"

"I thought I ought to."

"You thought you ought to sought me?"

Great-Uncle Humphrey smiled. "I was observing as you wandered the borderlands. You, my dear, are not very bright, but I'll give you points for audacity."

"Hey! I am *too* bright!"

"Let's see. You ran away with no destination in mind, right through a patch of land so loaded with traps that it's practically a land mine. You didn't carry a map. You had no buddy or backup to help you in case you ran into trouble. And you walked into a dark cave with a perfect stranger who claimed he was family. So . . . I'm going to have to go with *not very bright.*"

She folded her arms. "You don't even know me! And why are you here in the first place?"

"I could ask you the same question," he retorted. "Why are *you* here?"

"You're avoiding the question," Lennie pointed out.

Great-Uncle Humphrey put the teacup to his lips and sipped slowly, keeping his eyes on her.

They sat in silence under the light of the floating fires, which kept dazzling and blazing, as strong as ever. Lennie stared at them. What was keeping these fires alive for so long? There were no signs of flickering out, and Uncle Humphrey didn't seem to be sweaty or breathless or out of energy, like Lennie always was when she needed to recharge.

She stared at him, and he raised an eyebrow.

"Why haven't any of these fireballs blown out?" she demanded. "My mom is twice as powerful as me, but her power only lasts for thirty seconds. There's no way you can use your power for this long without resting if you're not a Prime Wizard!"

"You're very observant, aren't you?" And he didn't even wait for her answer before he continued. "Your power lasts for fifteen seconds, hmm? You should probably keep that to yourself. Just in case."

"Why?"

"You just let me know your greatest weakness, Lennie."

She slapped a hand over her mouth. *Way to go, dummy!* From now on, she had to be more careful.

Uncle Humphrey burst into rowdy laughter. "Don't worry—I was only teasing. Now tell me: Are you here because you've been eliminated from Wizardmatch?"

Lennie's mood instantly soured. She spun the silver spoon around in her tea, trying to keep herself from crying or getting angry. She was already starting to feel jealousy roar inside her chest every time she thought about the stupid competition.

"Are you not doing well in the competition?"

"I wasn't even allowed to compete!" Lennie said, throwing her hands in the air. "Poppop has this rule that siblings aren't allowed to compete against one another. And he wanted my mom to put my brother into the competition instead of me."

Humphrey frowned and sipped his tea again. "I know how you feel."

"How do *you* know how I feel?" she said. "You got to compete! Wizardmatch is so—"

"Unfair," her great-uncle finished. "Or perhaps you were going for unjust? Undue, undeserved, unwarranted, unreasonable, unjustifiable, unnecessary, unmerited, un—"

"I was going to say *dumb*."

Humphrey stared out at a spot beyond her head, a scowl forming on his weathered face. "Indeed," he nodded. "It is *dumb*, as you say."

His nostrils flared again as he stared off into the corner of the cave. He looked frustrated and exhausted: the sort of look you would have if you stepped in a wad of chewed-up gum every single day of your life. Lennie wondered if she looked like that, too.

"So tell me more," Uncle Humphrey said. "I'm here for you."

She told her great-uncle all about Wizardmatch—about Poppop, her mom, her brother, *everything*. She hadn't realized how much she needed to talk to someone. And he was an attentive listener—very quiet, but constantly nodding.

As she neared the end, Uncle Humphrey stood up and poured water into two glasses and began to rustle around in the pantry. "Breakfast time!"

"Breakfast? But it's midnight!"

"Not anymore!" Uncle Humphrey said. "It's morning now."

Morning! Lennie wondered, with a nervous shiver, if anyone had realized she ran away.

"I hope you like potato chips."

"Potato chips? *For breakfast?*" Lennie said. Her stomach gave a loud rumble.

"It's all I eat. Good for the mind, body, and soul. Also the wallet." He reached into a tiny cupboard and grabbed a few jumbo bags of chips. Then he handed them over to Lennie who yawned again, but carried them dutifully as Humphrey gripped the teacups.

She followed her great-uncle, her eyes watery from sleepiness.

Lennie wasn't even fazed when she crossed into the part

of the cave that was dark. She simply listened for the crunch of Humphrey's footsteps, so she could stay in his wake. And hopefully stay *awake* while she was at it. Once out of the rock, she looked around. It was still dark outside.

"It's not morning! It's still nighttime!" Lennie groaned.

"Follow me," Uncle Humphrey said, ignoring her complaint. He broke into a jog. And although he was holding two teacups, not a single drop spilled. Lennie scurried to keep up. They marched through the clearing, into a very wooded area with thick trees in a cluster, their trunks so close that their branches tangled up in one another.

Uncle Humphrey marched over a few roots, and disappeared on the other side of a thick tree that looked an awful lot like one of the redwood trees in her backyard.

"Ta-da!" Uncle Humphrey said.

Lennie had to squint to see it: There were footholds protruding from the tree, circling around the trunk in a spiral. A staircase!

"Where does it lead?" Lennie asked, looking into the canopy of leaves above.

Uncle Humphrey smiled slyly. "Up."

And so she followed Great-Uncle Humphrey up the never-ending staircase, the wood groaning with every step.

At the top, there was a small wooden platform, just big enough for the two of them to sit on. They put the tea and chips between them; then they dangled their feet over the edge, staring over the treetops. From this height, she could look down at the borderlands, the thick trees covering the booby-trapped area like a blanket.

But she *did* have the perfect view of Poppop's neighborhood, and though the estates were spread out as far as the eye could see, each castle was more beautiful than the next. There was one floating in the air, and another with tall spires, and another with a single bell tower, and the Oglethorpes' looked like it was made of starlight. In the quiet, shadowy morning, it twinkled and glowed.

"Eat," Humphrey said, pointing to the bags of chips.

She grabbed a fistful and began to munch. Humphrey, meanwhile, sipped his tea. Their legs dangled over the jagged edge of the platform. At first, it was so dark that Lennie could still see the stars, but eventually those faded out into a pale sunlight.

As she looked into the distance, she couldn't help but think of her family. She wished that her dad were here. Did her mom even notice she was gone? Did Michael? Her poppop? Would any of them even care?

"What aw you finking about?" Humphrey said through a full mouth.

She sighed. "I'm thinking about Wizardmatch. Again."

"You'll never stop thinking about it. It's all I think about. Well, that and potato chips." Humphrey licked the salt off his palm. *"What?"* he said at the sight of Lennie's scandalized glare.

"Nothing," Lennie said, turning to gaze out again. Some of

the castles began to stir. A windmill-shaped one began to spin; some of the chimneys on other mansions began to pump out smoke. "It's just," she hesitated, mulling over her words so that she said them just right, "you said you're the only person who knows how I feel. And I could use some advice."

"Hmm . . . Never sneeze on a circus clown. Always carry a snorkel. Don't fill your brother's shoes with oatmeal—"

"Not *that* sort of advice!" Lennie cried. "I want advice about Wizardmatch! What I should do. I want to know—what happened between you and Poppop?"

"I don't want to talk about it," Humphrey said brusquely. "I've filed that part of my life away. I'm over it."

"But clearly you aren't," Lennie said. "So just tell me what happened."

Her great-uncle bristled. Then he mumbled something incomprehensible.

"What?" Lennie said.

"I said ONCE UPON A TIME," he bellowed, and the sound of his voice echoed all across the tops of the borderland trees.

"Why are you starting with *once upon a time?*" Lennie said. "This isn't a fairy tale."

"Any story worth telling starts with *once upon a time*! Once upon a time," he began again, ignoring Lennie as she rolled her eyes, "my poppop, your great-great-poppop . . . hmmm . . . what do you call a great-great-poppop? A poppoppoppop? Poppoppoppop Pomporromp?"

"Stop stalling!"

"Once upon a time, my grandpappy decided he was going to host Wizardmatch. He was very ill and didn't have much time left, and all of us knew it. Whereas your grandfather can dillydally and shilly-shally all the livelong day because he doesn't *need* to pick a successor." He stroked his stubbly chin and got potato chip grease all over his face. "Winifred was fourteen, Mortimer was twelve, I was eleven, Bernadette and Ophelia were both eight. And we all had the same power—the ability to control fire for small amounts of time. Bernadette was eliminated first. That, of course, caused a big rift between the twins. They were very competitive with each other their whole lives—and continued all the way up until their simultaneous deaths in a duel."

"A duel? Is that . . . is that a thing that happens in Netherly?"

Great-Uncle Humphrey simply glared at her.

"Sorry," Lennie said. "Go on."

"As I was *saying*: After Bernadette was cut in the first round, Ophelia was eliminated next. It was hard for the twins to compete with Winifred, Mortimer, and me. We had many years of practice and training on them. Then Winifred was eliminated, which she was huffy about because she was the oldest of us all."

Well, Lennie sure understood *that*. And Lennie couldn't help but notice that all the girls got eliminated first in her poppop's Wizardmatch competition. She didn't know Winifred, but Lennie was sure—deep in her bones, *positively positive*—that this didn't escape her great-aunt's attention, either.

"In the final test, it was me versus Mortimer. We were so close in age—just nineteen months apart. We were best friends. Better than best! Better than better than best!" Uncle Humphrey snorted. "But your poppop was always the favorite, and Grandpappy chose *him* to be the next Prime Wizard. And so I was stuck with my limited firepower, while my brother had a whole world of magic available at his fingertips," he finished. "WOE! WOE IS ME! WOE IS WE! WOE IS US!"

"Woe is us," Lennie agreed. There were so many things unfair about Wizardmatch, from its sexism to its ageism to its straight-up favoritism. The competition was like a tornado that barreled through their family, leaving one person standing . . . and everyone else in shambles.

"The worst part was after the competition," Uncle Humphrey said in a low voice. "Mortimer gloated endlessly about winning Wizardmatch. Then, the moment Grandpappy passed, Mortimer kicked all four of us out of the house. Said the estate was *his* now, and we did not belong."

"That's horrible!" Lennie said.

Uncle Humphrey sighed sadly. "I'll never forget that rainy morning when he sent me and my sisters away. Alas— daybreak!" He pointed across the neighborhood. "Look at that sun . . . it's perfection! Like a glowing potato chip."

Lennie looked toward the horizon, where the sun was slowly rising. The morning light kissed the tops of all the estates and castles. It was beautiful, but also lonely. "It's very nice."

He put his hand on her shoulder. "Yes, I thought it would be the perfect send-off."

"Send-off?"

"Yes! I'm sending you back to the castle."

Lennie bristled. "What?! You can't send me back there! I just escaped!"

"Well, you can't stay here with me."

"I *won't* go back there! No! No, no, no!"

"No?" Uncle Humphrey scratched his head and flakes of dandruff sprinkled onto his shoulders like fairy dust. "You can't say no! I—I refuse your refusal!"

"Oh yeah? Well, I refuse your refusal of my refusal! I *have* to stay," Lennie said, stamping her foot onto the platform. "No one understands me—Mom, Michael, Poppop, my cousins, *no one*! I don't ever want to look at any of their faces AGAIN!"

"I could blindfold you, if that would help."

"That would *not* help!" she shrilled, her voice two octaves higher than normal. She'd run away again, if she had to— she was *not* going back.

Lennie got to her feet.

"Where are you going?"

"Back to the cave. I'm not leaving," she said. She stormed

across the wooden platform—and tripped over her own shoelace.

She tried to catch herself—but she couldn't stop. She lurched forward and tumbled right off the edge.

"AHHHHHHHHHHHH!" she screamed, closing her eyes.

The wind rushed around her, her stomach dropped—she was falling!

Plummeting!

Plunging!

Still plummeting! Still plunging!

Somehow, Lennie thought falling from a very tall height would be *faster* than this. She peeked an eye open—and gasped.

She was hovering in the air, halfway between the platform and the hard earth. But she wasn't falling anymore. Instead . . . she was *rising*. A burst of wind beneath her was pushing her back up to the platform—back to Uncle Humphrey.

Humphrey held out his hand to her. "GRAB ON, LENNIE!"

The expression on his face was of intense concentration—and maybe a bit of pain.

She took his hand, and he pulled her back onto the platform. Once she was safe, she lay down flat, a hand over her hammering heart. Uncle Humphrey sat down against the trunk of the tree and wiped his brow with his tattered coat.

"I told you to be careful," he growled.

Lennie's mouth hung wide open. It was *him*—he had conjured the air. But that was impossible! Humphrey's power was fire. No one except the Prime Wizard had more than one power.

"H-how!" she said, confused. "How did you do that?"

Humphrey's lips pursed together.

"You told me last night that your power was fire! You lied to me!"

"I wasn't lying. I *can* control fire. Oh, don't look so cross!" he said. "Of course I wasn't going to *lead* by telling you all the things I can do. I barely know you!"

"All the things you can do?" she said, and Humphrey's face scrunched up, clearly mad at himself for saying too much. "There's more," Lennie realized, her heart suddenly racing. "More than just fire and wind. What *else* can you control?"

". . . Water," Humphrey admitted.

"Water!"

"Earth."

"Earth, too!" Lennie repeated incredulously.

"How else do you think you got out of that moat last night?"

"But how?" Lennie demanded. She clutched both sides of the platform to steady herself, and she gazed at her great-uncle in shock. In awe. In wonder . . . as he was chewing a hangnail with his teeth. "How is this even possible?"

"I taught myself," Humphrey said, flicking his hangnail off the edge. "And it wasn't easy, I'll tell you that. It took forty years of grueling, backbreaking, sweat-dripping work. Unlike *Mortimer*," he said with a sniff, "who got all his powers handed to him on a silver platter. I've had to work for everything I've got. And I still don't have it all."

"What do you mean?"

"My powers are limited," he said, wringing his hands together in his lap.

"But you can do so much! And those fires! They haven't gone out once since I've arrived."

"Yes, but that's it, isn't it," Uncle Humphrey said. "I can make fire and water and ice. I can move rocks and blow air and even quake the earth. But I can't do anything other than elemental magic. I can't teleport or lift heavy objects or manipulate my body into different shapes. I can't go invisible—I can't do what you can do. My powers are stronger than they *were* . . . but I can only do so much."

"Who cares? That's way more than anyone else in the family can do!" Lennie gushed. "You have to tell me how you did it!"

"It doesn't come easy, and it doesn't come fast. It takes endless determination, drive, and grit to stretch your powers."

She had determination! She had drive! And, well, she didn't know what grit was, but if she didn't have it, she would get it!

"The first thing I had to do," Humphrey continued, "was to learn how to tease out my powers—pull it loose like putty. When I was your age, my fire only lasted for fifteen seconds. After I lost Wizardmatch, I had to push myself to stretch it to twenty seconds. Then forty. Then, over the course of many years, a minute. Five minutes. Ten minutes. And after a decade of increasing my stamina, I got to an hour. Five hours, ten hours . . . and after half a century of practice, a whole day."

"Wow!"

"Then of course, I need a much longer resting period. Many hours of no magic before I can start up again."

"That's still impressive," Lennie said, "to be able to do that with elements for so long!"

"And it's not just my endurance and stamina. I've improved my reach over the years—my fireballs can shoot farther. I can summon water from a distance. Using my special method and years of practice, I cultivated a whole buffet of powers from absolutely nothing. Nil, zilch, zero, DIDDLY-SQUAT! I worked for it. And worked hard."

Lennie's mind was dancing a jig. Just an hour ago, everything was THE WORST, and with one split-second realization it was now THE BEST. Her heart pitter-pattered and she was grinning—*beaming*—radiating with excitement.

"What?" he asked. "Why are you staring at me like that?"

"Because," Lennie replied, "I just had the greatest idea!"

"And that is?"

She smiled so widely her cheeks ached. "Humphrey de Cobblespork, *you* are going to train me!"

A Very Interesting Idea

Uncle Humphrey stood up. "What did you say?"

Lennie was giggling. Great-Uncle Humphrey could be her mentor! He could teach her to stretch her own powers and make her stronger. And maybe—just maybe—she could prove to everyone once and for all that she *was* worthy of being considered for Prime Wizard.

"I said I want you to train me!"

"What? Me?!"

"Yes, you!"

"You who?"

"Who? YOU!" Lennie said, pointing at him.

His mouth twitched, and he looked away. "No."

"Wait, *no*?!"

"No," Humphrey confirmed.

No.

Lennie sucked in a sharp breath. This couldn't be happening *again*.

"Well, why not?" she demanded.

Without a word, Uncle Humphrey stood up on the platform and began to walk down the footholds in the tree.

"Uncle Humphrey?" she called after him. "Uncle

Humphrey—wait up!" But he didn't once acknowledge that he heard her. She climbed down the steps after him.

Lennie thought he'd stop at the giant rock that led to his cave, but he kept marching—through the wooded borderlands, where it was still too dark for comfort, even in the morning.

"Where are you going?!" she asked again.

"I'm taking you back to the castle!"

Lennie stopped, firmly planting her feet in the dirt. "You can't take me back there!"

Suddenly, a strong wind blew at her back and she was forced to stumble forward.

"And you can't make me with your powers!"

"I don't have time to play around," Uncle Humphrey said, moving the earth to make his own bridge to cross over the oily moat. "I am not a babysitter."

"I don't need a babysitter! I need a coach!"

"No time for that, either," he said, sending another burst of wind to push her forward. It blew her hair right into her mouth.

Lennie spit out her hair. "Can't you even imagine what it's like for me?"

Uncle Humphrey sniffed. "I do not have to imagine. I know perfectly well, firsthand, the pain and suffering Wizardmatch inflicts."

Lennie folded her arms. "I wish I could just destroy

Wizardmatch, so no one had to compete! Then we'd all be happy!"

Uncle Humphrey stopped walking abruptly. "Now *there's* an idea," he said, an amused smile tugging at the corners of his mouth. "But can we do it?"

"Do what?"

"Destroy Wizardmatch."

Lennie furrowed her brow. "Wait, we're destroying Wizardmatch?"

"Isn't that what you just said?"

"I . . . I wasn't being serious. It just sort of popped out of my mouth."

"Well, why not?"

Lennie pondered. Could she destroy Wizardmatch? The more she thought about it, the more she liked the idea. By sabotaging the competition, Lennie could hurt Poppop like he'd hurt her, and prove to him and everyone else how good she was at magic.

Suddenly, there was a hunger inside her—and not just because she had barely eaten her potato chip breakfast.

"If we stop Wizardmatch," her uncle said, continuing the walk toward the Pomporromp property, "we stop all the injustice that comes with it." He smiled and rested a hand on her shoulder. "I want to help you. We will do it together."

Her heart jumped. "We can?!"

"You don't expect to take down Wizardmatch by yourself,

do you? Yes, I'll have to train you. But," he said, pausing for an *excruciatingly* long time, "before I do, I'm going to need to know you're serious."

"Seriously?"

"Isn't that what I'm asking *you*? I'm seriously serious about you being serious—"

"I'm serious!" Lennie cried. "Thank you, thank you, *thank you*!"

He squinted at her, his lips puckered tightly. "Don't thank me yet. Because I'm not ready to train you. If you're truly serious," he said darkly, "then I'm going to need you to *prove it*."

"But how?" Lennie asked.

"Think. What can you do to *show* me you mean business?"

"Well," Lennie said slowly, "the first individual test is tomorrow. At the pudding pool. What if I messed it up? I could throw garbage in there. Or cat litter."

"Yawn," he said with a yawn. "Mortimer could clean that with a flick of his staff."

"What if I brought you potato chips?" she offered.

"I'm going to make you do that anyway," Uncle Humphrey said, zapping a nasty spell with a fireball.

"I could steal the judges' scoring cards?"

"Is this really the best you've got?" Uncle Humphrey said.

They were getting close to the border of the Pomporromp property, and Lennie was out of ideas. She ran her hands through her hair, in a desperate attempt to shake a plan loose from her brain.

Could she do something with her powers, maybe? Uncle Humphrey didn't like her idea to mess up the arena. But maybe she could mess up one of her cousins' chances. That was something Poppop wouldn't be able to fix! And if she did her job right, no one would ever know she did it.

She met her uncle's flashing eyes.

"I could sabotage one of my cousins. Have them eliminated from the competition."

Uncle Humphrey stopped and stared. At first, Lennie thought he was going to tell her that this idea was stupid, too, but instead he began to clap very, very slowly. "Excellent, yes. And just so that I know it's fair and random and that you didn't preplan it with someone, I want you to ruin the last contestant's chances. That way, you only have one shot."

Lennie nodded. They were at the edge of the borderlands now. She could see the Pomporromp estate, but not perfectly: The empty grounds looked a little blurry and wobbly from this side of the border.

Uncle Humphrey hummed. "Yes, I like this plan. Whoever goes last, you wipe them out of Wizardmatch. And if you can do that, I will train you. Good luck!"

And he pushed her out of the borderlands.

Stumbling into the Pomporromp estate again was suffocating. The air on this side of the border was so thin and wispy—and the sun was so blindingly bright. She squinted as her eyes adjusted, and when they did, she found herself staring face-to-face with a tuxedo cat.

"Hey!" Sir Fluffington the Fourth hissed at her. The cat's tail was rigid. She realized she'd been looking to make sure the coast was clear for *humans*, but she forgot to consider that Fluffles might be out and about, and he was low to the ground. "What were you doing in the borderlands, Lennie?"

She was caught! *Stay cool!* she told herself. It's not like he knows about Uncle Humphrey. "I took a walk."

"How long were you in there?"

"I just went in!" Lennie lied.

"And where did you go?"

"Nowhere—I just wanted to see what it looked like!"

Fluffles's whiskers twitched. "A LIKELY STORY." He skirted behind Lennie, putting himself between her and the borderlands. "You were plotting with the Oglethorpes, weren't you? You sneaky, devious, sly, underhanded, duplicitous, tricksy little girl!"

"I've never even met the Oglethorpes!" Lennie said.

Fluffles bared his teeth. "And you better keep it that way. They are bad news. Once, I wandered into the borderlands, and Madame Oglethorpe turned me into a teakettle for stepping one foot on her lawn. If your poppop hadn't saved me, I'd still be in hot water! Or full of hot water!"

"Well, good thing I didn't run into Madame Oglethorpe!" Lennie said.

The cat regarded her with suspicion. "I don't believe you. You're up to something! You're . . . purrrrrrr," he said as Lennie leaned down and stroked his back to distract him.

Fluffles nuzzled her fingers with his face. "PURRRRRfect. Right there! That's the spot!"

She scooped the cat up in her arms. As she carried him back to the castle, she spotted Ethan and his father walking toward the Garden of Goulash.

Lennie said hi to Ethan and Uncle Philip #1 as they passed; her uncle smiled at her, but today Ethan's ginger hair was swept in front of his face. She wondered how he could see. When he walked into the Garden of Goulash and stubbed his toe on a gravestone, she realized he couldn't. He cursed, immediately uncovering his eyes by shrinking his hair into a buzz cut.

Lennie continued on her way with Fluffles. When she reached the door to the castle, her brother and her mom emerged.

"Len! We were just going outside to look for you! Where were you?" her mom demanded.

The cat stiffened in her arms, but Lennie continued to pet him hard. "What do you mean?" she asked.

"You didn't sleep in Cheeseburger Chamber!" Michael accused.

"Were you outside?" her mom said. "You didn't sleep outside, did you?"

"She was just in the borderlands!" Fluffles cried out.

Lennie dropped Fluffles on the ground, and he bared his pointy teeth. "HEY! YOU ARE NOT DONE PETTING ME, HUMAN!"

"I don't pet tattletales!"

"Or cat-tletales!" Michael snickered.

"Lennie!" her mom shrilled.

"It's not a big deal!" Lennie said. "I just poked my head in for a *second*."

"You are in big trouble! I told you not to go in there. It's dangerous!"

"It's not dangerous," Michael said. "I went in, too!"

"Okay," her mom said, rubbing her temples. "From now on, *no more borderlands*. Both of you. Promise?"

"Promise," Michael said.

"Promise," Lennie lied.

"If I catch you near it again—"

"I said I *promise*," Lennie snapped, whistling for a skateboard and rolling away. She headed back to her room to practice invisibling. She used the floor-length mirror to stare at her reflection—and then her nonreflection—and then her reflection again.

But then behind her shoulder, the tomato-red window began to steam up, so thick that it became suddenly dark in her room. Lennie turned to face it, and letters began to appear, as if an invisible finger was writing on her window.

You have five seconds to make sure you're alone in the room.–H

Lennie grinned, her heart fluttering as she dead-bolted the door, just to make sure Michael wouldn't come in while Uncle Humphrey was writing to her. Then more words began to appear beneath the other sentence.

Dear Lennie,

(Is that short for anything by the way? Perhaps Lenjamin, or Lentils?)

He thought her name was short for *lentils?* Lennie shook her head, then looked back toward the message.

From now on, this is how I will reach you.

Good luck tomorrow.

I will be watching.

Then the window wiped itself clean.

She was so close to having a mentor and growing her magic. Excitement prickled on her skin, like the chills she got whenever she went invisible.

Tomorrow, the first Wizardmatch test—and Lennie's first test, too—would begin.

The Pool of Pudding

The morning of the first test was frenzied. Everyone was running all over the castle; her cousins were stretching in the halls; her aunts and uncles were doting on their kids, making sure they looked presentable for Poppop; Fluffles was chasing a mouse; Estella was leaning over railings calling for Mortimer, who had disappeared somewhere in the castle.

But Lennie found him as she was skateboarding past the twenty-seventh floor.

"Poppop!" she exclaimed. "How—"

"Not now, Lennie—I am busy, busy, busy. Just *wait* until you see the first Wizardmatch test later! You'll be so impressed!"

"I—"

"NO TIME!" he said, skateboarding away. He held his arms out as he rolled along in a rather wobbly fashion.

Lennie sighed and continued into the dining hall. She grabbed her breakfast and saw—in the corner—Jonathan and Emma, huddled together. Maybe *they* would understand what she was feeling, since they couldn't compete either.

Lennie walked over, but as she got close, they immediately stopped talking and stared at her.

"Can we help you?" Emma asked, her green eyes piercing.

There was an excruciatingly long and awkward pause.

"It's okay," Jonathan said, kicking out a seat for Lennie. "Lennie's cool."

Lennie flushed. "I . . . I can go."

Emma studied her and sighed. "No, it's all right. Sit down," Emma relented, and Lennie took her chair faster than a blink. "We're talking about the big fight."

"What fight?"

"Were you under a rock last night?" Emma said. "The fight at dinner!"

"I ate in my room," Lennie said, looking between her two older cousins. "What happened?"

"Uncle Philip #3 was speaking badly about my brother," Emma said. "So my dad poured juice all over his head."

"And then Uncle Philip #3 punched Uncle Philip #1," Jonathan added.

"And then Uncle Bob used his stretchable arms to tear them apart."

"Wow," Lennie said. The competition had barely begun, and it was already heating up.

"Look!" Jonathan said, pointing to a table where Julien and his father were sitting. Uncle Philip #3 was hissing angrily into Julien's ear, and Julien looked more and more like he'd swallowed a frog.

"I, like, kind of feel bad for him," Emma said, biting on her black fingernails.

"I don't!" Lennie said loudly.

Julien looked up and caught them all staring. He stuck his tongue out at them.

"Come on," Jonathan said. "It's time to go. Lennie—want to sit with us? We're going to hang out in the back, so we can talk."

"Because this competition is *the worst*," Emma said.

Lennie hesitated. Sitting with her older cousins was, like, *beyond* cool. But at the same time, she needed to be close to the front, so she could be ready to sabotage the last competitor and prove herself to Humphrey.

"Actually, I want to wish Michael luck," she finally said.

They paused, and Emma shrugged. Lennie had a bad feeling that she failed some sort of unspoken test.

When they walked out to the pudding pool, there were no bleachers there. Just a mishmashed crowd of Pomporromps. Jonathan and Emma hung in the back, while Lennie wove her way through the crowd until she found her brother.

"Lennie!" Michael said. "I was worried you weren't going to come."

"I had to come."

"Oh," he said, shuffling his feet. "Aren't you going to wish me luck?" He looked at her, his brown eyes eager.

"Good luck," she said, but she didn't mean it. Or maybe she meant it. She didn't know. Lennie only just wished he could've said good luck back to her. Since her invisibility only lasted fifteen seconds, that was all she had to complete her mission *and* not get caught. Her stomach lurched at the thought, and she stood on her tiptoes to peer toward the borderlands—way, way, *way* across the estate. She couldn't see Humphrey de Cobblespork anywhere.

"What are you doing?" Michael asked her.

"Just . . . looking around," Lennie said. "Hey, do you have any idea what you're going to be doing today?"

"Nope!" Michael said with a smile. "But I'm still gonna crush it."

She sighed. *I could have crushed it, too. If I were allowed.*

No . . . she couldn't get negative. There was hope now! There was Uncle Humphrey and his special, top secret training method. And there was the plan to destroy Wizardmatch. She'd prove them all wrong.

The rest of the missing Pomporromps arrived, followed by Estella, Sir Fluffington the Fourth, and last of all, Poppop.

"HEAR YE! HEAR YE!" Poppop Pomporromp shouted. "And welcome to the first real test of Wizardmatch. This is the first time we will be doing eliminations. Let me reintroduce you to my fellow judges. Here we have Sir Fluffington the Fourth, the noblest guard cat I have ever known. And on my right is Estella Jane Wixson, the best human anyone could find."

Estella looked both surprised and touched at Poppop's words.

"Feast your eyes on my pudding pool! Delicious chocolate—I pride myself in it. Actually, I bathe myself in it, but that is neither here nor there." He cleared his throat. "What I want you to look at . . . are the diving boards."

Lennie did look. There were two diving boards—a low dive and a high dive—facing the pool. But then Poppop raised his magic staff, gave it a flick, and suddenly the diving boards popped out of the ground, like weeds being plucked. They floated across the pudding pool and then cemented themselves on the other side, facing out over the cliff. To jump off them now would be to dive hundreds of feet into the rough, black ocean.

Anya began jogging in place. Her curls bounced up and down around her workout headband. "Whatever the test is, I'm going to WIN! I'm captain of the swim team at school—*and* I have fifteen swim trophies!"

"You got this, Anya!" her dad said as he massaged her shoulders.

Perrie raised her hand, like they were all in a classroom. "Are we going to jump off the cliff?" her tiny cousin squeaked. "That's a deadly drop!"

"DEADLY INDEED!" Poppop said, glancing furtively at Estella. He coughed. "Are you feeling ill, Estella? I was very sure you were going to interrupt me or scold me or—"

"I thought I'd let you be dramatic today, Mortimer."

"You're the best best BEST!" Poppop squealed, clapping his hands together. "Okay, back to the test," he said, sounding giddy. "The *dangerous* test! At the bottom of the ocean, I've hidden a few items of mine. But be careful:

there's a three-headed shark guarding all of my possessions."

"A three-headed shark?!" Michael said. "That is AWE-SOME!"

"Yes, I created it!" Poppop said proudly. "'What's the one thing that's scarier than a one-headed shark?' I said to myself. A *two*-headed shark. And then I thought, what's scarier than a two-headed shark? A *three*-headed shark!"

"What about four-headed shark?" Julien asked.

Poppop's jaw dropped. "Four heads?! Why didn't *I* think of that? INGENIUS! Anyway, all you have to do is bring back any item, and you will pass. Let me stress this again: *the only rule* is that you must retrieve one of my items from the ocean. This will test your COURAGE. Your BRAV-ERY. Your METTLE. Your NERVE. Your VALOR. Your PLUCK—"

"*Someone* ate a thesaurus for breakfast," Ethan whispered.

Poppop leered at him. "It *seems*," he said, smacking his lips, "that we have a volunteer to go first."

Ethan's freckled face turned bright red—Lennie was sure he regretted speaking up. But he moved to the low dive nev-ertheless.

"One last thing," Poppop said. "You have only one minute to accomplish your task. When time is up, I will pull you back, whether or not you have anything in your hands. Try to get back on your own, as I will deduct points if I have to do it. Three, two, one, GO!"

Ethan got to work right away, growing his hair. And

growing. And growing. It extended past his shoulders, past his butt, past his feet. Then Ethan wrapped the ends of his hair around the diving board, tied a tight knot, and began to rappel down the side of the cliff, using his hair as rope.

Lennie and the entire Pomporromp family raced to the edge of the cliff, peering over to watch as Ethan descended into the ocean. And then he was gone.

Suddenly Ethan popped out of the water, and his hair began to slurp back into his scalp, pulling him up, up, up the cliff face. When he reached the diving board, he pulled himself up with one hand and held out the other to Poppop.

"Here," he said, handing Poppop something pink and soggy, "I believe these are your slippers."

Poppop clapped his hands together and laughed in delight. "Well done! That wasn't so bad, was it?"

"That water," Ethan said with a shiver. "It was cold and dark . . . like my soul."

"Indeed," Poppop said. "Next, we shall have . . . VICTORIA!"

Poppop waved his staff and levitated the baby right out of Aunt Macy's hands. Victoria soared to the diving board. She landed on her side and began to roll off; she plummeted to the depths of the ocean.

"MY BABY!" Aunt Macy shrieked. "PULL HER BACK UP!"

"Let's not ruin her chance," Poppop said. "Don't throw the baby out with the bathwater."

"BUT SHE CAN'T SWIM!"

"She can float."

"BUT THERE'S A THREE-HEADED SHARK!"

"A little shark bite never did anyone any harm! Well, except Sir Fluffington the *Second*, may he rest in peace."

Fluffles stiffened and backed away from the cliff's edge. "I thought Sir Fluffington the Second left to join the circus! You said he departed because he was forever in jest!"

"Yes, he departed because he was forever in*gest*ed."

The clock ticked on, and the waiting seemed endless.

"Time!" Poppop said, waving his staff. Victoria flew out from the water, and she appeared unharmed. She hiccupped as she sucked on a key ring. Lennie's eyebrows shot up. The baby actually found something!

"Beginner's luck," grumbled Uncle Philip #3.

"Of course she went for the shiniest object," Aunt Lacey muttered.

"You found my keys!" Poppop said. "And next up . . . Ellington!"

Ellington flounced her giant dress and curled a lock of her hair around her finger. She scrunched her face and leaned over. Something dark and brown rose out of the seawater: an old boot. It levitated upward, Ellington coaxing it up the cliff. But then, the boot quivered.

"OH!" Ellington said as her knees buckled beneath her and she swooned. The boot fell back to the ocean with a *plunk!* "The effort was just too much for me! I am too weak!"

She was *not* too weak. Lennie had seen her lift much heavier objects from much farther away for a much longer time. Lennie knew Ellington didn't want to be Prime Wizard, but it just felt like her cousin was spitting all over her dreams.

"Mmmm," Poppop said, frowning. All three judges were writing on their clipboards. "Well, thank you for trying. Now . . . Julien."

Lennie tried to hide her pout. She'd been hoping Julien would go last, so she could sabotage him.

He smiled, looked around—and Ellington came walking back to the cliff with a blank stare on her face. She clambered onto the diving board and leaned over the edge.

What is she doing? Lennie thought. *It's Julien's turn!*

Suddenly, a stuffed animal came flying out of the sea, straight into Ellington's arms. With a slack look on her face, she handed her prize to Julien. Lennie had never seen her cousin's eyes so dull or lifeless.

Mind control, Lennie realized, smacking her head. *Julien has mind control as a power.* She felt stupid for not figuring it out earlier.

"Fantastic display, Julien!" Poppop said with a wink. "Now . . . Bo!"

With every name that wasn't Michael, Lennie's stomach wrenched. What if her brother was the last contestant, and she had to destroy his chances? Could she do it? Would she?

As Poppop started the timer, Bo hopped right into the pool and spooned fistfuls of pudding into his mouth. He ate and he ate and he ate, faster than seemed humanly possible. Then Bo coughed up an enormous white bird as big as he was. He moved closer to the bird to hop on its back, but the bird kept trying to bite his fingers. They danced around each other in a wild goose chase.

"TIME!" Poppop called out. "You . . . you didn't even get down to the ocean!"

"I am afraid I cannot control the birds," Bo said breathily. "I only bring them to life, and that is the greatest power of all."

"The greatest power of all is *love*," said his sister Danielle.

"Peace, love, and spontaneously generating waterfowl," Bo agreed.

"The judges will deliberate on your effort," Poppop said. "Next up . . ."

Michael, Michael, Michael! Lennie chanted in her head.

"Perrie!"

Perrie ran up to the diving board, nervously running a hand through her short purple hair. But she had no reason to be nervous. She used her extendable arms to reach down into the water. With one hand, she restrained the three-headed shark. And with the other hand, she fished for an item: Poppop's spare dentures. She finished the task in a matter of seconds, and it was the best performance Lennie had seen yet.

"Very efficient!" Poppop said. "We have now come to our penultimate contestant."

Lennie suddenly felt feverishly ill. Next was either her

brother, Michael, or her cousin Anya. And whoever wasn't called, she'd have to destroy. "Next up is . . ."

Lennie closed her eyes.

"Michael!"

As Michael took his place on the diving board, she let out a sigh of relief. He looked so small up there. Lennie wished she'd meant it more when she wished him luck earlier.

"And your time starts . . . *NOW*!" Poppop said.

But Michael didn't move off the diving board.

"Your time is *going*," Poppop said, annoyed.

"I know," Michael said.

Most of the Pomporromps began murmuring to one another, but Lennie knew exactly what Michael was doing. His power only lasted for thirteen seconds. If he didn't wait until the last seconds to dive in, he'd be stuck in the ocean with the shark, totally visible, until Poppop could pull him up.

And sure enough, with seventeen seconds to go, Michael shouted, "SHARK ATTAAAAAAAAAAAACK!" and cannonballed hundreds of feet into the ocean. When the clock reached zero, Poppop pulled him back, and Michael proudly handed him a waterlogged book.

"I had my doubts," Poppop said with a smile. "But clearly you wanted to wait to the last moment to be dramatic. My, my—you might be the Pomporromp who is most like myself!"

Lennie's face twitched in rage.

"And the last champion . . . Anya!" Poppop said.

Lennie swallowed down her anger and wiped her sweaty palms on her shorts. Now was her time!

"Three, two, one . . . GO!" Poppop shouted, and Anya dove headfirst into the water, before Lennie could even think of a way to stop her.

What do I do?! Lennie rushed over to the edge of the cliff. There was *no way* Lennie could dive in after Anya without getting caught.

Lennie watched her cousin freeze the three-headed shark in place and dive into the deep for one of Poppop's belongings. And when the shark unfroze, Anya hopped onto its back and rode it—holding on to its fin tightly, even while it tried to buck her off. The whole family *ooooh*ed and *ahhhh*ed at her daring performance.

With only ten seconds left to Anya's test, Lennie began to panic. She scrambled away from the edge of the cliff. *How* was she going to sabotage her cousin?

Five seconds left.

Lennie invisibled.

Three. Two. One.

Poppop waved his staff, and Anya appeared just a few feet from Lennie, holding a toothbrush.

I have to get it from her! Lennie thought, racing closer.

She was right in front of Anya now. Her cousin looked so elated—her grin was wide and her dimple was deep, and Lennie felt sick. But she *had* to do this—it was the only way to convince Uncle Humphrey she was serious.

She reached an invisible hand forward, slid the toothbrush out of Anya's grip, and chucked it over the cliff. Anya was so busy making triumphant muscle poses that she didn't even notice.

"I WIN!" she gloated. "I'm the BEST, and don't you forget it! I *always* win!"

"Actually, you FAILED!" Poppop said.

"WHAT?" she choked. She stared at her hand, then scoured the ground. "But I had your toothbrush! I did! I swear!"

"Well, where is it, then?"

Still shaking from nerves, Lennie went visible behind the crowd and held her breath. None of the cousins noticed her. Not a single aunt or uncle blinked her way. Her mom and brother didn't even sniff in her direction.

But *the cat.*

Fluffles was staring right at her, his yellow eyes like two burning suns. Her chest tightened.

He doesn't know anything, Lennie told herself. *You're just nervous.*

She moved behind the crowd until Fluffles couldn't see her anymore.

Poppop clapped his hands together. "And now, Estella, Sir Flufflington the Fourth, and I will deliberate. When we return, we shall announce who won and who is eliminated!"

Poppop, Estella, and Fluffles formed a small circle and

began whispering together. Everyone started mingling, and Lennie wove her way to the edge of the crowd, looking toward the borderlands for Uncle Humphrey. Was he watching? Was he impressed?

Someone tapped her on the shoulder, and she whipped around.

"What are you looking at?" Michael asked.

"Nothing," she said defensively.

"Did you see me? Did you?! What'd you think?"

"You know you did great!" Lennie snapped. "You don't need me to tell you!"

And she stormed off, leaving Michael looking hurt and confused. *That wasn't right*, her gut told her. But she just couldn't get herself to apologize.

"HEAR YE HEAR YE!" Poppop said. "We are ready to start our eliminations!"

Everyone hushed.

"The first name I call is the best performer in this test. Drumroll, please!"

All the Pomporromps stomped their feet—

"JULIEN. Everyone give Julien a hand."

Julien's dad applauded wildly, but everyone else did a respectfully quiet clap. Lennie folded her arms—it was *Ellington* who did all of the work during Julien's trial.

"You are still in the running to become the next Prime Wizard." Poppop smiled. "In a close second, we have Ethan. Congratulations! Things are looking up for you!"

"For now," Ethan said gloomily. "But I'm sure things will suck again soon."

"Third, we have Michael, and fourth we have Bo. Congratulations! You two are both still in the running to become the next Prime Wizard! Now, there is only one spot left and four contestants remaining. Anya, Ellington, Perrie, Victoria. Who will it be?" Poppop paused. His mouth curled into a grin, and he was clearly enjoying the tension he was creating. "The last spot . . . in the first test of Wizardmatch . . . goes to . . ."

Perrie, Lennie thought. It had to be Perrie. She retrieved her object effortlessly! She was talented and smart and—

"Victoria!" Poppop said.

"WHAT?!" Uncle Bob said.

"THE BABY?" Uncle Philip #2 cried. "HER?!"

"She gave us a very dramatic moment," Poppop said. "Extra points for dramatic moments!"

The rest of the family clapped halfheartedly.

"I'm sorry," Poppop continued. "That means Anya, Perrie, and Ellington, you are eliminated."

Anya threw her sweatband off her head and stamped it in the ground, screaming until her cheeks were bright red.

Lennie bit her lips to keep from reacting. But inside, she was roaring with pride. After years of hearing Anya brag about all her successes and seeing all her trophies and feeling all the stress of Thanksgiving board games getting flipped across the room whenever Anya wasn't winning . . . *finally* Lennie put her cousin in her place.

Ellington, meanwhile, tore the ribbons out of her hair and used them like confetti.

Perrie frowned. "But I did so well!" she said disbelievingly.

Lennie couldn't help but agree—Perrie crushed it, yet Bo, who hadn't even completed the task, got to continue on in the competition. And—even though Lennie was glad she lost— Anya was the only one brave enough to ride on the back of a three-headed shark. Didn't Poppop say he was looking for adventurous and daring traits in this test?

The field cleared out, but Lennie lingered behind, hoping Great-Uncle Humphrey would make an appearance once everyone had left. But after an hour of picking weeds and aimlessly roaming around the grounds, she finally gave up. Hopefully he'd been watching, and hopefully she'd passed his test, and hopefully she'd find out soon.

Consequences

The cat cornered Lennie on the way up to her room.

"BOO!" Fluffles said, blocking her skateboard's path.

She skidded to a stop. They were on the twenty-fifth floor, just above the overzealous, book-pelting library.

"A word please?" the cat asked.

Lennie's stomach sank.

"This way," Fluffles said, leading her down a long hall. There were mostly guest rooms on this floor: Vegetable Villa, Quesadilla Quarters, and Bacon Boudoir. Lennie couldn't help but notice that not a single one of the guest rooms featured Filipino food.

Around a sharp corner, Fluffles ushered her into a room that was bare: white floors, white walls, no furniture, and a twenty-foot-tall domed ceiling.

"This room is so empt—"

Before she even had time to finish that sentence, she grew. And grew. And GREW. Her limbs not only stretched out—but they also got wider. Her whole torso expanded to the size of a tree trunk. By the time she stopped growing, she and Fluffles were both five times their normal size. Lennie had to crouch to keep her head from hitting the ceiling, and Fluffles looked like a lion wearing a tuxedo.

"What the heck?!" Lennie complained. "Did you have to talk with me *here*?"

"It's an enlargement spell, and you are trapped in here with me until you answer my questions. Now, what are you up to?!" Fluffles demanded.

"I *told* you—nothing!"

"I don't believe you." He bared his teeth, only this time, because of his size, he looked much more threatening. "I saw you today!"

The room suddenly seemed too cramped. She was caught. *No,* Lennie thought, *he knows nothing. Keep it together.* "Saw me what?" she said coolly.

"One minute you were over on the left side of the pudding pool. And the next minute, you were on the right side of the pool. You invisibled! I saw you!"

"You mean you *didn't* see me," Lennie corrected.

"Yes, I didn't see you! I mean, no, I saw that I didn't see you! I mean . . ." Fluffles scratched his ears with his paw. "You're trying to confuse me!"

"Is it working?"

"NOT IN THE SLIGHTEST! What are you plotting with the Oglethorpes?"

"For the last time, I've never even *met* the Oglethorpes."

"Well, if you're not plotting and scheming, then why would you invisible during one of your cousin's tests? What are you up to?"

"Nothing!" Lennie cried. She kicked at the door with her giant, car-size foot, and managed to squeeze out her big toe. The moment her toe left the room, she began to shrink. With unsettling creaking sounds, Lennie's limbs grew smaller and smaller until she was just the size she was before.

Fluffles stuck his paw out the door, but Lennie ran away before he could morph back to his normal size.

"I AM WATCHING YOU, ALWAYS!" he called after her. "AND CATS CAN SEE PERFECTLY IN THE DARK!"

Lennie ran until she reached the ramp, then whistled for a skateboard, and zoomed away. If Fluffles knew what she was *really* up to with Uncle Humphrey, he'd tell Poppop faster than Lennie could say *hair ball*.

Lennie skateboarded far away from that crazy cat, spiraling up the floors toward her room. But she stopped when she heard sobs echoing through the atrium.

She left her skateboard and carefully tiptoed to the source of the sound: a guest suite on the thirty-second floor called the Breadroom.

Lennie knocked.

"GO AWAY!" said a sharp voice.

"Anya?" Lennie said. "It's me . . . Lennie! Are you okay?"

"I'm fine! Please leave!"

Her gut clenched. *This is all my fault.* "I'm just going to sit at your door until you change your mind," she said.

There were footsteps, and then the door swung open. Anya's curls were even frizzier than normal, and her eyes were red. She snotted into a tissue as she let Lennie into her room.

"Your room smells *amazing*," Lennie said. "Like fresh bread."

"What kind do you smell?" Anya asked, sniffing. "I smell pumpernickel, and Mollie smells banana bread, and Jonathan smells pumpkin loaf."

"It's totally sourdough," Lennie said, feeling homesick for San Fran and her dad.

Anya hiccupped, which morphed into a sob.

"Are you okay?" Lennie asked. "Do you want to talk about it?"

Anya lay down on her baguette bed and stared up at the bagels painted on the ceiling. "It's over," she groaned. "Just like that, it's *over*." She paused. "I finally get how you feel."

Lennie dug her nails into her own skin to get out some of her own anger: Anya *didn't* know how she felt because Anya, at least, was picked. She wasn't rejected because of her identity, or her looks. Anya wasn't betrayed by her grandfather *and* her parent at the same time.

But just when Lennie was about to tell her off, Anya burst into tears. "Ohhhh, this is so *embarrassing*," Anya said, hiding her face under a pillow. "I broke my wrist last year in field hockey, and I didn't cry then. I got three stitches when Jonathan was teaching me snowboarding, and I was fine, but *this* makes me cry?"

Lennie softened. "There's nothing wrong with crying."

Which made Anya bawl even more. It was a disturbing sight—Lennie had *never* seen Anya cry before. It was like ten years of backed-up tears were flooding out of Anya all at once.

Guilt crept up and up and up on Lennie's spine, like a spider that just wouldn't quit. Any second now Anya was going to see right through her and know what Lennie did.

"It's not even the Prime Wizard thing that gets me!" Anya said. "I mean, yeah, it would have been sweet to have Poppop's powers. But it's the *losing*—I'm supposed to win! That's who I *am*!"

Lennie patted Anya's arm, feeling like she'd swallowed a bug. "I'm sorry," she muttered. She couldn't get her cheeks to stop burning up.

"You don't have to apologize!" Anya said, which made Lennie feel even *worse*.

They stayed together in silence for a while. Lennie thought about all their Thanksgivings: the times they built forts in the house, broke the wishbone together, rolled around in leaves, and the one year with exceptionally warm November weather—when their families took a spontaneous day trip to Ocean City, skipped on the boardwalk, and ate taffy.

Yes, Anya's competitive streak annoyed Lennie. But she still loved her cousin. And not because she was a "winner."

"You know," Lennie finally said to her cousin. "I don't even care about your trophies or medals or how many times you scored a goal. You're so much more than just a loser or a winner."

"Ha," Anya said. She sniffled, gave Lennie an affectionate nudge, then flipped onto her stomach. "Len, I can't stop replaying this afternoon in my brain. Don't you think it's ridiculous that Bo's advancing? He didn't do anything except eat some pudding and turn it into a bird!"

Lennie pressed her lips together.

She knew she was right about Wizardmatch and Poppop—after today, she was surer than ever that Wizardmatch was unfair. Not just to her, but to the other girls in the family, too.

Something had to be done. Poppop couldn't get away with this.

And Lennie would make sure he didn't.

Student and Teacher

In the late evening, as Lennie was crankily wondering whether Uncle Humphrey was even *watching* the first test, the window began to fog.

You have five seconds to make sure you're alone.

Lennie was already alone, but she dead-bolted the door to keep Michael from coming in.

Well done, my NEW PUPIL!

At midnight, go to the place where we last spoke, and I'll lead the way.

Bring potato chips.

Wear sneakers. Leave your glasses at home.

Seriously, bring potato chips.

—Your Dutiful Teacher

Her teacher!

Lennie smiled. She would have hugged that letter, if it weren't stuck to the outside of her window.

By the time she left to meet Great-Uncle Humphrey, Michael was fast asleep. She tiptoed out of her room and traveled the ramp by foot. Every so often, she had to hide in the hall to recharge her power.

And on the bottom floor, guarding the exit, was Fluffles.

Curse that cat!

He was pacing in front of the door. If she tried to tip-toe past him, she'd surely get caught. She had to get him to move. . . . But what could distract him? He was usually so watchful. In fact, the only time she'd ever seen him inattentive was when Michael dangled a shoelace in front of him.

That's it! She pulled the drawstring out of her sweatshirt and threw it across the lobby.

"What's that?!" Fluffles said, his eyes wide as he chased after the object. He slid across the floor and picked the string up in his mouth proudly, like he'd hunted a grand prize.

Lennie didn't wait—she invisibled and rushed out of the castle.

"WHO'S THERE?" called Fluffles from behind her.

She kept running invisibly, head down, trying to put as much distance between herself and the castle as she could.

In the dark of the night, it was hard to avoid the Garden of Goulash, and the stew sludged beneath her shoes. The night air was cool and foggy and still. When she reached the borderlands, she did not hesitate. And on the other side of the Pomporromp border, a message was waiting for her.

Avoid the bridge this time, okay?

It was written into the earth, before a trail marked by floating fires. Clearly a path left for her by Uncle Humphrey. So she walked along, following the fires, which blew out whenever she walked past—twisting this way and that as she avoided every booby trap that Poppop Pomporromp and Madame Oglethorpe had set.

The path led to a ring of trees, where the trunks stood separate and strong, but the limbs and branches were tangled together. Where the darkness was darker and shadows were shadowier. And there, in the middle of the clearing, Great-Uncle Humphrey de Cobblespork, sat pretzel-style. His eyes were shut, and he breathed in deeply and meditatively. Lennie could just tell he was about to say something profound.

"Where are my potato chips?"

Or not.

Lennie threw a bag of chips at him. He ripped open the packaging, grabbed a fistful, and began munching loudly. "Yum yum yum! I have never found a magic greater than that of fried potatoes." Humphrey frowned at her. "I thought I told you not to bring your glasses."

"I can't see without them."

"Yes, that's the point." Humphrey stood up and swiped the glasses right off her face.

"Why are you stealing my glasses?"

"You see—or perhaps, you *don't* see—this is all part of my foolproof one-of-a-kind method. All will be revealed in due time."

"What does that mean—"

"IN DUE TIME!" he bellowed.

"SHHHHHH!" Lennie hissed. "You're going to get us caught!"

"I will do no such thing!" Uncle Humphrey said. "No one comes in here. And even if they *do*, I am using my elemental powers to pay attention to the earth and the wind. If someone takes a footstep anywhere *near* us, I'll know." He knocked on the ground, and it cracked beneath his fists. He reached into the lightning-shaped crevice, pulled out a box, and placed it in Lennie's hands.

"What's this?"

"A wooden box."

"And what's *in* the box?" Lennie blindly felt around for the latch. When she opened the box, there came an unmistakable *hisssssssssssss.*

"Snakes!" Uncle Humphrey said.

"Snakes?!" she yelped, almost dropping the box.

"Relax," Uncle Humphrey said.

"How can I relax when there's a *snake* in here?"

"Three snakes, actually."

"Three," Lennie said, feeling a little ill.

"I'm going to wrap them around you . . . like so!" Uncle Humphrey said, curling a snake around each leg and one across her shoulders.

Their scaly bodies were cold and meaty and muscular as they crawled around her. "Th—they're not going to bite me, are they?"

"They might," Uncle Humphrey said.

When he said he was going to train her, this wasn't at all what she'd had in mind.

"This isn't at all what I had in mind," she said out loud.

"Of course not!" Uncle Humphrey said. "How could you've possibly hoped to foresee my genius? Now these snakes have a purpose, you know."

"I didn't know!"

"Well you should have known!"

"How could I have known what I don't know?"

Uncle Humphrey sighed loudly. "Here's the thing: It takes years to grow your endurance—in other words, how long you can use your power before getting tired. There's nothing I can do for you in the short time we have. But I can teach you something just as useful."

"And what's that?"

"The ability to transfer your invisibility to the objects you touch."

She squinted at him. "But that's impossible!"

"It is *not* impossible! You already do it! When you go invisible, your clothes turn invisible too, yes?"

Lennie nodded.

"VOILÀ!" her great-uncle said. "You already transfer invisibility to your clothes without even thinking about it. So I'm going to teach you how to share your invisibility with bigger objects. Or an animal. Or, say, another human."

Another human? She could turn other people invisible with her? How had she never known? Her breath caught in her chest. If she could make *another person* go invisible with her, even for a few seconds, it was more than her mom and Michael had ever done.

"Here's your problem, Lennie: You're so busy looking at yourself to make sure you're still invisible that you're not *feeling* the power inside you."

"And what are the snakes for?" she said with a shudder.

"You have to turn them invisible. Start small, and work our way up to transferring to humans." Uncle Humphrey smiled. "They also create a high-stress, high-intensity situation. Pressure increases your productivity and drive. Without it, you could train for years and never get anywhere, which is what happens with most of the Pomporromps, sadly. Now . . . START INVISIBLING!" he barked in her ear.

She went invisible—the telltale chills she always felt crawled up her arm.

"YOU HAVE TO PUSH!" said Humphrey. She could feel the breeze of his breath on her face as he hollered. "STAY DETERMINED! AND STAY HUNGRY!" It was hard to stay hungry when Great-Uncle Humphrey's breath smelled like sour milk.

She balled her hands into fists. *Stay invisible, stay invisible. You can do it!*

"Is this the best you can do?" he said. "You're showing me a namby-pamby display!" Humphrey yelled. "NO MORE NAMBY-PAMBY! Feel it burning! Do you feel it?"

"Uh-huh!"

"No . . . you don't. Not yet. Because I'm about to throw some fireballs at you. I need you to dodge them while staying invisible."

"WHAT?!" she shrieked. "WAIT, DON'T—"

"FIRE IN THE HOLE!" he shouted, and a ball of light zoomed her way.

She ducked, shielding her head for dear life. The fireball hit a tree trunk behind her, but it didn't set the forest ablaze—it simply snuffed out, like a dying candle flame. Still, the heat surrounded her like a wall, so thick and dry that she couldn't stop sweating. And the snakes began to circle around her tighter. They were getting scared or excitable—she couldn't tell which.

"MAKE THE SNAKES INVISIBLE!" Uncle Humphrey griped.

"I'm trying!" she yelled. "I think I'm out of magical energy."

"If you're in danger and run out of power, no one's going to let you take a break in real life!" He pelted a fireball at her stomach, and Lennie swerved to avoid it. "You have to keep on dodging until you can invisible again."

"WHAT?!" she said, ducking behind a tree. The snake on her shoulders squeezed her uncomfortably tight—her whole left arm was feeling numb.

"The only way to hide from my fireballs is to GO INVISIBLE!" Humphrey said, peeking around a tree and smashing a fireball at her legs. She skirted away just in time.

She took a deep breath, and even though she was tired physically, she could feel her magic swelling within her again. Droplets of sweat dripped down her forehead, and the snakes danced around her neck.

"Too slow!" he said, hitting her jacket with fire, just one second before she went invisible. Lennie quickly threw the jacket on the ground, where it burst into flames and smoke.

She was going to die training. Humphrey was going to kill her!

Whooosh! A fireball exploded near her elbow. She could feel the heat from it, and she screamed, "Ahhhhhhhhhhhh!"

"INVISIBLE PEOPLE DON'T MAKE NOISE!" he yelled. "If you can invisible your clothes, you can invisible the snakes! And if you can invisible the snakes, you can invisible *anything* you touch."

Two blasts came this time, both at her feet. One hit her shoe, and she had to kick it off before the fire swallowed it completely.

This was all *ridiculous!* How was she supposed to concentrate when fireballs were being tossed her way and snakes were doing laps around her limbs?

"YOU HAVE TO WANT IT MORE THAN THAT—YOU HAVE TO WANT IT WITH ALL YOUR HEART! DO YOU WANT THIS, LENNIE?" he bellowed.

More than anything! Lennie closed her eyes and took a deep, deep breath. Inhale. Exhale. *You can do this, Mercado,* she told herself. *Invisible, invisible, invisible. Come on.*

Stay invisible. With all my heart.

A few fireballs whizzed so close to her that they stung, and the snakes tightened around her thighs like a grandma's girdle. She was losing feeling in her toes, and the snake around her neck hissed in her ear.

Her magical energy was out; her fifteen seconds was over. She opened her eyes. Humphrey stood there, smirking.

"What kind of *insane* trick are you trying to pull?!" she yelled at him. "You're not training me—you're trying to get me killed!"

Humphrey folded his arms and harrumphed. "Well, my method is working, *thank you very much*. You made the snakes go invisible."

"I . . . I did?" She looked down at the snakes—but they were just as visible as ever.

"Just for a few seconds. Before you threw this little tantrum. I deserve a trophy."

"*You?*" Lennie scoffed. "*I'm* the one who did it!"

"And it was all thanks to *my* teaching methods," he said, uncoiling the snakes from around her limbs, one-by-one. "Without me, you would have gotten NOWHERE. Therefore, it is *I* who deserves a trophy, a plaque, a medal, a certificate, a cookie, a round of applause, and a standing ovation." He bowed. "But now, the ultimate test." Uncle Humphrey extended a hand to her.

Lennie sucked in a deep breath and grabbed his hand. She invisibled, and so did her clothes, but Uncle Humphrey did not. *If you truly believe that you would have been the best Prime Wizard,* she told herself, *then you can do this ONE LITTLE THING.*

Uncle Humphrey flickered for just a moment. "Don't worry. We'll work on that," he said. "We're going to practice every night until you can keep me invisible for at least ten seconds. I believe in you."

"WOOOOOOOOOOOOOO!!!!!" Lennie howled into the sky. She danced around the trees. She jumped up and down. She wanted to cry and sing and whoop all at the same time.

"Do you know what this *means?*" she kept saying over and over to Uncle Humphrey. "I'm going to be the strongest Pomporromp! Other than Poppop!"

"What am I, chopped liver?"

This was what she had trained for her whole life. This was what she *dreamed* of!

Michael could keep her mom as a trainer; Lennie had a way better tutor now. She was about to double lap her brother. And Uncle Humphrey, unlike the rest of her family, believed she could.

Take that, Mom! Take that, Poppop! TAKE THAT, WIZARDMATCH!

Ooey Gooey Icky Sticky
Double-Dog Dare

In the morning, Michael shook her awake. "Lennieeeee. Lennieeeeee."

"Erghhhh," Lennie groaned. She had been out training for most of the night, finally sneaking back into her room around dawn.

Michael began massaging her head. Though, it was really more like nudging her head with his fingers. "Are you mad at me?"

"Right now? YES!" she said, rolling over.

"Why?"

"You're waking me up early."

"Oh." He paused. "Are you mad at me for other stuff?"

"Yeah."

"Like what?"

"Like the time you continued to ask me questions when I was trying to sleep!"

"Are you mad at me about Wizardmatch?"

She sat up, finally, and rubbed her bleary eyes. She was surprised at the question—and even more surprised that she didn't have an answer. Was she mad at him?

"I think . . ." Michael hummed. "You're jealous."

"I am *not* jealous!" Lennie said.

"Jelly like the Jelly Floor!" Michael accused.

Her face grew hot. "I AM NOT JEALOUS!"

"That's what Mom says."

"Mom doesn't know anything."

"Mom is smarter than you! She has a masters plus fifteen!"

"You don't even know what that means!" Lennie said.

"Neither do you!"

Lennie gripped the edge of her bunk bed. "YOU ARE SO OBNOXIOUS!"

Michael frowned. "You were a better sister before Wizardmatch!"

Lennie hopped off the bed and stormed out of the room. Even though she was barefoot. Even though she was still in her pajamas. Even though she didn't even brush her teeth. She stomped along the cold floor, storming, fuming.

She shuffled around the ramp. Poppop liked to poke people not on skateboards, but let him *try* to poke her right now. She'd come at him with the bite of fifteen Fluffingtons—

"You do not know who you're dealing with!" snarled Julien, a few floors below her.

"Who cares?" Ethan shouted back.

Lennie turned invisible and crawled to the edge of the ramp—a perfect angle where she could spy. Julien, Ethan, and Bo were in a three-way standoff, aggressively scowling at one another.

"I just don't understand," Ethan said, his face sour, "how you won the first test. You and your dad have always acted like you're hot stuff, but you're not so great."

"That's not what Poppop says," Julien said smugly.

Ethan took a menacing step closer. "And when your dad said I was a two-bit haircut—"

"Shave and a haircut . . . two bits!" Bo sang.

"He didn't say anything that wasn't true!" Julien said, standing on his tiptoes to be even with Ethan.

"Let's all calm down," Bo said, gnawing on his sleeve.

"You're not going to eat that are you?" Ethan said.

"Your powers are disgusting," Julien said.

They both looked at Bo like he was contagious.

"Mother says I am a rare bird."

"More like *birdbrain*," Julien said. "No offense, but you can't possibly hope to win against me."

"Maybe he can't, but I can!" Ethan said as his hair began to morph into spikes.

"Whatever, Mr. Haircut."

"I like these nicknames! Call me Mr. Birdbrain!" Bo said brightly.

"It was supposed to be an *insult*, Bo!" Julien said.

"Up there!" Ethan said. "Lennie's spying on us!"

Ooops! She was so absorbed in their fight that she didn't even realize her invisibility ran out.

"Come down and face us! Don't spy like a creep!" Julien called out.

"If you don't want someone to hear, then don't fight in the hall!" she said, hands on her hips.

"Did I hear something?" Julien said, swiveling up the ramp toward her, Ethan and Bo close behind. "Must have been no one. No one *important*, anyway!"

Lennie folded her arms. "I could magic *circles* around you!"

Julien smirked. "If you're so good at magic, why weren't you picked for Wizardmatch?"

"Leave me alone!"

"*You're* going to be leaving, not me!" Julien said with a toothy smile. "When I become Prime Wizard, I'm not going to allow *bummers* to visit the estate. So take a long last look around."

Lennie clenched her hands into fists. "You can't ban me from the castle!"

"The Prime Wizard can do whatever he wants."

"Or she!" Lennie said.

"He." Julien smiled. "It's always been a he. It always *will* be a he."

Lennie flushed with rage.

"If you're really so special, Lennie, why don't you prove it?"

"What'd you have in mind?"

"Follow me." Julien smirked, rolling away on his skate-board.

Lennie whistled for a skateboard of her own and zoomed after her cousin. She bent her knees, skating so close to Julien's tail that she could have knocked him off his board. Ethan and Bo drifted a few yards behind.

Lennie skateboarded around and around the castle, down the ramp. She didn't know where Julien was taking her, but he finally slowed down at the twenty-second floor. The Jelly Floor.

It oozed and dripped and glopped and glooped. The hall-ways glistened with purple jelly; it bled out into the skate-board ramp, like snail slime.

"I dare you," Julien said, pointing to the hallway, "to go onto the Jelly Floor!"

Ethan gasped, and Bo hid behind his hands.

"No way!" Lennie snorted. "I'm not stupid! If I go in there, I'll get stuck!"

"Chicken!" Julien replied. "I *double-dog dare you!*"

"Ooooooooooh!" Bo and Ethan chorused.

"It's a double-dog dare," Bo said, his eyes as wide as sau-cers. "You can't say no to that!"

She peered into the hallway ahead of her—floor, walls, and ceiling all lined with jelly. It was glistening. Taunting her. *I'm going to glueeeee you to the wall,* it seemed to say. *I'm going to tangle your hairrrrr! I'm going to get stuck in your armpits and knee-pits and elbow-pits!*

She had no doubt she'd get stuck in the jelly. But she needed to prove she had what it takes to be a Prime Wizard. That even if she didn't have the *look*, she had the guts.

"Well?" Julien said.

Lennie's heart raced, and she took a step closer. She was disobeying her mom. She was breaking the rules. But it felt *good* to break the rules, especially since in the past few days, the rules had been breaking her.

She took a deep breath. *I can do this.*

She lifted her foot and took a step toward the jelly—

WHOOSH!

She went flying backward—tumbling back into Julien— like an invisible rope had yanked her.

"WHAT ARE YOU KIDS DOING?" bellowed Poppop Pomporromp, waving his magic staff at them, the rubber ducky sitting atop gazing at them with blank plastic eyes. Fluffles skidded to a stop next to Poppop.

"Lennie was going into the jelly, sir!" Julien said. "I tried to stop her!"

Lennie gaped at Julien. "That's not—"

"It's a very good thing I happened to pass by at the moment!" Poppop said. "If I didn't pull you back, you would have been stuck in there! You know, the last time someone went in, they were glued for a whole week! And I don't have time or energy to deal with this type of misbehavior when Wizardmatch is going on!"

Lennie glared at Poppop. But he barely noticed as he

turned his attention on Julien. "Oh, Julien, my dear boy, I can't wait for you to dazzle us again in the next test. I already know you're going to do very, very well in this competition," he said with a wink.

"Yes, sir!" he said.

Poppop nodded, satisfied. "Ethan, I'm looking forward to your performance, too. And, er, Bo. Uh . . . good luck. Come, Fluffles. Let's go."

Poppop stormed off, swinging his magic staff around as he skateboarded down the ramp.

Fluffles didn't follow. Instead, he walked up to Lennie. "I think you lost this last night," he said, dropping something at her feet. It was her sweatshirt string—the string she'd used to distract him!

How much did he know? Or did he only suspect? Heart thrumming, she looked at Fluffles—he had a suspicious gleam in his yellow eyes. "I don't know what you're talking about," she said coolly.

Fluffles squinted at her—then, without another word, he followed Poppop down the ramp. Once Fluffles was out of earshot, Julien grinned widely. And Lennie wanted, more than ever, to wipe that smile off his smug little face.

"See? Like I said, I visit here *all* the time. Poppop and I are really close. I'll always be his number one. Have fun playing catch up," he said to Ethan and Bo. "And *you* won't be playing at all," he said, as if Lennie needed any further reminder.

"GO AWAY!" Lennie roared.

He laughed as he skateboarded up the castle.

Lennie waited until Julien, Bo, and Ethan had gone before she let out a scream that echoed all across the Jelly Floor.

As she rounded back up the ramp, she thought only of Uncle Humphrey and their plan to destroy Wizardmatch. For the sake of *every* family, the sooner she ended the competition, the better.

A Plan

At midnight, Uncle Humphrey set a grizzly bear loose in the borderlands.

It was all part of her training, learning to stay invisible while she was constantly moving and dodging danger. She danced around the clearing, doing spins, leaps, cartwheels, hurdle jumps, stomach crawls—all while keeping away from the angry bear and remaining completely invisible.

"Good!" Uncle Humphrey said, from his tree bough. "Now keep moving—FASTER!"

She crouched down to catch her breath and recharge her power.

"CAREFUL! THE BEAR IS COMING!" Uncle Humphrey said.

She hopped up and ran. Just in time: The bear swiped the spot where she had been standing.

"DUCK!"

She ducked.

"CHICKEN DANCE!"

She invisibly chicken danced.

"Excellent," Humphrey said with a satisfied nod.

That little praise was all she needed to feel her spirits soar and her energy boost—even when her magical energy ran out, she wasn't tired. She was only ready for more.

They kept training for an hour or so—and as the night wore on, she felt more and more comfortable holding her power under extreme stress and avoiding a bear attack. Then, Uncle Humphrey lured the bear away from the clearing by hovering a ball of water—with a wriggling salmon inside—away from the trees.

When the bear was gone, he had her try to transfer her invisibility to him while running and hopping and moving. She wasn't as good at making her great-uncle completely invisible—sometimes he flickered back into sight, and sometimes she drained out too soon—but her muscles ached, and her skin tingled, and magic swelled inside of her. She took that as an improvement.

When she was soaked with sweat, too sore to even move, Uncle Humphrey finally called for her to stop. She sat down with him on the floor of the forest.

"So what now?" Lennie asked. "How are we going to bring down Wizardmatch?"

Uncle Humphrey tossed her some chips. "Yes, yes, good question. To rid the world of Wizardmatch, we are going to have to get rid of the Prime Wizard position."

"What do you mean?"

"I mean . . . we won't *have* a Prime Wizard. The whole Pomporromp family can share Mortimer's power. Equally."

"That's an option?" Lennie asked. "But . . . if the power can be shared, why hasn't anyone done it before?"

"Because Prime Wizards are selfish," Humphrey spat. "They want to hoard power for themselves—and then pick a pupil who's going to hoard power. And so on and so on and so on. People who have power *never* give it up voluntarily." Uncle Humphrey paused. "But just because it's always been done a certain way doesn't mean it's the *right* way."

Lennie twisted her ponytail around her finger, deep in thought. It seemed like this was one of those things that went on for generations—something that was so entrenched in tradition that it was nearly impossible to fix the problem. But they *had* to fix it. "So how are we going to convince Poppop to change his mind?"

"Convince?" Uncle Humphrey scoffed. "We're not going to *convince* him. We're going to do it *for* him. By taking his staff."

"Taking his staff?! But . . . but isn't that dangerous? What would that even do?"

Uncle Humphrey sighed. "Your powers lie dormant in you. When you become Prime Wizard, your magic gets activated—like a little jolt of lightning that awakens all of your powers, whether or not you are holding the staff. The magic staff amplifies those powers, but it's not *all* the staff can do. If you or I touch the staff, it would increase our powers, as long as you or I were holding on to it. Haven't you ever wondered why Poppop won't let anyone else handle the staff?"

She thought back to that time she confronted Poppop in his bedchamber. "Poppop told me it was really dangerous. That I shouldn't touch it. It could burn my eyeballs out."

"AN INSIDIOUS, BALD-FACED LIE!" Uncle Humphrey said, and his voice was as steely as a silver filling. "He just doesn't *want* anyone to have amplified powers. But if we take the staff, we can use it to share Mortimer's powers evenly among the whole family. We'll make everything equal. I just need you to get me to that staff."

It seemed like a complicated task. "How do we get it? What do we do?"

Uncle Humphrey's downturned mouth suddenly curled up into a smile. "This is why I am so excited about your powers, Lennie. You will transfer your invisibility to us both, and we will borrow Mortimer de Pomporromp's staff when he's not paying attention." He closed his eyes and took a deep, satisfied breath. "I will finally be able to right the terrible wrong that was done to me when I was a child. And to you, of course. Together, we will stop Wizardmatch."

She jumped up to give him a high five, and he sent a burst of air to clap against her palm. "It's time for you to go back to the castle," Uncle Humphrey said.

She wasn't ready to go back—she never was. But she sighed. "All right." She gathered her jacket and looked at the opening of the clearing. There, between two trees, a familiar pair of yellow eyes stared at her from the darkness.

Fluffles had been watching them.

AFTER HIM!

Lennie and Fluffles stared at each other for a solid second. "FLUFFLES?!" she cried.

"IT'S SIR FLUFFINGTON THE FOURTH TO YOU!" he screamed.

Then he ran.

"That's Poppop's guard cat!"

"AFTER HIM!" Humphrey cried, and he and Lennie charged. They jumped over fallen logs, ducked under booby traps, and hopped around the ground as cautiously and quickly as they could. Lennie was running faster than she ever had before—faster than any drill she'd ever done. Her legs ached, but she pushed forward, behind the cat who was quick as a breeze.

They followed the sound of Fluffles's swift pads on the ground. But he was getting away! They were so close to the border of Poppop's property that Lennie could feel the air thinning.

Suddenly, the earth in front of them shot up—a giant wall erupting from the ground. It blocked Fluffles's exit. Panicked, the cat scampered around, unsure of which direction to run.

And that's when Humphrey turned the ground beneath

Fluffles's paws into putty. Fluffles's legs sank into the earth, and Humphrey hardened the ground again. Fluffles was stuck.

"HELP!" Fluffles screamed. "INTRUDER! TRES-PASSER!"

"Shhhhhhhhhhh!" Lennie said. "Fluffles, keep your voice down!"

"I AM A GUARD CAT, SWORN TO PROTECT THE PRIME WIZARD POMPORROMP, AND I WILL NOT BE SILENCED!"

"We have to take him to my place," Uncle Humphrey said, fishing through the pockets of his tattered trench coat. "Ah—found it!" he said, pulling a cloth bag out of his left inside pocket.

"HELP!" Fluffles yowled. "I'M BEING CATNAPPED!"

"You mean *kidnapped*," Lennie said.

"CATNAPPED!" Fluffles cried. "I'm not a goat!"

"Sorry," Uncle Humphrey said as he popped the block of earth out of the ground and dropped it—with Fluffles still stuck—straight into the bag.

Lennie winced as she heard Fluffles meowing and trying to bite the bag. But what could she do? It wasn't like they could let Fluffles go—he'd tell Poppop all about their secret plan!

This was the only option, she told herself over and over again as she followed Uncle Humphrey back to his Secret Cave of Secrets. Once they were inside her uncle's fire den,

Humphrey gingerly placed the squirming bag on the table and frowned.

"Aren't you going to let him out?" Lennie said.

"I can't let the cat out of the bag!" Humphrey said. "He'll let the cat out of the bag!"

"I'm just saying to let him breathe!" Lennie said.

Great-Uncle Humphrey opened the bag and placed the slab of earth trapping Fluffles on the table.

"YOU . . . YOU . . . YOU DOG!" Fluffles said, like it was the worst insult imaginable. "I KNEW IT, I KNEW IT, I KNEW YOU WERE UP TO SOMETHING! AND NOW I HAVE PROOF! I followed you, and *oh* how I'll be rewarded with catnip and treats!" Even the thought of treats made Fluffles start purring.

"I thought you said you weren't followed!" Uncle Humphrey said.

"I thought *you* said you'd be able to tell if anyone got close from the ground and wind!"

"For humans, yes," Uncle Humphrey said. "But cats are light-footed! They're paw-sitively nimble."

"What now?!" Lennie said, pacing around Uncle Humphrey's small room. "Fluffles is a judge! Poppop will notice if he's missing from the Wizardmatch festivities!"

"I *will* tell Mortimer what you're up to, whoever you are!" the cat said. ". . . Or is it *whomever* you are?" Fluffles glared at Uncle Humphrey.

"Wait, you don't know who this is?" Lennie asked. But

then she realized—why would he? Sir Fluffington the Fourth was *her mom's* childhood cat. Uncle Humphrey was long gone by then.

"Have you," Uncle Humphrey finally said, "ever wanted a pet?"

Not quite the question she was expecting. "Yes . . . I've always wanted a puppy."

"Those slobbery things?!" scoffed Fluffles.

"Good," Uncle Humphrey said, and he gestured widely to Fluffles. "This is your new puppy. Every day when you come to train, you will meet me here. You'll feed your puppy some food, and we'll work on your magic."

"You have insulted me, sir!" Fluffles said coldly.

"And what about Poppop?"

"Let's just hope he doesn't form a search party in the borderlands. And if he does? I will sink this cave even further beneath the ground, create a labyrinth of tunnels, and hide."

Lennie frowned deeply.

"Don't look so worried, Lennie. In three days, this will all be over. We will have magic beyond our wildest dreams! Not to mention, we'll have something even better than that."

"And that is?"

He smiled. "Justice."

Every night, Lennie snuck out of the castle. She trained with Humphrey for hours, each session more grueling than the last. But she liked it that way—she could feel herself growing stronger and bolder. Even though they'd only been training for four days, she felt like it was more effective than her entire year of practicing by herself.

Of course, training wasn't the only thing she did. She always took care of Fluffles, stroking his back until he purred and feeding him all sorts of people food: apples, string cheese, cold French fries, and bologna. She *did* try looking for cat food, but she couldn't find any, and she didn't want to raise eyebrows by asking where it was kept, as Poppop was distraught at Fluffles's disappearance. He searched high and low in the castle and on the grounds, performing summoning spells and luring charms, but it did nothing. He even checked inside the three-headed shark's stomach chambers, but Fluffles was nowhere to be seen.

"I'm sure he'll turn up," Estella said to Poppop as he cried over a bowl of oatmeal on the third day of Fluffles's disappearance.

"O-o-oatmeal was his favorite fooooooood!" Poppop sniveled.

"I'm not sure that's true . . . but Mortimer, Fluffles steps out all the time! This isn't the first time he's gone somewhere."

Poppop sniffed. "But the second Wizardmatch test is *tomorrow*!"

"If he doesn't show up by Saturday, we'll sound the alarm," Estella reassured him.

Lennie snuck a little extra food in her pocket and tried not to feel guilty. It wasn't *her* fault that Fluffles wasn't here. She didn't ask Fluffles to follow her—he was being nosy! Clearly, it was curiosity that catnapped the cat!

On her way out of the dining hall, a bird darted in front of her face.

"What the heck?!" she said, jumping back. She looked around. It wasn't just the one bird; there was a swarm of them zipping and darting and circling around Perrie, who was using her long, wiggly arms to swat them away.

Lennie ran over to her cousin. "What is going on?!"

"It's Bo," Perrie said, catching a hummingbird in her hands, extending her arms, and letting it go outside the dining room. "He's angry with me because my dad challenged him and his family to a game of trivia last night. Daddy and I crushed them—in front of an audience, too—you weren't there? Anyway, serves them right."

"Why, were you mad at them?"

"Of course! Bo's whole family was gloating about how I was cut from the competition—and bragging about how Bo is still in it. Aunt Lacey was especially . . ."

"Annoying?"

"Insufferable," Perrie said, catching another bird in her hands and flicking it away.

Meanwhile, from across the room, Ellington waved at Lennie, but Lennie kept her head down and ignored her.

"That's not all," Perrie said, not noticing Lennie's discomfort. "All of the Uncle Philips have been bickering about the results of the first test. Julien seems to be mad at everyone.

And Anya and Michael are mad at each other because he farted on her, and she said he was too immature to be in the competition."

"Surprise, surprise," Lennie said, just as Ellington called her name from across the dining room again. Lennie looked away.

Perrie squinted at Lennie. "And judging from the way you keep avoiding Ellington, I'm guessing you're mad at her, too."

"Wow," Lennie said. "You're good. How do you even know about all of this stuff?"

"People think I'm too wrapped up in my books to be listening," Perrie said slyly. "But it's my *job* to know. I know everything! Except maybe astrophysics, but give me a year and I'll get there." A bird hit her cheek, and she scrunched her nose. "I will get Bo back for this!" she whispered.

"Then he's going to come back at you with an even worse bird!" Lennie said. "He'll get an ostrich to sit on you or something."

"Well, he started it!" Perrie's cheeks flushed with anger. "This isn't my fault. And I have to retaliate."

Lennie could understand that. *After all*, she thought as she left the dining hall, *I'm retaliating, too*. She could hardly wait. Tomorrow, she'd finally get the recognition she wanted, and the payback she so desperately needed. Justice, Uncle Humphrey had said. Sweet, sweet justice.

And it was going to taste *so good*.

The Garden of Goulash

It was the morning of the second Wizardmatch test, and Lennie was more ready than ever to *end* it.

She popped out of bed and began to prepare for the day. Michael looked up at her from beneath his covers. For a moment, she thought he was going to say something, but they hadn't talked since their last fight. It was the longest she'd ever gone without speaking to him, and she hated it. And she hated herself for hating it.

"Lennie," Michael said softly. For a second, she thought he was going to apologize, but that was crazy talk: No one in the Mercado family *ever* apologized. "I'm nervous."

In surprise, she stopped brushing her hair midstroke. From the way he had been acting, she didn't think he was worried at all. "You are?" she said, walking over to his bed.

"What if I mess up? What if I fall on my face? What if I get eliminated? What if I *die*? What if I accidentally eat the mystery meat in the goulash? What if Julien gives me a wedgie? I was up all night thinking about it!"

"You'll be fine," she promised him. "Nothing to be nervous about." Especially since, after today, she and Humphrey would put an end to the competition.

He patted his bed, and she sat down beside him.

"What do you do when you're nervous?" he asked.

"I take a deep breath . . . and go invisible."

Michael rubbed his hair sheepishly. "Yeah, I thought you'd say that. I guess that's good advice."

Just then, Lennie saw the window behind Michael starting to fog, and her stomach tightened.

You have five seconds to clear the room.

Michael's back was to the window. He hadn't seen the message, but if she didn't get him out *now,* he might see the next. That couldn't happen!

"Michael, up!" she said, pulling him out of bed and dragging him to the door.

"HEY! OW! YOU'RE HURTING ME!"

"GET OUT!" she said, pushing him outside the room.

"HEY!" he shouted. "MY KEYS ARE INSIDE! LET ME IN!" He pounded again. "WHAT THE HECK, LENNIE?!"

Michael beat on the door, keeping time with her heart. She almost got caught *again* . . . as if Fluffles wasn't a big enough problem!

The writing on the window began to appear:

Good Morning, Lennie!

Although, I am composing this message just after midnight, so is it morning? Or still night? Is tomorrow today? Or is today still today until I wake up into tomorrow? How will I know when today has become tomorrow if I don't go to sleep? But don't be preposterous, Humphrey—I must go to sleep, for we have a big day tomorrow (today?).

Meet me. Two p.m.

Need I even ask for potato chips? POTATO CHIPS!!!

When the message disappeared, Lennie sighed and unlocked the door.

Michael's nose was all scrunched up.

"HEY!" he said. "YOU CAN'T JUST KICK ME OUT OF MY OWN ROOM! What's going on?!"

"Sorry," she said. "You can come back in now."

"No! You hurt my arm before the big test today!" He rubbed his shoulder. "From now on, I'm sleeping in Mom's room!"

"Good! I'll finally have some space to myself!" Lennie said as he grabbed his pillows and blanket off his bed.

"You can have a whole *life* to yourself!" he said, stomping out of the room and slamming the door behind him.

She sat down on his bed and collapsed facedown onto his mattress, her glasses pinching into her nose. If it weren't for Wizardmatch, she'd still be best friends with Michael. If it weren't for Wizardmatch, she wouldn't be fighting with Ellington. If it weren't for Wizardmatch, she would be talking to her mom. She wouldn't feel like a reject in her own family.

The more she fumed about Wizardmatch, the more resolved she was to end it. *Today.*

In the afternoon, she invisibled as she ran across the

Garden of Goulash before the family was due to arrive. Then she slipped into the borderlands, coughing in the intense smoggy air and blinking in the darkness.

"You're here! Excellent," Uncle Humphrey said, emerging from behind a tree.

"How's Fluffles?"

"Our furry friend is . . . *impatient.* As am I."

"Me too," Lennie said. Her skin was practically itching for this day to be over.

They sat pretzel-style near the edge of the borderlands while Poppop and Estella set up for the big event. Peering into the Pomporromp property was like looking through a one-way mirror. They could see the grounds perfectly, but no one could see them.

"Where are my po—"

Lennie passed him a bag of chips, and Humphrey squealed.

"So we're just going to wait here?" Lennie said.

"Precisely. We are waiting for the perfect moment to pounce." He licked the salt off his fingers. "Do you think anyone will notice you're gone?"

"No," Lennie said bitterly. But then that wasn't entirely true. "Mom will notice, but she'll just wait until later to yell at me for missing *Prince Michael's big moment.* And maybe Ellington will realize I'm missing, but she's not going to say anything about it."

"Let's hope not," Uncle Humphrey said. And then they waited.

Her heart thudded in fear and leaped in anticipation. *I know I'm just as good as everyone else . . . now's the time to prove it.*

Peeking out of the borderlands, Lennie could see four of the remaining contestants standing in a particularly deep, goulashy area, their shoes entirely sunken in the chunky sauce. And the fifth contestant—Victoria—was rolling around in the stew.

"HEAR YE HEAR YE!" boomed Mortimer de Pomporromp from his elevated judges' podium. He was wearing a poncho, and so was Estella. Whatever crazy scheme Poppop had planned, it was sure to be messy. "WELCOME to the second test of Wizardmatch. First off, I wanted to see if anyone has any information on Sir Fluffington the Fourth's whereabouts. Anyone? I am desperately despondent!"

There was silence in the stadium, and Lennie guiltily looked down at her shoes. She had no idea how much Poppop would miss Fluffles.

"If anyone knows *anything*, please let me or Estella know right away! I am very close to declaring a state of emergency on the Pomporromp estate!" He sighed deeply.

"You have to continue on without him, Mortimer," Estella said. "Sir Fluffington the Fourth would understand."

Poppop frowned. "In honor of Sir Fluffington the Fourth, the missing and dearly departed, though hopefully not *departed* departed, if you know what I mean—"

"Mortimer!"

"—we will embark on a little Ghoulish Goulash."

Humphrey sighed. "Of *course* he'd select that as one of the tests."

"What is it?" Lennie asked, but her words were cut off by Poppop's.

"Before I explain, please give a round of applause for your remaining competitors!" He gestured to the contestants, who were all huddled together in the middle of the Garden of Goulash.

Julien smiled in that self-satisfied way he always did.

Bo stretched his jaw, probably preparing for all the upchucking he was about to do.

Ethan scowled as he looked around, his magical red hair styled in a pompadour.

Victoria, lying on her stomach, was getting goulash all over her face.

And Michael chortled as he kicked around in the messy stew.

Envy and hurt gnawed in Lennie's chest. She couldn't watch Michael prance around the field to thunderous applause any longer. At that very moment, she loved him and she hated him and she rooted for him and she was mad at him and she wanted him to win and she wanted him to lose.

Uncle Humphrey watched her carefully. "Michael! That's your brother, eh?" he said, putting an arm on her shoulder. "He's kind of a pip-squeak."

"Well, he's only ten," Lennie said.

"And he's got *enormous* ears."

"They're not *that* big . . ."

"And what's with those gapped teeth?"

"Stop it!" she said, feeling suddenly protective.

"Oh, sorry, I didn't realize we were Team Michael here. Shall I get out my pom-poms?"

"We're not Team Michael!"

"Could have fooled me," he said, squinting.

Lennie glared at her great-uncle. "I want to do this! Really, I do!"

Poppop had begun speaking again. "The task is simple. Each of these tombstones behind me represents a Pompor-romp who has died! And today . . . I am going to reanimate their spirits. Oh, if only Sir Fluffington the Fourth were here to see this! He loves chasing their ghostly wisps! At least, until they start chasing him back . . . *then* he becomes a scaredy-cat."

All of her aunts, uncles, and cousins began whispering to one another. "Aren't the ghouls dangerous?" Julien called out.

"*Of course* they're dangerous!" Poppop said. "That's exactly the point! They're searching for warmth, but if any touch you, you'll DIE."

Estella elbowed Poppop in the side.

"Okay, not die, but you *will* be knocked out. Sometimes for an hour, sometimes for a day, sometimes for years! In fact, I got ghouled once," Poppop added, "and I don't think I've ever fully recovered."

"You're just fine, Mortimer," Estella breathed.

"Would a *just fine* person sneeze whenever someone says the word snickerdoodle?"

"Snickerdoodle," Estella said.

"AAAAAH—AAAAHHH—ACHOOOOOOOOO!!!!" Poppop wiped his nose on his sleeve and shouted, "CURSES, ESTELLA! A POX ON YOUR HOUSE!"

Years in a coma seemed like a very dangerous thing. Lennie edged toward her brother, even though he couldn't see her or hear her from her spot beyond the Pomporromp property's border.

Poppop continued. "Your goal is to get these ghouls out of the garden and over to the grass—without ever stepping out of the goulash yourself. If you step out of the goulash, you are AUTOMATICALLY DISQUALIFIED." Poppop laughed maniacally for a moment, then cleared his throat and moved on. "Now, your body heat is like a magnet to these ghouls, so you're going to have to be creative in how you get them out of the garden area. Once all the ghouls are out—or all the players are comatose—we'll stop the test. And now," Poppop said grandly, holding his wizard staff high in the air, "we are going to wake the ghouls! Brace yourselves!"

Poppop twirled the staff like it was a baton and slammed the rubber ducky's head on the floor. It squeaked and emitted a purple beam of light—which zapped right into the ground in front of the tombstones.

Out of the graveyard came floating apparitions. They were silver and shiny, like strands of spiderweb that had come together in the shape of a wobbly human. They were not invisible, but not entirely solid, either. Their eyes were like black sockets, and their mouths were foaming with drool. They bobbed above the earth, slowly, waking up from a long slumber.

"THEY'RE ALIIIIIIIIIIIIIVE!" Poppop cackled. "No, THEY'RE DEAAAAADDDDD! No, wait, THEY'RE UNDEADDDDDDDD!"

Uncle Humphrey shifted beside her.

"You okay?" Lennie asked her great-uncle, searching his face as he stared at her poppop. Uncle Humphrey's expression looked rather dark.

"I'm fine," he said.

"Is it the ghouls?"

"I said *I'm fine*," Uncle Humphrey said.

Lennie let it drop and turned her attention back to the ghouls who were circling the contestants.

S-s-sooooo c-c-c-cold! they chattered.

H-h-h-humansssssss! they shuddered.

B-b-b-bodiesssssss! They shivered.

Lennie looked at Michael, who was jumping up and down in the goulash. He was so excited, which made Lennie feel bad. But she and Uncle Humphrey were doing a good thing. At the end of this test, there would be no winners, but there would be no losers, either. Everyone would be equal.

"Wait for my signal," Uncle Humphrey said. "We don't have that much time to get from here to Mortimer's podium."

Estella blew a whistle, and the second test began.

The ten ghouls circled the competitors, while the competitors pressed their backs together in a smaller circle. It was like they were in a ballroom, a ring of ghosts twirling around a ring of Pomporromps in a silent dance.

Then, the ghouls began to moan—softly, at first. Then louder and louder: unsettling guttural noises, echoing across the estate.

Silently, Ethan's hair started growing to the ground. Bo crouched down and began shoveling goulash into his mouth. Michael and Julien were frozen, never once taking their eyes off the ghouls. Victoria splashed around in the meat stew, giggling like she didn't have a care in the world.

Then two ghouls moved abruptly, swooping down low and quick. Ethan stepped forward and used his hair as a whip to keep them at bay.

Three swooped for Michael, but he went invisible to avoid them. They could still feel his body heat, but they seemed to have a hard time detecting *exactly* where he was while he was invisible.

Bo coughed up three wild turkeys and a cockatoo. He zigzagged through the goulash to escape the ghouls as they confusedly went after the birds. Victoria was splashing around in the goulash, but the ghouls weren't getting her. Maybe she was just too small for them to pay her any attention.

A ghoul dipped down for Julien. He stood still—until the last second, when he dove to the side. He quickly began to panic. "IT'S NOT LISTENING TO MY MIND CONTROL!" he shouted.

"Probably because they don't have minds!" Michael shouted back, turning visible again.

"That's *unfair!*" Julien whined.

"Get creative!" Bo suggested, and then he coughed up a duckling.

"And stop complaining!" Ethan added.

Lennie would've enjoyed continuing to watch Julien struggle, but Michael was on the move! He hopped across the garden and slid through the goulash as a ghoul hunted him. Then he went invisible, but the confused ghoul kept floating—right out of the garden.

"OUT!" Estella shouted waving a flag. "One ghoul down, nine to go! Point Michael!"

Go Michael! Lennie thought. Then she remembered she wasn't supposed to be rooting for him.

The ghouls pounced again. Two of them tried to attack Michael, who ran in circles while flickering in and out of invisibility to confuse them. One was chasing Bo around, who waved his arms in the air and screamed wildly, "GO FOR THE BIRDS, GO FOR THE BIRDS!"

A ghoul went for Julien, but he was saved by Ethan's hair, which formed a protective cocoon around Julien at the last second.

"Thank you, mind control!" Julien cried gleefully.

Ethan snapped his hair back from Julien and glared. Then

he looped his locks into a lasso. Spinning his hair around, Ethan caught a ghoul in his mane and tossed it out of the garden.

"Point Ethan!" Estella called. "Two ghouls down, eight to go!"

"HELP!" Julien shrieked as three ghouls dipped toward him. Ethan's hair began zooming over to protect Julien again, but the ghouls were faster. *Whoosh, whoosh, whoosh*—one right after another, they flew through Julien's chest. His skin turned bluish and cracked like it was a piece of dried-out clay. He wheezed one last breath—then fell forward like a plank, facefirst into the goulash. Completely fainted. Out cold. Stiff as a stiff.

Lennie gasped.

"JULIEN!" Uncle Philip #3 hollered from the bleachers.

The parents of the remaining four Wizardmatch contestants began to cry out to their kids. The cousins sitting on the bleachers blinked in horror.

Michael's powers finally returned to him, and he went invisible, dodging yet another ghoul and jumping over Julien's body. Wasn't anyone going to stop the game? Or carry Julien off the field? How could Poppop allow something like this to happen to one of his own grandchildren?

"Point Michael again!" Estella said. "And point Bo! Four down, six to go!"

Uncle Humphrey put a hand on her back. "It's time."

Her stomach bottomed out from under her.

"See where Poppop is watching, across the Garden of Goulash?"

Lennie nodded.

"We have to get to him, and we have to be invisible. Now, we're going to run around the garden." Uncle Humphrey pointed to the left edge, where the goulash met the grass. "We don't want to get ghouled."

Lennie's stomach turned.

"You can do this. I believe in you," Uncle Humphrey said, and just hearing those words—knowing that *someone* believed in her—made her feel like she could fly.

Uncle Humphrey helped her up. Lennie turned them invisible, and they crossed the border into Pomporromp territory.

Then they sprinted. Treading on the grass, Lennie pumped her one arm and held tightly onto her great-uncle with another. They were running right next to the Garden of Goulash, beside all the contestants and the ghouls. She could have been one of them . . . if only.

Don't think about that!

Poppop and his staff were just ahead of them—only a few more seconds. Lennie squinted, eyes on the prize. *I have to get there!* she said to herself as the sweat dripped down her face, as her arms prickled with pain. She was running out of time.

All too quickly, her energy drained and she tugged on Uncle Humphrey's sleeve. They were going to get caught— they were going to be seen—

With a flick of his wrist, Uncle Humphrey expanded a hole in the ground in front of them—big enough for them both to jump into. She hopped in, just as she released a breath that made her visible again. The ground closed in around them on all sides; there was no room to move beneath the grass. No sounds to be heard—not of the ghouls or the contestants or the rowdy audience.

It was dark and silent and cold.

"Do you think Poppop saw us?" Lennie shivered. She could only imagine what sort of horrible punishment he would dream up for them if he caught them. Maybe make them clean the skateboard ramp with their tongues. Or hit them with a giggle spell, which would make them laugh until they cried.

"No," Uncle Humphrey said at last. "I don't think he saw us. Or else he'd open up the ground with his staff and yank us out of here like weeds."

Lennie closed her eyes and let out a slow breath.

When her energy returned, Lennie invisibled herself and her great-uncle as Humphrey popped them both up out of the ground. Uncle Humphrey was right—Poppop *didn't* seem to notice. He only had eyes for the Garden of Goulash, where Michael and Ethan had teamed up to bait and attack three ghouls. Where Victoria was sliding through the goulash on her butt. Where Bo was hiding beneath an ostrich.

But Lennie kept her focus on Poppop's staff. *The key to equality is right behind Poppop.* It was what she needed for her voice to be heard—for *all* of their voices to be heard.

Her heart was racing.

When they were no more than a hundred feet away from the podium, Uncle Humphrey was practically soaring every time he leaped. *Almost there!* she thought.

But then! Michael slid across the garden—landing in the goulash right near her. From across the field three ghouls came barreling toward him, spinning in a vortex of white smoke. They were headed directly for Michael's back. But he was distracted getting to his feet. And he didn't see them coming.

Michael!

She wrenched her hand away from Uncle Humphrey and ran to her brother. She tackled him around the waist and they both went flying into the ground. They slid across the goulash, meat sauce getting *everywhere*. But the ghoul had missed her brother. She'd saved him from being in a coma for days. Or months. Or maybe even years.

I did it, she thought in sheer relief.

And then the relief was gone.

"Lennie?" Michael said, confusedly wiping the meat off his face.

She looked down at her hands—fully visible. *No, no, nooooo!*

She scrambled to her knees and glanced at the shocked, angry faces of her family in the bleachers.

Lennie tried to invisible and dash off, but Poppop waved

his staff and she froze. It was the same sensation she felt whenever Jonathan, Anya, or Mollie used their powers on her. Then Poppop made the ghouls disappear with another flick of his wrist.

"WHAT IS GOING ON HERE?" Poppop thundered.

Lennie looked for Great-Uncle Humphrey to save her, but he was nowhere to be seen.

She was on her own . . . and in big trouble.

"LENNIE, WHAT ARE YOU DOING?" her mom screamed.

Lennie's face grew hot. A little *thank-you* would be nice from her mom—she just *saved* Michael from getting ghouled! Wasn't that a little more important than some stupid competition?

All the aunts, uncles, and cousins were yelling at her simultaneously, so loudly that she couldn't even make out who was screaming what.

Poppop raised his hands for quiet, but everyone ignored him and continued spitting choice words at Lennie.

"LISTEN TO ME, YOU WEASELS!" Poppop cried. "SILENCEEEEEEEE!" He stamped his rubber ducky staff, and everyone stopped hollering midword. "Let the girl explain herself." He turned to Lennie with a glance so cold it could've frozen the goulash solid. "Well, *go on*," Poppop said.

"I was saving Michael," she said.

"I call foul!" Bo said, and he coughed up a chicken. "I call *fowl*, too!"

Poppop's beard twitched as he glared at her. "Cutting off your face to spite your nose, are we?"

"Mortimer, it's cutting off your nose to spite your face."

"THAT'S WHAT I SAID!"

He looked at Lennie. They all looked at Lennie.

"No, that's not—" Lennie began, but she couldn't finish. The words stuck to the roof of her mouth, like peanut butter. "I just don't think it's very fair—"

Poppop got up off his throne and leaned forward, amid hisses and whispers from the family. "YOU ARE TRYING TO RUIN THIS TEST, AREN'T YOU?"

"I'm *trying* to get you to see reason!" Lennie shouted, her temper flaring. "All of you! This has gotten out of control! Everyone's fighting—and everyone's miserable! And nearly all the girls are eliminated—"

"I don't see gender," Poppop said, which was a statement so ridiculous Lennie's jaw actually dropped. "Boy or girl, everyone in this competition has trained hard and earned their spot! Are you saying your competing cousins don't deserve my title?"

"That's *not* what I'm saying!" Lennie fumed. "But you clearly have favorites—"

"Jealousy," Poppop said, frustratingly calm. "Exactly the sort of thing I wanted to avoid." He shook his head at her, *tsk*ing with his tongue. It was so . . . so . . . so *belittling* it made Lennie want to scream. Her mom gave her the *I'm-very-disappointed-in-you* face, which was almost as bad.

And everyone else surveyed her with disgust and anger.

Michael's face, though, was worst of all. His bottom lip wobbled. He didn't look mad. He looked *devastated*.

"Why?" Michael finally said.

Lennie never—in a million years—thought he'd be so crushed. *She* was the one whose dreams had been dashed.

The family grumbled from the bleachers as they looked down at her with disdain.

"Now what?!" Aunt Lacey said. "She's ruined everything!"

"You have to do something!" Uncle Philip #1 demanded.

Everyone murmured in agreement.

"If you don't mind," Lennie's mom said to Poppop, "I would like to have a talk with my daughter."

He thought for a moment. "Very well. I will let you handle the *troublemaker*."

"Are we going to redo the Ghoulish Goulash Test?" Aunt Macy asked hopefully.

"Hardly," Poppop Pomporromp said. "We were nearly done anyway. The judges shall deliberate, and we will let you know our decision tonight at dinner. Oh, and someone carry Julien up to his room and get him some smelling salts. Hopefully he'll wake up in a day or two."

Uncle Philip #3 let out a distressed cry as he made his way down the bleachers to his son.

"That will be *all!*" Poppop said, stomping off toward the castle.

The second Poppop left, the spell was broken; she could move again. So she clomped off to the garden, letting the sauce splatter everywhere with every stomp of her foot.

"Lennie, stop!" her mom said. "Come back here!" She grabbed on to Lennie's arm and whipped her around.

She glared at her mother.

"Don't be disrespectful, Lennie! I don't like that look!"

"Why, because it's not a *Prime Wizard look*?" she bit, and in her mother's stunned silence, Lennie wrenched herself away and ran invisibly into the castle.

Done

Lennie retreated to the Cheeseburger Chamber, but she knew she couldn't hide for long. After a half hour of staring at the ceiling, her mom came into the room and locked the door behind her. Lennie assumed this was to keep Michael from barging in. Or maybe her mom didn't want any witnesses when she murdered Lennie for the stunt she pulled today.

"Lennie, what is going through your head?" her mom asked. "I'm trying to understand your actions, but I just can't. How would you feel if *you* were Michael, and he had messed up *your* Wizardmatch test?"

"Well, that would never happen because I'm not allowed to participate in Wizardmatch. As you know."

Her mom frowned. "I thought we talked about not letting life get you down!"

"It's not life," Lennie said. "It's Poppop, and it's you! How *could you*, Mom?" Lennie said. And for the first time since she'd met Uncle Humphrey, she let the tears flow. "You knew magic was my dream! You should have chosen me, and you know it!"

Her mom flushed. "Your Poppop had very strong opinions—"

"But they were the wrong opinions!" Lennie said. "You knew he was interested in Michael for all the wrong reasons. If I were a boy, I would've had the *look,* and you would have picked me over Michael."

Her mom shifted uncomfortably. "I understand how hard this is, Lennie, but there were a lot of things to consider. When you grow up, you'll see that life isn't always fair, but we have to learn to roll with the punches."

"But the punches shouldn't come FROM MY OWN FAMILY!" Lennie said.

Her mom's lips pressed together in a thin, tight line. "You're angry. I get that. But this isn't Michael's fault, and you've taken your anger out on him. You have to apologize to your brother."

Lennie nearly choked. She couldn't be serious!

"Apologize?" she said. "For what?! I was trying to save him from being ghouled!"

"You didn't give him a chance to save himself," her mom said. "It was his time to shine. You can't keep going around doing whatever you want to do, whenever you want to do it. Your actions have consequences, Len. And you might have gotten him eliminated. So you're going to have to say you're sorry."

"Now?" Lennie said.

"Now," her mom insisted, opening the door and calling down the corridor. "Michael! We're ready for you!"

Footsteps thudded down the hall, and Michael walked in. Like he'd been waiting obediently for this very moment.

His eyes were puffy. Lennie's heart tugged, and she even felt a little bit sorry. But still not enough to actually *apologize*. Out loud.

She turned to her mom. "I can't do it."

"*Lennie*," her mom said in a warning tone.

"I forgive you," Michael said stiffly, "because I know you're just jealous."

"For the last time, I am *not* jealous!"

"Yes you are!"

"NO I'M NOT!"

"YES YOU ARE!"

"WHAT DO YOU EVEN KNOW?" Lennie cried. "YOU'RE JUST A SPOILED, SELFISH BRAT!"

Michael's face twisted up. "TAKES ONE TO KNOW ONE!"

They both lunged at each other, quick and furious; it was impossible to tell who threw the first punch. Lennie smacked Michael's head; Michael grabbed ahold of her arm and squeezed it so hard that it was like he was wringing out a lemon; Lennie clawed at him—

"NO!" their mom roared, and she grabbed Lennie and dragged her away from Michael.

Lennie was panting and sweating, her heart beating a million miles a minute. She wanted nothing more than to smack Michael again. Her arm was throbbing, and when she looked down, she saw the outline of his fingers. He left his mark, and she—apparently—had left a few scratches on him.

"I'm never going to talk to you AGAIN!" Michael shouted.

"GOOD because I'm never talking to *you*, either!" Lennie replied.

"I won't talk to you for longer!"

Her throat was sore. Her pulse was hammering in her ears.

"Get *off* of me," Lennie said to her mom.

She wanted her mom to say *no*—to hold her tight, to dry her tears, to make everything all better.

But her mom let go, and Lennie left.

Lennie weaved through the castle, flickering invisible whenever she neared any of her extended family. After what she'd done, it would be risky to move about the castle and leave the grounds, but Lennie *needed* to see her great-uncle right away. He would know how to make her feel better. He would fix everything. They would come up with a new plan to destroy stupid Wizardmatch, and everything would be okay again.

Her arm was still smarting from where Michael had grabbed it; she cradled her arm to her body and gently rubbed it with her other hand.

"It's all RUINED!" came Poppop's voice.

Lennie's heart caught in her chest; she pulled herself to the side of the ramp and invisibled just in time as Poppop and Estella skateboarded past.

"Sir Fluffington the Fourth, missing! And my dear Julien is in a coma! And Lennie is plotting behind everyone's backs! It's all too much, Estella!" Poppop sniffled, before circling out of Lennie's earshot.

As Lennie tiptoed around the Jelly Floor, avoiding the bits of jelly that had stretched onto the ramp, she thought about how she and Michael used to be like peanut butter and jelly, like French fries and ketchup, like pretzels and ice cream— they just meshed together, the perfect combo. Siblings who were also best friends.

Would she ever have that with Michael after this competition was over?

For the first time since arriving in Netherly, she wanted to go home. Not just back to San Francisco, but back to school and her friends and her church and the pretty good life she had before Wizardmatch screwed everything up.

At last, she was out of the castle, undetected. Outside, the sun had just set. Early evening shadows cloaked her as she made her way to her uncle's cave in the borderlands. When she reached the clearing, she knocked on the big boulder like she always did. But instead of opening up for her, it stayed closed.

"Uncle Humphrey! Let me in!" She knocked again. "I have food for Fluffles!"

"It's not going to open," Uncle Humphrey said from behind her.

She pivoted around. His eyebrows converged together, his forehead was all scrunched, and his mouth was twisted into a scowl.

"Are you mad at me?" Lennie asked.

"You dropped my hand today! You almost got me caught!" he said angrily. "You abandoned me in the middle of our mission!"

Her stomach dropped. "I—I'm sorry," she said. "I thought—"

"No, you *didn't* think. That was the problem."

Lennie took a small step toward her great-uncle, but his nostrils flared dangerously.

"I told you we needed the staff. I told you we couldn't stop Wizardmatch unless we had the staff. I *told you* our objective was *the staff*." Uncle Humphrey's nostrils flared. "We were SO CLOSE to the staff, and you just *blew* it! All because you couldn't let your brother *faint*."

"I know, I'm . . . I'm sorry," Lennie whispered. "I just couldn't help it."

"I'll just have to try again," Humphrey muttered to himself.

"Yes! We can—"

"We?" Humphrey said. "No, no, no, my dear. Just me. You're done."

"Done?"

"Through! Finished! Kaput! Outta here!"

She blinked. For a second, she'd thought he might be

joking, but his mouth was puckered, and he glared at her with loathing. It wasn't a kidding face. "You can't—"

"Oh, believe me, I can," Uncle Humphrey said, his mouth twitching. "You've almost cost me *everything*, and if you're going to be a liability, I can no longer afford to mentor you. Go away, Lennie," he said in disgust.

Lennie couldn't stop the tears now—she threw the bag full of food for Fluffles at Uncle Humphrey and sprinted back to the castle, her face dripping. The fury in his expression, the disappointment in his eyes . . . it was too much to bear. It was the same look she got from her brother, her mom, her poppop.

She let herself into the castle and slumped against the door. Her whole body felt heavy; her heart ached. All the fight seemed to leave her in one breath. She was just so tired. If she weren't positive that a search party would come after her, she would have skipped dinner and gone right to bed. She felt like she could sleep for days. Or years.

She wiped her eyes with her sleeves and shuffled toward the bottom of the ramp. A skateboard ushered her to the dining hall. Her head hung low as she lumbered inside. No one talked to her or acknowledged her or even glanced in her direction.

Except Ellington, who cornered her while she was getting her food.

"A-are you mad at me?" Ellington said timidly. Her eyes filled with tears, which began to escape down her cheeks.

"You *are* ignoring me, aren't you? I thought it was in my head, but then every time I try to talk to you . . ."

"Of course I'm ignoring you!"

"Well, *why*?" Ellington said.

Lennie simply folded her arms.

"I'm mad at you, too," Ellington said so softly that Lennie could barely hear her over all the noise in the dining hall. "You've been so mean to me for no reason at all. It's not fair."

Lennie scoffed. "Fair?! Don't talk to me about fair!"

"You're not mad at me; you're mad at your mom. If you and your mom just apologi—"

"NEVER!" Lennie fumed, grabbing a seat in the far corner of the kids' table and moving it even farther away.

Ellington really thought two little words could solve all her problems? An apology wasn't big enough for the hurt she was feeling.

"ATTENTION, ATTENTION!" Poppop Pomporromp said, standing up on his chair and waving his hands. "The judges have deliberated! And we are pleased to announce the three children who will be moving on to the finale. Congratulations . . . *Michael!* You are still in the running to become the next Pomporromp Prime Wizard."

Lennie sunk even further in her chair, while Michael spit his water across the table. "Really?!" he said.

"Really," Poppop answered. "The next person who is still in the running is . . . Victoria! Well done, Victoria."

"Victoria?" Anya's dad, Uncle Philip #2, said. "Are you kidding? She sat there like a lump!"

"DON'T QUESTION MY AUTHORITY!"

"He's easy on judging Victoria since she's a baby. I wish *I* was a baby," Anya muttered.

There was one spot left, and three people Poppop still hadn't called: Ethan, Bo, and Julien. Ethan stared hungrily at Poppop, and Bo kept his head down.

"And the final person who will be competing in the last round of Wizardmatch is . . . Julien! I'm sorry, but that means Ethan and Bo, you are eliminated."

Bo stuffed a scoopful of potato chowder into his mouth and coughed up a swan. "My swan song!" he cried.

"Are you kidding me?!" said Ethan's dad, Uncle Philip #1.

"Julien is unconscious!" said Bo's mom, Aunt Lacey. "He got ghouled! He failed the test!"

"Shut up, both of you!" Julien's dad snapped.

"Make me!" Uncle Philip #1 retorted, and suddenly he slapped his own cheek.

"Stop hitting yourself," Uncle Philip #3 jeered, using his mind control to make Uncle Philip #1 continually smack himself in the face. "Stop hitting yourself! Stop hitting yourself!"

Uncle Philip #1 grew his hair out, long and pointy, like a spear—but just as he was tilting his head in the right angle, Uncle Bob sliced his hair off with a steak knife.

"THAT'S FOR WHAT YOU SAID ABOUT PERRIE!"

"DON'T YOU TOUCH MY DAD!" Ethan shouted, growing his hair.

Perrie grabbed Ethan with her long, noodly arms. "Don't you touch *my* daddy, you hair ball!" she said, dangling him up high.

"LET GO!" Emma said, using her hair to pelt potatoes in Perrie's face—only she missed and hit Danielle instead.

Then Michael went invisible, and food from his plate started flying everywhere: bananas, apricots, peach slices, mashed yams. Uncle Philip #1 tied Uncle Philip #2 up in his chair. Mollie hid under the table with Raina, who was using her powers to make food fly away from them both. Bo was coughing up hawks, falcons, and eagles, which circled menacingly around the ceiling. Victoria was shrieking so loudly that it was like she had fifteen lungs inside her.

Lennie sat in her seat in complete shock, watching food and birds sail past her. Her dad always taught her not to waste food; he would be *horrified* to see this.

"This is all your fault, Estella!" Poppop cried.

"Me?!" she said. "*You* were the one who insisted on hosting this competition!"

"HOW DARE YOU! WHOM DO YOU THINK YOU ARE?"

"*Who* do you think YOU are?!"

"Don't correct me!"

It was chaos. Absolute chaos. Food flying everywhere, birds pooping on people's heads, limbs and hair tangled, cousins roaring, aunts and uncles screaming.

This was what Wizardmatch did.

Estella was right—it *was* all Poppop's fault. The food fight, the competition, her misery, *everything*!

Lennie jumped up, mashing bread in her hands and rolling it between her palms—tighter and tighter until it made a giant bread ball. Then she *pelted* it across the room toward Poppop.

The bread hit him in the chest, and he stopped shouting, looking at it in shock as it bounced away.

All at once—like a switch had flipped inside her—Lennie grabbed everything she could see and started throwing it at Poppop: creamed spinach, rice pudding, napkins, soup, cheese wheels, a slab of steak. She smashed plates on the floor—shattered glasses, too. Every throw, every broken shard of ceramic on the floor, was a release.

She hurled pasta at Michael, for being so stuck up. She flung hardboiled eggs at Mom, for not understanding. She threw salmon at Ellington, for telling her to apologize and *get over it*. She attacked Anya, Ethan, Perrie, and Bo, whose birds kept pecking her head, trying to eat the food that covered her head-to-toe.

And they pummeled her right back with all combinations of nasty, smelly foods. But every hit jolted her. She was *awake* and *alive* and *angry*—

"THAT'S ENOUGH!" Poppop shouted, stamping his staff down so hard that the rubber ducky on top actually squeaked. A sparkly dust settled over the dining hall, and a film descended over her eyes. She was light-headed. Dizzy. Slowly, Lennie dropped the baked carrots in her hands.

Everyone quietly shuffled out of the dining hall to their bedrooms. The spell wore off once Lennie got back to Cheeseburger Chamber. She was caked with cake, crusted with crust, pickled in pickles—but she couldn't stop shaking.

It was *over*.

Done.

She had nothing left—no great-uncle to train with. No mission to work for. No chance at being the Prime Wizard. Just this morning, she had hope and purpose, but not anymore.

As she tucked herself into bed, the food still stuck to her skin, she thought about Wizardmatch. When she had overheard that awful conversation between her mom and Poppop, she remembered thinking that her life couldn't get any worse. But now she knew . . .

She was wrong.

Last Chance

The final Wizardmatch test was approaching. The days ticking up to that last hurrah were some of the most miserable of Lennie's life.

Her mom was still treating her like a baby who couldn't be left alone. The rest of the family either ignored her completely or gave her the stink-eye whenever they passed her in the hall. And Julien—who didn't even wake up until two days later—whispered snide comments to Lennie whenever she was nearby.

And she and Michael remained frigidly silent. Whenever he wasn't around, Lennie ached to talk to him. And whenever he *was* around, she only wanted to smash her fist into his face.

On the day of the third and final Wizardmatch test, Michael was gone before Lennie had even woken up. The castle was abuzz. Estella and Poppop were running about, hanging more MISSING FELINE posters all over the walls of the castle: *Answers to Sir Fluffington the Fourth, Fluffles, or Fluffy Fluffy Poo Poo! Looks like a furry penguin! Will not come when you call him. Will not play fetch either (believe me, I've tried)!*

While Poppop was distressed, it seemed like everyone else

was excited for the final test. People were rushing to and from the dining room. Julien was stretching in the halls. Aunt Macy was feeding Victoria spoonfuls of mashed carrots and cooing, "Who's my wittle-bittle champion? You are!"

"Len!" her mom called from seven stories up. "WAIT THERE. DO NOT MOVE. You need to be chaperoned!"

But Lennie didn't wait for her mom to catch up. She skateboarded down as fast as she could and was out the door before her mother could shout *LENNIE!* yet again.

Outside the weather was hot and dry; the sun beat down and warmed her black hair. Lennie walked along the edge of the Pomporromp property, starting at the cliff where the first test had taken place—and strolling toward the borderlands. She sighed with every step and flashed invisible at random moments, in case her mom was watching. But she suspected that Mom had given up on her—and was getting Michael ready for the final round of Wizardmatch. That would certainly take precedence over babysitting Lennie.

Today was the day when a new Prime Wizard would be declared. And Lennie had utterly failed in her mission. Wizardmatch would just keep happening—again and again and again—from now until the end of time. She had no effect on the system. She changed nothing.

She wasn't going to be the first female Prime Wizard. There probably wouldn't be one in her whole lifetime. Poppop would get away with discriminating against her and the other girls. He *already* got away with it. Because he was in power, and everyone in the family wanted to stay on his good side.

Lennie trudged past the Garden of Goulash and wandered to the edge of the Pomporromp property. As she walked along the border, she thought about Great-Uncle Humphrey. She hadn't heard from him since their fight. She doubted she'd *ever* hear from him again.

Maybe I should try to talk to him again, she thought. She reached a hand through the border—into the fuzzy darkness ahead. Then she took a steely breath and plunged forward, carefully scanning the ground for any new booby traps.

"Mortimer, you can't be serious!" came Estella's voice from some yards away. Clearly from inside the borderlands, too.

"I am as serious as a head injury after suffering a heart attack after breaking your arm."

Lennie invisibled instantly. And a moment later, Poppop Pomporromp and Estella came strolling from around the bend.

"It's so musty! We can't have the third test in here! And besides, it's too late to change the location. We've already told everyone that the last event is taking place inside the castle," Estella said.

"We *have* to change it!"

"I'm just concerned you haven't thought this through. If you haven't found Fluffles, what makes you so certain *they* can? We don't know if Fluffles is even in the borderlands! And what if one of the competitors falls into one of Madame Oglethorpe's booby traps? Or one of yours?"

"Then they'll have to escape," Poppop said. They edged so close to Lennie that she held her breath. "If they want to be Prime Wizard, they have to know how to escape one tiny little booby trap, Estella! But we need to search for Sir Fluffington the Fourth. I am desperate! Whoever finds him truly deserves to be the next Prime Wizard!"

"And you're sure you want to put a full mute on the candidates?" Estella said.

Poppop nodded. "Of course! It's the only way to guarantee a fair test."

Lennie's fifteen seconds were up, and she tucked herself behind a tree.

"Then who will you follow?"

"Julien, of course," Poppop said. "He's the favorite to win."

Lennie clenched her jaw and kept walking forward. She didn't stop until she was at Uncle Humphrey's Secret Cave of Secrets. Knocking on the rock wildly, Lennie shouted, "I have important information for you! Things you *need* to hear about the third Wizardmatch test! Open up!"

For a moment, she thought he was going to keep ignoring her. But at last, the rock split open in the middle, and Lennie scampered inside. She weaved her way through the geode, avoiding stalactites and stalagmites. And she reached the fire den at the end of the tunnel.

When her eyeballs adjusted, she saw Fluffles in a cell made of hard earth. And Uncle Humphrey frowning at her from a beanbag chair.

"Well?" he said. "What is this important information?"

"Don't tell him, Lennie!" Fluffles cried. "Don't reveal any of Mortimer de Pomporromp's secrets!"

Lennie smiled at her great-uncle. "The third task is taking place in the borderlands."

"Here?"

Lennie nodded. "They're going to be looking for Fluffles!"

"Little ol' me?!" Fluffles said. "I am so honored! Mortimer *does* care!"

Humphrey frowned. "Hmmm . . . that may present a problem. Anything else?"

"Uh . . . they are putting a full blind on the contestants."

"A full mute," Fluffles and Humphrey both said at the same time.

"That! What is that?"

"My brother will use his magic to prevent the contestants from being able to see, hear, touch, smell, or interact in any way with anyone else. It's so everyone can follow close by and watch without helping the competitors cheat."

"And Poppop's going to follow Julien."

"LENNIE, HISSSSSSSSSS!!!!" Fluffles said.

"Which one was Julien? Was he the goth kid with the wild hair? Or the one with all the birds?"

"I know which one Julien is. I can lead you to him!" Lennie blurted.

Humphrey eyed her warily.

"I know what you're going to say, but please let me team up with you again! I want to end Wizardmatch more than anything in the world. I just want Poppop to listen—I want to be heard!" she insisted.

"That's what you said last time."

"I'm sorry about last time," Lennie said. "I really, really am! But I'm here now. If you don't trust me, then . . . then I could just steal Poppop's staff on my own and then bring it to you. That way you don't even have to worry about me letting go of your hand."

Humphrey rubbed his stubbly, spikey chin. "That's a thought."

"It is?" Lennie said.

"Your best skill is sneaking. My best skill is camouflaging myself with the elements."

"Don't do it, Lennie!" Fluffles pleaded. "As a Pomporromp descendant, it is your duty to help protect Mortimer de Pomporromp's secrets!"

"Shush, you," Uncle Humphrey said, feeding the cat a potato chip.

"Why should I care about protecting Poppop's secrets, Fluffles?" Lennie said fiercely. "Poppop's never cared about me." She turned to Uncle Humphrey. "You're the only one who's cared enough to believe in me."

He patted her on the head. "There, there, you sappy sap. Let's get ready."

She waited for Wizardmatch to commence at the edge of the borderlands. She considered hiding inside the borderlands until the time was right to execute Uncle Humphrey's plan . . . but she knew that if she didn't show up to the test again, everyone would notice right away. She was on a short leash.

She walked along the edge of the Garden of Goulash. Running her hand over the warm gravestones, she thought through their plan. And thought again. And thought a third time.

Poppop would never let his guard down for long. Lennie probably only had seconds to work with, when his hands were off the staff, but she was used to doing effective magic in mere seconds. She'd been practicing all year for this.

I have to be brave. I have to be sneaky. And most of all, I have to be quick.

Poppop announced the new event venue just ten minutes before the third test was about to start. And as her extended family started arriving, little by little, they were all grumbling about the last-minute change of plans. With no stadium to sit in, they all huddled awkwardly together, waiting for further instructions from Poppop. Most of them—maybe *all* of them—had no idea the test was going to take place inside the borderlands.

Michael was one of the last people to arrive. She didn't look at her brother because she *couldn't* look at him. Maybe they'd never speak again, like Poppop and Great-Uncle Humphrey.

She took a deep breath. *I have to stop thinking about Michael.* As Uncle Humphrey reminded her over and over again, Michael was just a distraction. And she couldn't afford to be distracted again. Michael was on his own today.

"Lennie," her mom scolded. "I told you to stay put this morning—and you skated off! You *disappeared*!"

"In case you forgot, I have that power," Lennie grumbled.

"I haven't forgotten," her mom said. "That's why I'll be keeping a very close watch on you this time around."

Shoot, Lennie thought. That wouldn't do. *I have to get her off my back.*

"I-I've been doing a lot of thinking this morning," Lennie lied, "and I wanted to say I'm sorry." The words tasted bad in her mouth. She was *sure* she puckered her face as she spoke, but her mom didn't seem to notice.

Her mom's jaw fell open. "You are?"

She choked out another lie. "I feel bad for everything. I forgive you." That was the biggest lie of all. Her mom didn't even say she was sorry! She *did not* forgive her mom and saying *I forgive you* out loud made her stomach churn.

Her mom kissed the top of her head. "Oh, Len, I'm so glad we're all coming together to root for your brother."

At that moment, a bugle sounded and Poppop sauntered over, in shiny robes of turquoise.

"HEAR YE HEAR YE," he said, wrapping his beard around his neck like a scarf, "and welcome to the final challenge. Julien, Michael, Victoria: You three are the only remaining contestants in Wizardmatch. For your ultimate test, we are going across the border of my property. Your job . . . is to find Sir Fluffington the Fourth!"

"You want the contestants to find your lost cat?" Uncle Philip #2 said.

"You don't understand!" Poppop said petulantly. "Sir Fluffington the Fourth is my best friend, and he is GONE! I've looked everywhere—he has to be in the borderlands! He could be in danger! There are hundreds of booby traps in this forest . . . *deadly* booby traps. Not only will the Wizardmatch contestants have to defy these obstacles, they'll have to use their unique skills to track down my dear beloved Fluffles. FLUFFLESSSSSSS!" Poppop cried, dabbing at his eyes with his beard. "Whoever—whomever?— wins this challenge might very well find themselves the next Prime Wizard of the Pomporromp estate, and will forever have my gratitude."

Julien looked determined. Michael looked excited. Victoria looked like she spit up all over herself. All the other cousins glared at them with envy. Lennie looked deep into the borderlands, and though she couldn't see anything, she knew that Uncle Humphrey had his eye on her. She wouldn't let him down this time!

"Mortimer is about to put a full mute on each of the contestants," Estella explained. "You will be able to see and hear them, but they will not be able to see, hear, or touch any of you. So, you can follow whichever contestant you want, but you won't be able to interact with them."

"Once I complete the spell, you three are free to go into the borderlands and hunt for Sir Fluffington the Fourth," Poppop said. "Ready? BEGIN!" He waved his staff, which emitted black fog. Michael's, Julien's, and Victoria's eyes began to glaze over, and then it was as if they were staring directly through Lennie and the rest of the family. "And the test is afoot!" Poppop shouted as Michael and Julien trudged into the borderlands. Victoria crawled. Poppop hurried after Julien, using his staff as a walking stick.

Lennie eyed the staff hungrily, but her mom pulled on her arm and dragged her in the opposite direction: after her brother.

She needed to stay close to Poppop—and to his staff. If only her mom wasn't babysitting her! If only she didn't get caught during the last test!

"Isn't this nice?" her mom said, squeezing her hand so tight that Lennie thought it might fall off.

"Great," she said, and it was a real effort not to roll her eyes.

I'll just have to escape her grip, Lennie thought as they followed Michael into the thicket. The thick, heavy air was familiar to her, and the cracked earth groaned beneath her feet as she walked on.

She was helpless as Julien was getting farther and farther away, headed in the direction of the trap-bridge, and soon she could barely see the enormous group that went with Pop-pop to watch Julien's assured victory.

Michael invisibled and crept around. Lennie knew to watch the ground for his footsteps; with every step, the dust swirled a bit around his invisible shoe.

Suddenly Michael visibled again, his head smacking the ground. In a blink, he was completely upside-down, held by the ankles with a rope and bobbing in midair in front of a tree.

"MICHAEL!" her mom cried.

"Wheeeeeeeeeeeeeee!" Michael said, bouncing up and down.

"Michael! Don't just stay there! Keep moving—"

As her mom ran forward, she dropped Lennie's hand.

Lennie stood for a moment, her chest tight. Michael was in trouble. She couldn't just *leave* him.

But she couldn't abandon Uncle Humphrey and the Plan. And who knew if she'd have another opportunity to escape, once her mom grabbed her hand again?

She hesitated, running her hands through her hair. But then—with a resolved breath—she turned and invisibly sprinted away. Toward Julien. Toward Poppop.

Mom is there for Michael, she assured herself as she skirted around Victoria, who was crawling through a patch of neon-glowing lollipops with a sign that read EAT ME, YOU KNOW YOU WANT TO. *Someone has to be there for me. And that someone is MYSELF.*

The woods were dense, and it was dark, even though it was the middle of the day. The thick borderland trees were like a tightly woven basket above her head, and there wasn't a single place where the sun bled in. The inky moat stretched out before her, and the air was muggy, and every few steps, there seemed to be another trap beckoning her into its clutches.

But she'd tread this path so many times on her way to see Uncle Humphrey that she knew exactly which dirt patches to avoid, which roots to jump over, and which tree boughs would fall on her head if she walked under them.

When she finally reached the oily moat, she heard Poppop squealing with delight—and the sounds of a crowd up ahead. Julien was tiptoeing around a small patch of tangled yo-yos, and everyone was following with whispers and cheers.

Lennie went visible and stopped running. She needed to save all of her magical energy—and nonmagical energy—for the moment she *really* needed it. Everyone was so absorbed in watching Julien that they didn't even notice her approach, anyway.

Poppop was in the front of the crowd. She had to get close to him. But if Poppop realized what she was doing . . . that would be it for her. She had one chance. One shot. One singular opportunity that she *could not mess up*.

She wiped her sweaty palms on her shorts. If she failed, this might be the last day she ever spent at the Pomporromp Castle. And if she succeeded? She smiled thinking about Uncle Humphrey's idea—to share all the powers evenly, among the whole family. Finally, they could all stop fighting. Everything could be fair and equal.

But it all came down to Lennie and her invisibility.

Julien reached the trap-bridge that Lennie herself had fallen for, but Julien ignored it. Instead, he crossed the moat by swinging across on a vine. Poppop swung his staff around to create a safe path for the audience to follow.

They were very close to Uncle Humphrey's secret cave . . . *too* close. Uncle Humphrey had assured her that Fluffles was well hidden and well protected—but what if he was wrong? She became more and more anxious with every step closer to Humphrey's hiding spot.

She had to get the staff—and *fast*.

SNAP!

Julien had just stepped on something. He froze, looking left, right, forward, and backward, for whatever horrifying trap was about to come his way. At last, he breathed a sigh of relief—

PLUNK!

A bug's nest landed on Julien's head.

Out came hundreds of centipedes and millipedes—no, wait *centicentipedes* and *millimillipedes*. Lennie stared, horrified. They were brightly colored and enormous—each one the length of a ruler—with sharp pincers and thousands of legs. More legs than she'd ever seen on one bug. More legs than she even thought possible. They crawled all over

Julien, swarming him, covering every inch of him—until she couldn't see anything but legs.

"HELP!" Julien cried. "MMMMM!"

"DAD!" Uncle Philip #3 shouted. "DO SOMETHING!"

"Nothing I *can* do!" Poppop said. "This is Wizardmatch!"

The centicentipedes and millimillipedes crawled all across Julien's face, the back of his neck, on his arms and legs. He was totally motionless—as solid as if Anya herself had frozen him.

Poppop was watching, mouth agape, and Lennie edged closer to her grandfather. This was just the distraction she needed. His staff was *right there*. The rubber ducky on the front was grinning at her. Taunting her with its shiny orange mouth.

Lennie maneuvered through her cousins, aunts, and uncles. She was close enough to touch Poppop.

"Oh boy! This is exciting!" Poppop said, exuberant. "Estella, I am glad I changed this third test after all!"

Now was her chance!

She invisibled and reached forward.

Her fingers curled around the staff, and she wrenched it— only Poppop's grip on the staff was *tight*.

"WHAT WAS THAT?!" Poppop exclaimed.

What could she do? If she visibled, he'd see her and know what she was trying to do. But she couldn't keep up her power for much longer!

Sweat beaded on her forehead.

"HEY! LOOK OVER THERE!" Anya cried.

"IT'S FLUFFLES!" Ethan shouted.

"Found him!" Julien mumbled, blowing a bug away from his mouth.

"MORTIMER!!!!!!!!!!!!!" Fluffles called from a distance. Lennie's heart dropped as she visibled again. How did he escape? The cat was out of the box, and he was about to let the cat out of the bag. Fluffles knew too much about their plan—he would ruin *everything!*

"SIR FLUFFINGTON THE FOURTH!!!!!!" Poppop cried, turning around. "OH HAPPY DAY, MY BEST FRIEND—"

"—MORTIMER—"

"—HAS RETURNED HOME TO ME AT LONG LA—"

"There's a wicked plot!" Fluffles howled.

"WHAT PLOT, FLUFFLES?"

Without a breath, Lennie invisibled and crouched beside Poppop.

Now!

She grabbed Poppop's staff, and it—like her—became invisible.

"WHAT IS GOING ON?" Poppop said. "WHERE'S MY STAFF?"

"I don't see anything, Mortimer!" Estella said, panicked.

Poppop's grip on the staff loosened. Just a little bit. Just enough.

Lennie yanked it and ran, dodging her family members and hopping over anything that looked suspicious on the ground. She darted through trees, toward Uncle Humphrey's secret cave, skirting around Fluffles as they crossed paths.

"IT'S LENNIE!" Fluffles shrieked from behind her. "MORTIMER, IT'S LENNIE!"

Her heart thrummed, and her pulse pounded in her ears.

"LENNIE?" Poppop cried.

"SHE'S BEEN WORKING WITH A STRANGE MAN. THEY CATNAPPED ME! THEY FED ME *BOLOGNA*! THEY ONLY PET ME FIVE TIMES A DAY! IT WAS TORTURE!"

"FIND HER!" Poppop bellowed. "SEIZE HER!"

Lennie nearly dropped the staff. Pomporromps were spreading out behind her, fast on her trail. And her skin began to prickle with the first signs of magic fatigue.

Not now! Please, please, please.

She flickered, slightly, before pushing herself to invisible more—she was sweating. Soaked. "Humphrey! Help!"

"HERE I AM!" Out of the hollow of a tree, Humphrey de Cobblespork emerged. He was far—all the way across the three clearings, a tiny figure under distant trees. Her heart beat fast. She couldn't reach him in time, but could the staff?

Lennie leaned forward and threw it like a javelin. The moment the staff left her hands, it went visible, soaring through the air. And just when she thought it was about to fall fifty feet too short, a strong gust of wind picked it up and kept it going until it flew right into Uncle Humphrey's arms.

Lennie couldn't hold out any longer. Exhausted, she went visible, and was quickly frozen into place by Anya.

"YOU!" Poppop Pomporromp cried, but he wasn't talking to Lennie. He was glaring at Humphrey de Cobblespork, his long-lost brother. "WHAT ARE *YOU* DOING HERE?"

Uncle Humphrey smiled. "Let's gather the whole happy family together, shall we?" He flicked the staff, and suddenly, Michael, Victoria, Julien, and everyone else came flying across the borderlands—like they were being dragged by an invisible hook. They all collided together in a *thump* in front of the oily moat.

Michael and Julien were especially confused, looking around wildly. Victoria was drooling. Lennie realized they still had the full mute on them, and couldn't see anyone else there. Uncle Humphrey waved the staff again, and Michael jumped.

"Oh! Is it over? Is there a winner?" Michael asked.

"Did I win? I found the cat!" Julien exclaimed.

"Actually, *I* found Fluffles, AND I froze Lennie, so I win!" Anya said.

"Let's get our facts straight," Uncle Humphrey said. "None of you found the cat. I released the cat on purpose. He played his part perfectly."

"Who is this guy?" Aunt Tracy demanded, clutching Ellington and Raina protectively.

"THAT'S MY BROTHER!" Poppop Pomporromp hol-

lered. "DON'T TRUST HIM! HE'S A FIEND! A MEN-
ACE!"

"Takes one to know one!" Uncle Humphrey shouted.

The magic restraining Lennie wore off, and she could move
again. "This," she said, turning to face her entire extended
family, "is Great-Uncle Humphrey. And we're here to end
Wizardmatch . . . forever!" Lennie announced grandly.

"GASP!" the family gasped.

"It's an unfair contest," Lennie continued. "We want the
family to *share* the Prime Wizard power, so we can stop all
this fighting."

Lennie beamed—this was the moment she'd been dreaming of. She flashed a thumbs-up at Great-Uncle Humphrey,
who nodded back in encouragement.

But her family had a different reaction: confused, bewil-
dered, uneasy.

"Share the powers?" her mother said. "Len, what are you
talking about?"

Poppop Pomporromp looked murderous as he glowered at his brother. "YOU KNOW WE CAN'T SHARE
THE—guh!"

Uncle Humphrey swung the staff, and a ball of glowing
light burst forth from Poppop Pomporromp's chest. Everyone watched, jaws open, as it hovered in the air before
zooming over to Uncle Humphrey. Her great-uncle caught
the ball of light hungrily. The moment it touched his skin,
his body twitched, his face contorted, and his skin glowed

white. Then—when the light subdued—Humphrey sighed. "Ahhhhhhh," he said with a smile, stretching out his hands. "Yessssssssss."

Poppop's knees buckled beneath him, and he sagged to the ground like a wilted rose. All of Lennie's aunts and uncles cried out and rushed to Poppop's aid as he lay still on the ground.

Is he okay? Lennie thought, taking a worried step closer.

But then Poppop's body shuddered, and he coughed wildly. "Estella! F-fetch me a barf bag!" he croaked as he crawled across the ground.

Great-Uncle Humphrey grinned as he swung the staff around casually. There were some sharp breaths from her family. They all stood protectively in front of Poppop, shielding him from view.

Lennie excitedly examined her hands. Did Uncle Humphrey share the magic yet? She didn't feel any different—was she supposed to? Taking a step forward, she stared at her great-uncle. "Did we complete our mission? Do we all have Poppop's powers now?"

Uncle Humphrey caressed the staff for a moment before looking firmly at Lennie. "I completed *my* mission," he said. "I took all of Mortimer de Pomporromp's powers. I am the new Prime Wizard."

The New Prime Wizard

Lennie's heart dropped into her stomach. Frightened whispers erupted from behind her, but she couldn't focus on her family right now. She blinked at her great-uncle; the lines in his face looked harsher.

"What do you mean—you're the next Prime Wizard? I thought you didn't believe in a Prime Wizard! You said you wanted our family to share the powers!"

"*Please,*" Uncle Humphrey snorted. "You really thought I would share these powers? The powers that *should* have been mine from my own Wizardmatch?!"

Lennie's head was spinning. "But you said . . . you told me . . ."

"I told you what you wanted to hear. You, my dear, were easy to manipulate."

Manipulate? Her fingers curled into fists. "You *used* me?"

"Don't sound so scandalized," Great-Uncle Humphrey said. "We used each other. I helped train you to be more powerful—what *you* wanted. And you helped me get the staff—what *I* wanted."

"But—*why?*"

Humphrey de Cobblespork stretched his neck to the left,

then to the right. "My powers," he said, breathing in deep, "are more FORMIDABLE than ever. My sixty years of hard work have made me strong. But with the magical energy that comes from being Prime Wizard, I can do magic I only dreamed of." Humphrey waved the staff and invisibled his arm. He extended his neck and wiggled it like a snake. He made his eyes pop out of his head and then back in again.

Poppop moaned, and Estella helped him to his feet as his knees threatened to buckle beneath him. The rest of her family huddled together, trembling.

This is all my fault, Lennie thought, and her cheeks grew hot. She'd fallen right into Humphrey de Cobblespork's trap. She believed everything he said—ate it up with a spoon—and never even considered that he might be tricking her. *Stupid! I'm so stupid!*

"Y-YOU FIEND! YOU USURPER! YOU TOTALITARIAN DESPOT!" Poppop bellowed. "I'LL SHOW YOU!" He shot a fireball at Humphrey, but it fizzled into steam halfway there. Poppop tried again, but the flame pooped out a second time. Then he squatted and scrunched his face up real hard. "FIRE!" he shouted, but this time only a puff of smoke erupted from his fingers.

"BAHAHAHAHAHA!" Uncle Humphrey laughed, clutching his stomach. "You are not the Prime Wizard anymore. The powers are inside of *me* now, you miserable lump of rotting oatmeal—"

"You listen here! I won that competition fair and square!" Poppop spat.

"YOU DIDN'T, YOU DIDN'T! YOU KNOW YOU DIDN'T!" Humphrey said, stamping his feet. "YOU WERE ALWAYS GRANDPAPPY'S FAVORITE! IT WAS UNFAIR!"

Poppop stamped his feet right back. "I CAN'T HELP IT IF I'M ADORED BY ALL I ENCOUNTER, LOVED BY EVERYONE, REVERED BY AN ENTIRE—mmmmmf!" Poppop's mouth closed like a bear trap. He tried to pry his lips open with his hands, but they were sealed shut.

"Much better," Uncle Humphrey snarled. "As I was saying—since I am Prime Wizard, the powers and estate are mine." He gestured across the forest, toward the border of the Pomporromp property in the distance. "Unfortunately, I don't want my brother's offspring in my new castle. I dislike guests who are constantly plotting to overthrow me. But I *do* like potato chips." Uncle Humphrey smiled wickedly. "How would you like to be a potato chip?"

"Y-you're going to turn us all into *potato chips?*" Perrie squeaked.

Lennie's stomach was icy.

A hand grabbed hers—and when she looked beside her, Michael was squeezing it. He was standing with her, defiant and determined, just as she was. She hadn't even realized he'd been by her side. Then, moments later, Ellington put a hand on her shoulder, and Lennie thought of the advice her cousin had tried giving her.

"Please!" Lennie cried out desperately. "You have to let all this roll off your back—or it will eat you up inside. You have to forgive Poppop."

Humphrey's downturned mouth grew even frownier, and his eyebrows moved down over his eyes. "Lennie . . . if you're not with me on this, then I'll be forced to see you as an enemy."

"LENNIE! HIDE!" cried Estella.

"Thanks for the help. Couldn't have done it without you," Uncle Humphrey said, raising his staff. "Now, good-bye."

And he shot a beam of purple light right at her.

Invincible

Uncle Humphrey's spell landed right in the moat.

Did he miss? was Lennie's first thought. But then, as the dark water rose like a tidal wave, Lennie realized that he *meant* to hit the water. He was going to take all of them out at the same time!

The water rose higher and higher, so tall that it seemed to brush the tops of the trees. Her invisibility was useless—her brain was frozen.

WHOOSH!

The moat came racing toward the family.

But then, something jerked around her navel, and she started flying *up*, hovering in the air, along with her brother and a handful of cousins.

"GO!!!!!!" Ellington shouted as she floated them toward the border of the Pomporromp estate. And in a breath, the wave crashed over the family, and the water froze around them—keeping them perfectly in place.

Lennie cried out—but it was too late. They were frozen: her mom, Poppop, Estella, Fluffles, Ellington, half her cousins, and all her aunts and uncles. She couldn't believe it—

Ellington sacrificed herself, just to buy her cousins a little extra time.

We have to move!

"Come on!" Lennie shouted to the group. She knew Michael was with her, but didn't even have time to see who else was, or whether her mom was okay. Her brain skirted in panic as she ran away from Uncle Humphrey, who laughed maniacally behind them.

They burst through the border of the Pomporromp property. Now Lennie could see that—in addition to Michael—Anya, Bo, Perrie, Ethan, and Julien, holding baby Victoria, were all with her.

"Ellington is so, so brave!" Perrie said.

"And so, so frozen!" Ethan added.

"We have to get to the castle!" Anya grunted, stumbling forward.

All the breathless running triggered a memory in Lennie. "Everyone! Grab on to me," she said sharply, and she transferred her invisibility to her cousins as they darted across the grass.

"So what do we do, Lennie?" Julien panted as they ran.

"How should I know?!" Lennie cried.

"You *have* to know! You're the only one who knows him!"

"You're our best chance of stopping him!" Anya said.

Lennie combed her brain for an idea, but she couldn't think of anything. "I have no clue!"

"You can do this, Lennie!" Michael said.

"You're very smart, even if you don't know calculus!" Perrie added.

Far in the distance, the castle stood, tall and crooked. But first, they had to get through the Garden of Goulash, which was fast approaching.

"SURRENDER!" Uncle Humphrey bellowed from behind them as he strode across the borderlands into Pomporromp property. "This is your last chance!"

"Keep going!" Lennie whispered as they dashed across the goulash. Feeling her cousins' hands all over her shoulders, side, legs, and back, Lennie hustled and hurried and . . .

SLIP! She slid in the sauce and went gliding across the field away from her cousins. In an instant, they all were visible.

"Aha! There you are, you little brats!" Uncle Humphrey said. "You've made a *grave* mistake."

He wiggled the staff, and wisps of black smoke shot toward the graveyard.

All at once, the ghouls began to wake.

"S-s-s-s-s-souls!" they chattered.

"B-b-b-b-b-bodies!" they moaned.

They smacked their ghostly lips together as they descended in a row in front of them. Their silvery bodies wobbled, and their mouths were dribbling with spit. Lennie could see through their bodies to the castle, but now it seemed even farther away than ever.

With Humphrey behind them and the ghouls before them, Lennie didn't know which option was worse.

"We beat these ghouls before," Ethan said, twirling his hair menacingly in his hands.

"But what about Humphrey?" Perrie asked.

The ghouls swooped down.

They snapped into action: Ethan shaped his hair into an enormous baseball bat, and Bo began to shovel down fistfuls of goulash, coughing up birds faster than Lennie had ever seen. Perrie flung goulash with her super long arms, and Michael went invisible, distracting and confusing the ghouls around them. And though Lennie knew Julien would never admit it, he looked at the ghouls with an expression of pure terror, his eyes bulging, his mouth in a perfect O shape.

"LENNIE!" Uncle Humphrey bellowed from the edge of the Garden of Goulash.

She whipped around.

Uncle Humphrey raised the staff, and Lennie braced herself—but just before he gave his wrist a final flick, he froze into place.

"Anya's doing it! She's holding him!" Julien said in awe.

"Agggagggggaggg," Victoria babbled, spitting up on Julien.

Anya's face was screwed up in concentration. "Not for long!" she said, through gritted teeth. "He's really strong, and my power is draining!"

"Let me take over!" Julien said, and the moment Anya's power ran out, Uncle Humphrey began smacking himself in the face with the staff.

"Keep doing that!" Lennie exclaimed. An idea was forming. The answer was right in front of her eyes—*the staff*! "Anya, Julien, keep switching back and forth—if you can keep him stuck in a loop, maybe I can get close."

"Why would you want to get close to him?" Julien said.

"We have to separate Uncle Humphrey from the staff! Cut him off from Poppop's powers!"

And before her cousins could respond, Lennie darted forward.

As she hurried toward her great-uncle, she was practically skating in the slippery goulash.

Uncle Humphrey stood on the edge of the goulash—now completely frozen. Lennie invisibled as she approached. He stood very still—but then Humphrey *actually dropped the staff*.

"THAT'S ME!" Julien crowed, delighted. "I'M DOING THAT!"

For the first time in her life, Lennie wanted to hug him.

But she had to end this. She dashed forward. The staff was so close! *Almost there,* she thought desperately, arm outstretched—

WHOOSH!

She flew backward with so much force that she slid fifty feet across the goulash garden. Meat sauce was *everywhere*. She scrambled to her feet, frantic. Her cousins rushed to her side.

How did he do that? She'd separated him from the staff!

"I DON'T NEED THE STAFF TO DO MAGIC!" Humphrey shouted, levitating it off the ground and snatching it with his hand. "It makes me stronger, but the magic is *inside me* now!" Then he waved the staff, and a ray of glowing red light beamed their way, straight out of the rubber ducky's mouth.

It was quick. Lennie huddled together with her cousins, closed her eyes, and—

BOING!

The red light bounced off of them and hit the goulash, which exploded from the ground like a saucy fountain.

Uncle Humphrey looked confusedly at his staff and tried again.

BOING!

The red light bounced off of them and flew into the air, disintegrating one of the ghouls.

"NICE SHOT!" Michael called.

What's happening? Why can't Uncle Humphrey hit us?

It was almost like they had a protective shield around them. Something in the goulash, maybe? Or had Uncle Humphrey's spell backfired?

BOING! BOING! BOING!

Uncle Humphrey fired spell after spell as he stormed toward them, looking angrier by the second.

"QUICKLY!" Lennie shouted, and she grabbed her cousins. She turned them all invisible again, and together they pushed through the goulash, arm in arm.

"S-s-s-s-s-souls!" four ghouls shivered, swooping down and blocking their path.

"What now?!" Perrie shrieked.

"They're surrounding us!" Anya said. "Nobody touch them!"

Ethan stepped forward, letting go of the group and becoming visible. "Go to the castle without me. I'll keep them from following you. Remember me if I get ghouled!" he cried. Then he morphed his hair into the shape of a giant butterfly net and charged at the spirits.

Lennie hesitated—could she really leave Ethan behind?—until Uncle Humphrey shot a spell that landed at her invisible feet. "GO, GO, GO!" Lennie cried, grabbing her other cousins and dragging them toward the castle.

Lennie and her cousins stumbled onto the grass. As they ran, they could hear the sounds of Ethan battling the ghouls: snarls, grunts, shouts, and shrieks.

Just get to the castle, she repeated with each step. *Just get inside!*

They hurried and scurried and scuttled and scampered. Someone stepped on Lennie's ankle, and she tripped a bit—but her cousins kept her from falling.

At last, every detail of the patchwork castle, every carving of the wooden door, was finally in view.

GURGLE GURGLE BLOOP!

The pudding swelled out of the pool and quickly encircled them, spinning like a tornado. It was taller than all of them *combined*, blocking their view of the castle—and even of the sun. Dark, thick, and impossibly high. It smelled so sickly sweet that Lennie nearly choked.

The pudding swirled faster and faster and faster, constricting tighter and tighter around them until they were so squished together they could barely breathe.

Lennie shuffled closer to her brother and cousins—all of them were on top of one another. Someone was stepping on her toes, and she could feel someone else's breath on her neck. There was nowhere left to shuffle—nowhere to go. If the eye of the cyclone got any smaller, they'd be drowning in pudding.

"SOMEONE DO SOMETHING!" Michael cried.

"There's no going around it," Bo said.

"Or over it!" Anya added.

"Under?" Lennie asked.

"Through!" Perrie said triumphantly. "I can push you all through to the other side. My arms are long enough and strong enough to handle it!" Perrie put her hands on Julien's hips as he clutched Victoria. "Hold your breath!" she warned him, then she extended her arms and pushed Julien and Victoria right through the pudding to the other side.

Then went Anya, then Michael, then Bo. At last, it was just Lennie and Perrie left, the cyclone so tight around them that pudding splattered on her glasses.

"How will you get out?" Lennie asked.

"I'll push you through first," Perrie said. "Then I'll extend my arms through, and you guys can pull me out."

Perrie put her hands on Lennie and pushed. The pudding was thick around her, and her glasses were being smashed into her nose, and she couldn't see or breathe, and it felt like forever in the dark—

Until, at last, she *burst* through to the other side. She coughed for air, her lungs on fire.

"Grab—Perrie's hand!" Lennie panted.

But when Perrie shot her hands through, she got swept up in the tornado. Her body whipped around and around and around. Her arms wiggled, and her legs flailed, but she was stuck inside the vortex of pudding.

"She's going to drown!" Lennie shouted.

"We're a team," Anya said. "We can't leave her!"

"But our powers are useless against a pudding tornado!" Julien said.

"NOT MINE!" Bo said, unhinging his jaw. "I can rescue her, and the proof is in the pudding!" He reached into the pudding with feverish speed, taking scoopfuls of pudding in his hands, eating faster than humanly possible.

Suddenly, a streak of blue light came flying their way. It flew right into the tornado of pudding and exploded—bits of chocolate drizzling all over them. And then: the telltale cackle of Uncle Humphrey.

"LENNIE! WE HAVE TO GO!" Michael cried.

"It's okay—I can do this!" Bo said, then he choked up a puffin.

Lennie tore her eyes away from the pudding. *I have to trust Bo,* she thought. Just like Bo was trusting her to stop Uncle Humphrey.

She grabbed her cousins and invisibled, and Michael went invisible, too. They ran together toward the castle entrance— that beautiful wooden door! Almost there. Once they made it inside, they could hide and think of a plan. They just needed some time.

Sweat beaded down Lennie's face. *We're going to make it!* she thought, squinting at the entrance through her pudding-clouded glasses.

A cloud of smoke poofed in the doorway, and Lennie stopped, so surprised that she went visible again.

As the smoke cleared, she saw a long tattered coat, a wizard staff, and familiar gleaming eyes: Uncle Humphrey.

"You can hide . . . but you can't run," he said with a wicked smile.

Lennie could feel Julien and Anya stiffen on either side of her. "But how?! You were behind us!"

"Please, Lennie," Uncle Humphrey scoffed. "You didn't think this would be an actual chase, did you? What part of *unlimited magic powers* don't you understand? I can raise ghouls from the dead! I can create tornadoes of pudding! And I can teleport! I am," he said, grinning widely, "*invincible.*"

All That, and a Bag of Chips

This was bad, bad, bad. No, worse than bad. Impossibly insanely worst-thing-in-the-world *awful*. Uncle Humphrey was just too powerful. There was no way to stop him.

"Leave us alone!" Lennie shouted.

"You can try to resist," Uncle Humphrey said, waving his staff, "but I'll *chip* away at you!" A blast of purple bubbles zapped Anya in the chest, and a poof of smoke surrounded her. When the smog cleared, Anya was gone. And where she had been standing was a bag of sour cream and onion potato chips.

"NO!" Lennie screamed.

"Anya?!" Michael whispered.

Uncle Humphrey raised his staff again.

But suddenly, he began to scratch his butt. Then he mooed like a cow. Then he crossed his eyes and jumped on one foot.

"GO!" Julien said, handing Victoria off to Lennie. "My powers won't last much longer!"

"What about you?"

"I'll find you later!" Julien said. "I have to stay in range for my powers to work! You get a head start—"

"But why?" Lennie said. "You hate me!"

"You're family," Julien said. "Family always comes first. Now go!"

Lennie held Victoria close to her chest and invisibled. Michael invisibled, too. They slipped under Uncle Humphrey's arms, opened the door, and stepped into the castle . . . just as Uncle Humphrey started to fight Julien's power.

"LOOK OUT!" Julien cried.

A wayward spell was headed toward them. No time to run or hide or duck—

BOING!

The spell hit Victoria square in the chest . . . then ricocheted off her and hit one of the banister posts, which splintered into pieces. Lennie shut the door quickly before any more spells could sneak in.

Then she held up her cousin. Was she hurt? Victoria baby-babbled happily. Lennie and Michael looked at each other—and then at Victoria. It was the same thing that had happened in the Garden of Goulash.

"It's Victoria!" Lennie gasped. "She has force-field powers!"

But there was no time for awe. Lennie whistled twice for skateboards, and she and Michael hopped on.

"Where are we going?" Michael asked. "How can we stop him? What are this guy's weaknesses?"

"He *has* no weaknesses," Lennie said as they zoomed along the ramp. She held on to Victoria extra tightly. "Didn't you hear him? He's invincible, with and without the staff!"

"No one's invincible," he replied.

Below, there was the unmistakable sound of the front door opening. "Lennieeeeee! Ready or not, here I come!" Uncle Humphrey called out, and shivers went up Lennie's spine.

"Pull over!" she hissed.

Lennie yanked her brother into the closest corridor. They found themselves in the library, where the books were so eager to be read that they pelted library guests with their requested genre. *At least there are hundreds of shelves to hide behind,* she thought as she and Michael ran through rows and rows of books. She clutched Victoria and didn't stop until they were all tucked away in the corner, far behind a bookshelf.

"Are we safe here?" Michael asked.

"I don't know. I hope so."

There was a tired pause. Lennie's heart beat too fast and her limbs were shaking too much to even process what had happened—to the family, to her cousins, probably to Mom.

"Michael, I don't think we have a lot of time left," Lennie said, grabbing his hand. "And I just want to say . . . you were right all along. I was jealous."

"You were?" Michael whispered, his brown eyes growing wide. "Because that's how I feel about you all the time!"

"What? You do?"

"Well, not *all* the time," Michael said. "It's pretty awesome being me."

She rolled her eyes. "You are gloating again! You keep throwing Wizardmatch in my face—"

"I'm sorry. I just wanted you to be proud of me." He looked down at his shoes.

Michael . . . apologizing? Shock radiated through Lennie. Shock and guilt and love. She squeezed his hand. "I am so sorry, too . . . for everything. And I *am* proud of you," Lennie whispered fiercely. "I know it wasn't your fault I wasn't picked."

Michael grinned. "You were jelly like the Jelly Floor!"

Lennie smiled weakly. "Jelly like the—"

She perked up.

Jelly like the Jelly Floor.

"The Jelly Floor!" Her heart skipped a beat. "Michael, follow me. I have an idea!"

With Victoria in her arms and Michael on her tail, Lennie tiptoed out of the library and invisibled, keeping their eyes peeled for any sign of Humphrey. They sneaked around the ramp, making their way down.

The Jelly Floor was the one place Uncle Humphrey didn't know about, because he'd left the castle before it was created. And it was so sticky that even Poppop, with his Prime Wizard magic, couldn't get rid of it.

Which meant that Humphrey wouldn't be able to, either.

They reached the twenty-second floor, just as their magic drained.

"We'll take a moment to recharge," Lennie whispered,

shifting Victoria onto her other hip. The baby was heavier than she looked.

The jelly glistened a deep reddish-purple, and Lennie and Michael stood dangerously close.

She sucked in a deep breath. For once, her powers weren't going to help her. She needed to be seen.

"I have to call him," she said. "He'll teleport to us, if he knows where we are."

"Are you *insane?*" Michael whispered. "You can't!"

"This is the only thing that will trap him! You go invisible. While I distract him, you push him in, and I grab his staff. Maybe a non–Prime Wizard *with* the staff can compete with a Prime Wizard *without* the staff."

"I can't do this."

"Yes, you can."

"But—"

"Michael, it has to be you," she said firmly. "He wants to catch *me* right now. I have to show myself. I believe in you."

Lennie put Victoria on the ground. She needed both hands if she was going to try to take the staff.

"Ready?" she said. And before her brother could respond, Lennie yelled, "I AM ON THE TWENTY-SECOND FLOOR!" Her voice echoing around the Pomporromp Castle. "I AM READY TO SURRENDER! I AM SCARED!" She nodded to Michael, and he disappeared.

POP!

Uncle Humphrey appeared. He stood between her and the

jelly, looking all around at the purple jam, at her, and right through invisible Michael. "Where's your brother?" he asked suspiciously.

Lennie invisibled and lunged forward.

Uncle Humphrey looked ready for her—but seconds before she reached him, he swayed, as if some other invisible person had tackled him around the middle.

Go, Michael! Lennie thought, and she reached forward to wrench the staff away from him.

But Uncle Humphrey sent them both soaring across the room without even a blink.

Michael crashed against the floor, becoming visible, but his left foot got stuck in the jelly. He pulled and pulled, but he couldn't move.

"MICHAEL!" she cried.

"LENNIE!" he called back, his panicked eyes on Uncle Humphrey.

Uncle Humphrey came trudging toward her. Every step of his boots rattled Lennie to her very core.

"This was your big plan?" he laughed. "Your brother was going to push me, while you tried to steal the staff . . . and *then* what?"

He hovered over her like a hungry vulture, leering.

"LENNIE!" Michael shouted.

Humphrey waved the staff.

"Aaaaaggg gaggggg!"

The noise came from behind her—the baby! She was strong enough to protect them both!

Lennie grabbed Victoria, held her out in front of her, just as the light burst out of the rubber ducky's mouth—

BOING!

The spell ricocheted off of Victoria and bounced right back into Humphrey—and he flew backward and landed in the jelly with a *splat!*

Uncle Humphrey lay in the middle of the hall, purple jelly quickly engulfing his arms and legs. "WHAT IS THIS STUFF?" Humphrey de Cobblespork bellowed, every vein in his neck bulging. The more he thrashed, the more the jelly stuck to him, congealed to his clothes—until at last, he could barely move. His fingers twitched as he desperately clawed for the staff, trying to wrench free of the jelly.

But not even magic could get him out of this jam.

The Decision

While Uncle Humphrey continued to howl, Lennie hugged Victoria.

"You did it!" she said to the baby, kissing her round, soft cheek. "You defeated Uncle Humphrey!"

Victoria tugged on her hair in response.

"Ow!" she yelped, disentangling herself from Victoria's tiny fingers. Then she rushed over to Michael. "Are you okay? Can you take your shoe off?"

Michael carefully untied his shoe and wiggled his foot out. His sock was covered in jelly, and he peeled that off, too. "It was almost between my toes . . . toe jam!"

"GET ME OUT OF HERE!" Uncle Humphrey snarled.

Lennie looked around. Uncle Humphrey was glued so firmly to the ground that his arms and legs and torso were completely purple. Only his face was jelly-free, and he screamed and raged and cursed and spit.

Lennie ignored him. Instead, she went for the staff, which was lying on the floor. The rubber ducky was dangerously close to the edge of the jelly.

She bent down to pick up the staff—the wood was smooth and surprisingly warm in her hands.

"You have to use it to fix everyone," said Michael.

"Me?"

He nodded.

Lennie nervously cleaned her glasses, which still had flecks of dried pudding on them. In their imminent doom, she had been too preoccupied with defeating Uncle Humphrey to wonder what she was going to do about the cousins. The staff felt like an anvil in her hands—the weight of it! The pressure!

As they made their way outside, they found two bags of potato chips on the ground, right outside the door to the castle: sour cream and onion and bacon cheddar.

She paused. Uncle Humphrey had told her that as long as she was physically holding the staff, she'd be able to do more than just go invisible—that it would help stir up some of the dormant power inside her.

"Please work," she said out loud. Then she closed her eyes and waved Poppop Pomporromp's magic staff over the bags of chips.

Nothing happened.

"It's not working!"

Michael gripped her by the shoulders. "That's not the Lennie Mercado I know!" he said loudly. "The Lennie I know never says die! The Lennie I know believes in her magic! Now, WAVE THAT STAFF!"

She took a deep breath. *I can do this,* she repeated to herself, a chant, a whisper.

Warmth bloomed inside her stomach, like she'd just drank hot chocolate. *This* was what her mom had meant when she said the power was inside her all along—the staff helped amplify it.

The rubber ducky on the top erupted green slime out of its mouth, which got all over the potato chip bags that were her cousins. The potato chips remained still. Lennie looked at the staff. Did she do something wrong? But then, at last, the bags began expanding, growing arms and legs—until *POOF!*

Anya and Julien were restored!

"Thank you, thank you!" Anya said. Then she sniffed around. "Why do I smell like onions?"

Michael helped Anya to her feet, while Lennie bent over Julien.

"You did it!" Julien said as she grabbed his hand and yanked him to his feet. "Of course, no one would *need* saving if it weren't for you, bummer!"

Lennie punched his arm.

"Lennie! Michael!" Bo called from the grass, waddling over to them.

"Where's the pudding?" Michael asked, looking around.

Bo patted his stomach. "In here. And out there!" He pointed up at the sky to a flock of geese.

"What about Perrie?" Lennie asked.

"She's fine! She went to help Ethan." Bo pointed across the estate. The ghouls were nowhere to be found, but Perrie and Ethan were lying in the goulash. Perrie was shaking Ethan's shoulder, and Ethan was emitting a low moan.

"What happened?" Lennie asked as she rushed over.

"Ethan got ghouled!" Perrie said. "He's been out for ten minutes, but he's finally waking up."

His eyelids fluttered, and he stared up at the sky, "This is so much worse than . . . everything. I'm never going to complain about anything ever again!"

"Glad you're okay. I know what that feels like," Julien shuddered, hoisting Ethan to his feet.

"Let's go save our family!" Lennie said, rushing toward the borderlands. She gripped Poppop's staff with white knuckles, trying not to think about the worst-case scenario. What if she couldn't revive them? What if they were hurt?

And if she *did* revive them, how could she ever explain away what she'd done?

When they arrived, the scene was more ghastly than she had imagined. Everyone was completely frozen in the dark moat water, like figurines in a snow globe.

Maybe they wouldn't forgive her. But she was responsible for this mess, so she had to be the one to clean it up. Lennie took a deep breath and waved the staff, and the familiar sensation of warmth bloomed in her navel. Bubbles rolled out of the rubber ducky's mouth, and the water melted.

It seemed like the family took one collective gasp before each one started panicking.

"HELP!" Poppop croaked. "HEEEEEELLLLLPPP!"

"I'm all *wet!*" Fluffles sobbed.

"What happened?" her mom cried.

"We got him!" Michael said. "In the jelly!"

"Lennie and Michael did it," Perrie added.

"It was actually Victoria," Michael said, holding the baby up in the air.

"It was a team effort," Lennie said. "All of us." She slung her arm over Michael's neck. She truly couldn't have done it without *everyone*. Not just Victoria and Michael, but Julien, Anya, Ethan, Bo, Perrie, and Ellington, whose butt-length hair was sopping wet.

While Michael returned Victoria to Aunt Macy, and as all her cousins went to exchange hugs with their own families, Lennie found her mom.

"I'm sorry," Lennie blurted. She buried her face into her mom's shirt. "I'm so, so sorry."

"I'm sorry, too," her mother said, tears welling in her eyes as she stroked Lennie's hair. "I was so concerned with what your poppop thought and what he wanted . . . And when he said all those hurtful things, when you overheard . . . I didn't know what to do. I *still* don't know what to do."

"You can *listen* to me," Lennie said. "And next time, you can stand up for me."

Her mom tucked a lock of hair behind her ear. "From now on, and always," she said softly. "I hope you know that I believe in your magic."

When Uncle Humphrey had told her that, it made her feel special. But now? The words felt hollow.

It seemed, after all that, she still *was* angry about Wizardmatch. And worst of all: she still empathized with Uncle Humphrey more than anyone else. Which was the most disturbing thought she could think—and that included the one time she had a nightmare about a cockroach sandwich.

"You're with him! SEIZE HER!" Poppop bellowed. He pointed at Lennie and flapped his arms wildly. "Where is my brother?! LET ME AT HIM!"

"I'm not on his side, I swear!"

"WHY SHOULD I TRUST YOU?"

"I promise I had no idea," Lennie said. "If you'll just let me explain—"

"HALT!" Poppop said, his beard twitching as he looked around at his family, spread out across the clearing. He clapped his hands twice. "GATHER AROUND! IT'S STORY TIME!"

"Oh, er . . . okay. When I first met Uncle Humphrey—"

"NO!" Poppop whined. "Every good story starts with *once upon a time*!"

That's what Uncle Humphrey said, too! He and Poppop were more alike than either one probably realized.

"Once upon a time," she said, indulging her grandfather, "I met my great-uncle Humphrey for the first time." She described his house in the borderlands, and their conversations, and her training, and his plans to split the powers evenly.

"Is he cuckoo bananas?" Poppop interrupted. "He knows

there's no sharing the power! If you divide the magic up, it disappears completely. We'd *all* lose our powers. But continue, Lennie."

And she did, telling everyone about how Humphrey betrayed her, and how she—and everyone else—managed to defeat him.

When Lennie finished, Poppop squinted at her. "There is much to consider. On the one hand, you saved everyone. But on the other hand, you brought danger to our doorstep. But on the other hand, you didn't know you were bringing danger to our doorstep. But on the other hand, you knew you were doing wrong. But on the other hand, you didn't seem to know what right was—"

"This is making my head spin," Ellington groaned.

"My head only spins when I turn it three hundred and sixty degrees," Bo said airily. "It's my special talent. Besides turning things into birds."

"What I don't understand is *why*," Poppop continued. "What would make you want to join Humphrey in the first place?"

Lennie took a deep breath. *Here it comes,* she thought. This was the moment she was working up to—the thing that was *really* on her mind. And though it was difficult to say out loud, she swallowed down her fear and drummed up her courage. "I was *there*. During your meeting with Mom, when you told her to choose Michael over me. I heard . . . I heard you say that I don't have the Prime Wizard look. And that . . . and that I'm too different." Lennie had to blink to hold back tears. Her family shook their heads and gave Poppop disapproving looks. Poppop flushed.

"You heard all that?" he said. "I am horror struck! More horror than struck." He paused, sighing. "I never meant to hurt you."

Lennie's tears started to shake loose, so she stared down at her feet.

"Lennie," Poppop said, and she looked up into his hazel eyes again. "I was insensitive! Tactless! Thoughtless! A complete cad! I am truly and deeply sorry. And I do love you very much—I love *all* of my grandchildren very much," he said, looking around at all the Pomporromp grandkids. "From now on, I'm going to work very hard to make sure you all get the love, attention, and respect you deserve."

Though it didn't erase all the hurt he caused, her whole chest felt lighter. And she realized—Poppop wasn't the only one who owed an apology.

Lennie shuffled her feet. "I want to say—I'm sorry to all of you. Sabotaging Wizardmatch wasn't the right thing to do. I hope you can forgive me." It felt uncomfortable to apologize, like using a muscle she hardly ever flexed. But strangely, it felt good, too.

She looked around at each of the families, hoping they knew how much she meant it. The silence was charged.

But then Ellington inched closer and threw her arms around Lennie, and the whole family thawed.

"Lennie, we forgive you," Uncle Bob said.

"We love you!" Aunt Macy said.

Lennie melted in relief. As she looked up across the borderlands, toward the castle, she wondered if Uncle Humphrey deserved some of that same forgiveness, too.

"What's going to happen to Uncle Humphrey?"

"OFF WITH HIS HEAD!" Mortimer cried.

"If you can forgive me, maybe you can forgive him, too," Lennie said.

"Forgive!" Mortimer said. "I'm going to freeze him in a moat! How's *that* for forgiveness?"

"He's kidding!" Estella said.

"I AM NOT!" her poppop shouted. "I have never been, nor will ever be, a goat. But perhaps," he said, drawing out a very long and very dramatic pause, "I should call my sister Winifred and apologize. After all these years, maybe we can put the past behind us. And . . . I shall probably leave Humphrey in the jam for a week. Then I'll dig him out and try to make amends."

"I thought magic doesn't work on the Jelly Floor!" Lennie said.

"It doesn't," Poppop said. "But a spoon and a stomach work perfectly well. I've had to eat my way out of that blasted place before. I'm sure I'll do it again."

Lennie smiled, but there was something still gnawing at her. Even though she'd gotten Poppop to apologize for the hurtful things he said, she didn't actually change Wizardmatch. She didn't stop the system. It had hurt Uncle Humphrey, it had hurt her, and if she didn't do something about it, Wizardmatch would probably hurt someone else in the future.

"I know you have to pick a Prime Wizard now," Lennie said carefully.

"Yes!" Poppop said with a giddy squeal. "Whoever—whomever?—I pick is going to be a very lucky Pomporromp!"

"I just need to say something first."

Poppop looked surprised, but he did not interrupt.

"The thing is . . . Wizardmatch is unfair to everyone," Lennie said, remembering how she and Uncle Humphrey had talked about this very thing. "At the end of the day, you're just going to pick your favorite, not the most talented or deserving. And the thing is: There's no reason why people over fifteen can't try for the title."

"Exactly!" shouted Jonathan, and Emma grinned.

Gaining confidence, Lennie continued. "Did you even notice that three girls were eliminated first, right off the bat, no matter how they performed? And that the only girls in the competition are from families who had no eligible boys to choose from? And why do you think that is? All the past Prime Wizards have been boys! And the next one will probably be a boy, too. It's a pattern that you just can't break from!" she said loudly.

"And I . . . I know you said I didn't have the *Prime Wizard look*. And I just have to wonder . . . if I wasn't *both* a girl and half-Filipino, maybe you would have given me a more serious shot. All I want is to have the same chance as everyone else—"

"Life is inherently unfair," Mortimer said, stroking his beard. "But I see your point."

"You do?" Lennie said.

"Indeed. And I must say! I never understood how you felt . . . until now." He paused. "To this effect, I am ready to select a Prime Wizard. One that breaks this so-called pattern. One that has impressed me beyond all reason. A young lady."

Lennie's heart began to beat wildly.

"Victoria de Applegrove!" Mortimer cried. "You are the next Prime Wizard!"

"YAY!" Aunt Macy cheered. But she was the only one.

"Victoria?!" came a few cranky voices.

"Seriously?"

Could someone be both surprised and not surprised in the same breath? Lennie wondered.

Mortimer de Pomporromp twirled his beard. "She's been very impressive to me, and I can just tell that she is wise beyond her years. Well, wise beyond her nine months. Besides, her name already has the word *victor* in it."

"More importantly," Estella added, "Victoria made it through all three of the Wizardmatch rounds. With her force-field powers, the three-headed shark didn't bite her, and the ghouls couldn't touch her. *And* her shield was the only power that held up against Humphrey de Cobblespork's magic."

Mortimer clapped his hands. "Yes, yes, congratulations, Victoria. You are the worthiest wizard of us all. You'll do great!"

Victoria drooled.

"But I was so close to becoming Prime Wizard!" whined Julien.

"So close, and yet SO VERY FAR," Poppop Pomporromp said.

"The rest of you can PET ME!" Fluffles suggested.

"And come back to visit us soon," Estella said.

"Yes! From now on, family is *always* welcome at the estate. And," Poppop added, "you and your family can all go back to exactly the way you were, like none of this ever happened."

That, Lennie knew, was impossible. There was no going back. Lennie turned to Michael, knowing that he was different, too. They'd weathered the worst sibling rivalry and come out the other side stronger.

Lennie pulled him into a tight hug, and he—for once—melted into her embrace without fidgeting.

Michael broke away first. "For a second, I really thought he was going to pick you! He *should* have picked you."

"No, he should have picked you," she said. "You were so good during the competition!"

Michael beamed.

"Are you kids okay?" their mom said. "Are . . . are we all okay?"

It was hard. Lennie was still so angry. She wasn't okay . . . Not by a long shot. But she was going to try to be. Lennie knew there was nothing left but to forgive Mom and Poppop and move on. Being angry forever was too painful. And she didn't want to end up like Uncle Humphrey.

"I'm not ready yet," Lennie said to her mom. "But I will be. I . . . I just need more time."

Her mom nodded. "I understand."

"We'll be okay," Lennie said, and her mom kissed her forehead.

"So what now?" Michael said to her. "What about our magic?"

"Uncle Humphrey said he spent years training to expand his powers, so I thought you and I could—"

"YES! YES! YES!" he said, and he flashed his gap-toothed grin.

"It won't be easy, you know. It will be really difficult. And slow going."

"So?" Michael said. "I'm not afraid of hard work. I bet I can learn magic faster than you!"

"Cannot!"

"Can, too!"

"Cannot!"

"Can, too!"

"Well, whoever learns faster has to promise to teach the other what they learned. From now on, we're on the same side . . . always."

"Deal!" he said, and they invisibly high-fived. Of course, he missed her hand and smacked her glasses.

"OW!" Lennie howled, massaging the bridge of her nose.

"We're going to be so strong! LIKE AN ELEPHANT! LIKE A HERD OF THEM!" Michael said, flexing his muscles. Then he began popping invisible and uninvisible again, his tongue sticking out in the silliest of expressions.

Lennie laughed, and for the first time in weeks, she felt hopeful. So what if she didn't get unlimited powers handed to her, with a single wave of a magical staff? She could earn her magic. She was ready to break her back, bust her hump, and sweat rivers. Anything worth having was worth working for, and she understood that in a way her poppop never would. It was the one thing Uncle Humphrey got right.

And, she thought as she looked at Michael—her brother, her blood, her sometimes rival, her greatest friend—*the best part is we're doing it together.*

Acknowledgments

I am grateful to a handful of extraordinary wizards who gave this book a bit of their own spark and razzle-dazzle!

Thanks to the Penguins with powers: Stacey Friedberg, Lauri Hornik (the Prime Wizard of Dial Books), Namrata Tripathi, Katie Quinn, Rosanne Lauer, Vanessa Robles, and the marketing and sales teams.

Thanks to the wizards of art: Natalie Andrewson, Dana Li, Theresa Evangelista, and Mina Chung.

Thanks to those who lent their editorial superpowers to this book: Anu Ohioma, Jewel Benton, Shaina Verma, Kathrene Faith Binag, and Caitlin Whalen.

Thanks to the Writers House wizards: Brianne Johnson and Allie Levick.

Big hugs and chocolate pudding to my big, fun, loving family. Aunts, uncles, and cousins: forever and always, family comes first. (P.S. I know who will play Uncle Randy in the movie.) Special shout out to my bubbie, Florence Gold, the ultimate matriarch of the family, who rules over us all with warmth and spaghetti sauce. With fond memories of my super poppop, Sidney Gold, who was far kinder and more progressive than Poppop Pomporromp . . . but who really did stick his dentures out at me.

To the Magaziners—Robin, Neal, and Michael—you are way better than the families I write. You three are *my* superpower.

Lastly, thank you to all the powerful women role models in my life, both imaginary and real. Most especially: Hillary Rodham Clinton, who is persistently strong and gracious and unwavering in the face of outrageous sexism. Thank you for inspiring this story. Your wizard power is an epic shimmy that stuns everyone in proximity for twenty seconds.